# Gabriel's Sacrifice

## CB Halliwell

Copyright ©2024 by CB Halliwell

All rights reserved.

No part of this publication may be reproduced, distributed, or transmitted in any form or by any means, including photocopying, recording, or other electronic or mechanical methods, without the prior written permission of the publisher, except as permitted by U.S. copyright law. For permission requests, contact [include publisher/author contact info].

The story, all names, characters, and incidents portrayed in this production are fictitious. No identification with actual persons (living or deceased), places, buildings, and products is intended or should be inferred.

# Contents

Important Notes — VI
Trigger Warnings — VII
Quote/ Dedication — VIII
Prologue — 1
1. Chapter One — 2
2. Chapter Two — 15
3. Chapter Three — 21
4. Chapter Four — 30
5. Chapter Five — 40
6. Chapter Six — 49
7. Chapter Seven — 56
8. Chapter Eight — 67
9. Chapter Nine — 86
10. Chapter Ten — 96
11. Chapter Eleven — 106
12. Chapter Twelve — 111

| | | |
|---|---|---|
| 13. | Chapter Thirteen | 123 |
| 14. | Chapter Fourteen | 133 |
| 15. | Chapter Fifteen | 143 |
| 16. | Chapter Sixteen | 152 |
| 17. | Chapter Seventeen | 161 |
| 18. | Chapter Eighteen | 169 |
| 19. | Chapter Nineteen | 176 |
| 20. | Chapter Twenty | 186 |
| 21. | Chapter Twenty One | 197 |
| 22. | Chapter Twenty Two | 209 |
| 23. | Chapter Twenty Three | 216 |
| 24. | Chapter Twenty Four | 233 |
| 25. | Chapter Twenty Five | 237 |
| 26. | Chapter Twenty Six | 245 |
| 27. | Chapter Twenty Seven | 251 |
| 28. | Chapter Twenty Eight | 260 |
| 29. | Chapter Twenty Nine | 271 |
| 30. | Chapter Thirty | 277 |
| 31. | Chapter Thirty One | 285 |
| 32. | Chapter Thirty Two | 298 |
| 33. | Chapter Thirty Three | 304 |

| | | |
|---|---|---|
| 34. | Chapter Thirty Four | 316 |
| 35. | Chapter Thirty Five | 323 |
| 36. | Chapter Thirty Six | 332 |
| | Acknowledgments | 341 |
| | About the Author | 345 |

## Important Notes

This book ends on a cliffhanger and is the second book in my Fire and Ice Series, so please ensure you've read book one - Gabriel's Salvation first.

As you'll remember from Book One we left on a heartbreaking cliffhanger. Just when we finally thought our poor, broken bad boy had found his happily ever after with his Little Firecracker, everything was cruelly ripped away from him.

Just like Gabe, this book is broken and bruised. It's full of bad language, smut, and so many morally gray moments. But just like our favorite 'villain,' if you take a chance on this book, it will open your eyes up to a whole new perspective and a whole new level of emotions.

Please ensure you read the trigger warnings... unless like me, you are a wild child who thinks trigger warnings are spoilers and prefers to dive in blind.

# Trigger Warnings

Child abuse (in flashback memories)

Alcoholism and drunk driving

Physical violence and bullying.

Drug abuse- including potential overdose.

Drugging and attempted sexual assault. (non-graphic)

Lots of smut including some spanking and choking kinks.

Self defense, accidental death and possibly even some Unaliving.

Thug's for hire, who mention rape and abuse (talk only)

Domestic violence (not between MC)

Death of a family member.

Read at your own discretion.

Your mental health matters!

"Not all girls like the hero. I was fated to fall in love with the villain. Because I know, I just know that he'll put me ahead of everyone. Himself included." - Rina Kent

"Just because he can't love you the way you want him to doesn't mean he doesn't love you with everything he has" - Anna Todd

## Prologue

*It's been said a hero would sacrifice the one he loves to save the world, whereas a villain would sacrifice the world to save the one he loves.*

*But what happens when to save the one I love, I have to sacrifice myself? What do I do when the only way to protect her, is to destroy her?*

*She crashed into my life a year ago, and like a tornado she flipped everything upside down, breaking down and destroying every wall I'd spent a lifetime building.*

*From the moment I met her, she set my world on fire. But like a phoenix rising from the ashes of my pathetic existence, my future finally looked like it could grow and evolve into something wonderful.*

*Until the day the sins, or should I say Sinners from my past, came looking for retribution. And just like that the love and happiness I finally had within my grasp was cruelly ripped away from me.*

*I was pulled back into the darkness, forced into a life of pain and suffering, a small price to pay in exchange for her life though.*

*So now here I am, alone, in pain, and soon to be hated by all those I care about. Back to playing the role of the villain in everybody else's story, the devil in disguise.*

*But what people seem to forget is, even the devil was an angel once.*

# Chapter One

# Gabe

Walking away from Riley was the hardest thing I've ever had to do, but I knew I needed to do it. As long as she's with me, she'll never be safe. Not from me, not from the Sinners, and not from the other monsters who may be lurking in the shadows.

No, I have to do this. I have to make sure she's safe. And if that means I have to break my own heart in the process, then so be it.

I hop on my bike and make my way towards work, knowing that no one else will be there at this time. Once I arrive, I park my bike around the corner, out of sight of any passersby, and slip in the side gate. I spot John's truck still sitting out front in its usual place and pray just once that he ignored my many attempts to get him to stop leaving his keys in the damn ignition. *Thankfully the stubborn old fool never learns.*

Tugging open the door, I see that god awful lucky 8-ball keyring just dangling from the ignition and shake my head, equally grateful and annoyed that his truck has been sitting in the parking lot all night, unlocked and with the keys right here, just begging to be stolen.

I make my way inside and pick up some supplies. *I need to go get John's body, I can't bear the idea of his body just left rotting, like discarded trash. Either that or for someone else to find it, and for his family to have to know what happened to him.*

Rummaging around, I try to decide what I need, still unsure if my plan is to bury the body or to move it and make it look more like an accidental death. *Perhaps I could make it look like he'd just crashed his car? Had a heart attack at the wheel or something?*

I manage to find some plastic wrap, the sort we use to cover furniture when we're working in someone's home. As well as a shovel in case this turns into a bury the body in the woods kind of deal. I then head to John's office, fill up a thermos of boiling water, grab a bucket and some bleach, as well as some old towels. Not really sure what I may need but wanting to be prepared.

As I'm about to leave, I spot some of John's old work gloves, sitting on top of his desk, as well as one of John's hoodies poking out of the drawer of clothes he keeps here for the nights he gets too drunk to go home, and an idea hits me. I remove my own jacket and throw his on, pulling the hood up to cover my hair. Next, I carefully put on his work gloves. If I'm going to make it look like he crashed alone in his car, I can't risk any of my DNA being found on the driver's side. If nothing else, TV has taught me a few tricks on how not to get caught. *I hope!*

I quickly check that the coast is clear, which given the fact that it's barely even six a.m. on a Sunday, is almost a guarantee, then jump in his car and make my way toward the barn.

As I'm driving I get an uneasy feeling in the pit of my stomach. At first, I assume it's just nerves about what I'm planning on doing, but as I get closer an unexpected feeling of sadness and loss overwhelms me. I find myself thinking back to what I felt like watching my mother die. The empty look on her face that last time I saw her laying in the hospital, the ice cold touch of her hands as my father was pulling me out of her clasp.

Next memories of John flood my mind, him sneaking a young me sweets and chocolates occasionally as he and my father would disappear on another dodgy job leaving me playing lookout in the car. Him coming around to teach me how to fix a fuse box and rewire faulty electrics after finding out I'd had no electricity for almost a week after a huge storm hit not long after I moved back. How excited but also frustrated he got teaching me to drive a car and then bike. How he'd taken me to a strip club and paid for me to get my first lap dance after finding out I had turned eighteen a few days before and hadn't told anyone.

I know he could be a little rough around the edges, and wasn't exactly what most people would describe as a good guy, but he was to me. Without him allowing me to work to pay off my father's gambling and drug debts as a child, and giving me a job when I came back, who knows where I would have been? Probably dead myself, spending eternity rotting just like my father. In some unmarked grave somewhere.

I finally turn down the road towards the barn and that uneasy feeling in my stomach morphs into full on dread. I pull up outside, take a few moments to compose my thoughts, and take some deep breaths then make my way inside.

I walk past the blood splattered floor from mine and Marko's fight, and the broken chair, still covered in the rope they'd used to restrain me, and make my way toward the tarp, mentally preparing myself to see John's cold lifeless body. But as I get closer I see it's now flat, I pull the tarp back, lifting it into the air and my suspicions are confirmed. His body has been moved.

I look around again, just in case I am confused and maybe his body was under a different tarp, but no. This is it; no other tarps in sight.

*What the fuck?!? Have Marko and the Sinners already been here? Have they already disposed of his body? Was it all a trick? An illusion? Was John in on the plan? No, surely not, he may be a twisted son of a bitch but even he wouldn't do this to me, would he?*

A familiar sound of music breaks me from my own mind, but the sound stops before I have time to register where it's coming from. *Strange!*

I look around quickly, looking for any sort of radio that could be playing music. The sound starts again, this time though, it's obvious it's a phone ringing. I reach for my own and then it dawns on me, *that's not my ringtone, it's John's.* I've heard and mocked him for that stupid Elvis Presley song more times than I can count. *Shit!*

The sound of Can't Help Falling in Love With You, John and his dead wife's wedding song, finally ends. I begin hunting for his phone and find it on top of some hay bales.

*How did it get here? The Sinners must have taken it from him. But why?*

I see that he has over ten missed calls and countless voice messages from his daughter and his latest fuck piece.

*Fuck! Fuck! Fuck! What am I going to do now? They obviously know he's missing so are probably calling the cops. Or maybe his whore will turn up at work and then everyone will know he's missing. What the fuck do I do?*

I pull out a smoke from my back pocket and light it while I try and think what to do next.

*I can't be caught up in this because what if I somehow end up getting the blame. But at the same time, where is his body?*

I decide to quickly search around the building. What if the Sinners just left him here, or buried him on the farm grounds? After all, it makes sense. It's secluded and run down, so I doubt anyone comes here often.

*But then I don't want his family to spend the next however many years thinking he's run out on them or worse, involving the police and having them poking around and uncovering lots of things we'd both rather keep buried.*

I may not have been able to do much to help him in his final moments but my plan was to ensure that in death he at least got some dignity. No one could be mad or investigate further if he'd simply died in a car crash, it would be upsetting but pretty much a simple cut and dry case. But now with no body, we're all screwed.

*Was this the Sinners' plan? To steal his body as an extra insurance policy? To ensure I stayed in line or the police would receive an anonymous tip of where to find his body and somehow it would all lead back to me?*

I light up another smoke as I try to get my head into gear. My phone buzzes and I see Riley's picture pop up and a whole new wave of guilt and pain hits me. I let it ring out, just staring at her beautiful face until it's cruelly ripped away from me and replaced with the words '1 missed call'

I look at my phone at 8:15am. *She's up unusually early. Must be for another one of her study sessions with the rest of the group. My girl is so smart, she's gonna ace her exams and then hopefully leave this godforsaken town.*

My mind drifts back to my current dilemma, if the Sinners are gonna try to incriminate me somehow, then I have to make myself look as innocent as possible. So I begin setting the scene. I collect all my discarded cigarette butts and put them in my pocket, careful not to risk leaving any DNA at the scene they can use later. I pull out my own phone, take a calming breath, and then call John.

"Hey boss, where are you?" *shit that sounds too weird, make a joke, be sarcastic.* My brain screams. "Are you fucking around, or some shit old man? Thought we were supposed to be starting work on that new place today?"

Next, I retrieve the chemicals from the back of the truck, strip down to my boxers while carefully placing both mine and John's clothes on a hay bale, and begin trying to scrub as much of the blood off the floor as possible. Once I'm content that all evidence of anything is removed I throw on both sets of clothes again, grab the tarp and chair, and sling them into the back of the truck. I also carefully pick up John's phone, again careful not to touch it with my bare hands, and wrap it in some of the plastic wrap I brought with me.

I get in the car and drive back towards work, deciding I'll find some way to dispose of all of this evidence later. But for once the gods are on my side as, in my preoccupied state, I end up taking a wrong turn, finding myself at a run down house that looks like it either needs to be demolished or made into the setting of some horror movie.

I quickly look around for cameras or people, and when it becomes very obvious this isn't the sort of place you'd find either, I grab the stuff from the back of the van. Including the spare gas cans John keeps in his trucks for emergencies and dump them in the garden, before setting them all on fire, I step on John's phone a few times, ensuring it's properly broken then throw that into the fire too.

Getting back into the truck, I drive to the shittest neighborhood I know and leave John's truck there, knowing it will be stolen or burned out within a few hours.

Once that's done I begin walking, hoping to spot a pub or something else since my nerves are shot. Eventually, I spot one and make my way inside.

"Give me a double whiskey." I snap.

I see the bartender give me a strange look as he looks at his watch, probably about to chastise me for ordering hard liquor at 9:30 a.m., but luckily he doesn't say a word and just pours me a drink.

He hands me my drink and I down the whole glass, taking pleasure in the burn I feel as it slides down my throat. "Hey you got a phone I can use?" I ask, as the guy stares at me as if I just grew a second head.

"Down there, near the toilets" the guy replies as he points, before turning away from me and busying himself again.

"Nate, I need you to come pick me up, now!" I say quickly. "I'm at a bar. If you drive towards..."

"Gabe?" Nate says through a yawn. " Where are you?"

"If you'd shut up and listen I could fucking tell you." I snap before giving him directions as best as I can. "Now get here ASAP I fucking need you, no joke. I don't care what you're doing, I don't even care if you're balls deep in little Miss Perfect, pull out and get here ASAP!" I snap.

"I'll be there ASAP," Nate says, sounding equally as panicked as me now.

I order another drink, this time taking my time a little more with it. About thirty minutes later I go back to the pub phone and call my brother again.

"Where the fuck are you Nate?" I say when he finally answers.

"I'm about ten minutes out Gabe, I've been trying to call you but your phone is off. What the heck are you doing all the way out here?"

"I'll tell you everything when you get here," I say even though I've no idea what the fuck I'm going to say because I can't exactly tell him the truth, *can I?*

I pay for my drinks, finally remove John's clothes and discard them in a goddamn garbage can in the shared bathroom. I then head out onto the street to look for Nate. Just like he said, just under ten minutes later I see his car driving towards me, I wave him down and climb inside.

"Oh my god Gabe! What the fuck happened to you?" Nate gasps as I get into the car.

"I got jumped by some punks" I lie.

"Do you wanna go to the emergency room? That looks really nasty," he says, worried and concern lacing his tone.

"Nah, it's fine; looks worse than it is." I say as I try not to whimper when I take a deep breath.

"It looks really bad, Gabe, you really should see a doctor."

"I'm not a fucking child Nate. I'm more than able to know if and when I need medical attention. I'm used to taking a beating." I snap. Feeling even worse about myself when I realize the way Nate is going to interpret that sentence.

*I can see on his face that all he's thinking about is the beating we received growing up, instead of realizing I'm referring to the fact that I've always loved the thrill of the fight to relieve some tension.*

"What the heck are you doing here?" Nate questions a little while later.

Unsure what to say, I just say the first thing that comes to my head. "I was at some girl's house."

"A girl? Riley doesn't live anywhere near here!"

"A different girl," I say absentmindedly before the realization of my words hit me. *Fuck!!*

"A different girl?" Nate snaps, his tone a mixture of confusion and anger. "What other girl?"

"You don't know her," I say, as I continue to dig myself a bigger and deeper hole.

"Just some girl, some girl I don't know?" Nate says, as his voice gets angrier. "You were just with some random girl, some girl that isn't your girlfriend?" he fumes.

"No it wasn't like that, not a girl like that. I wasn't fucking someone else." *Seriously, could I be making this any worse?*

"Really?" Nate asks dubiously. "So what the heck are you doing sneaking out of some girl's house this early on a Sunday then?"

*Fuck! I'm making a total mess of this; what the heck do I say next? I don't want him to think that I'm cheating on Riley. I don't want Riley to think that's why I left her, but at the same time, I have to say something otherwise he'll never shut up.*

"Well?" Nate snaps as we continue driving.

"Oh it was for work. John sent me to get some details for an extension she wanted to do but then he didn't show up." I reply, happy with my excuse. That is until Nate asks his next question.

"So where's your bike then? If you were meeting John here then where's your bike? You must have driven here?"

*Seriously, who is my brother? Fucking Sherlock Holmes all of a sudden? Why won't he just drop this? And why am I so bad at lying today?*

"No, erm, I came with John, we came together but he left to get some supplies and never came back."

"Oh, how strange! And he's not answering his phone?" Nate continues to question.

"Nope called him a few times and no answer"

"Strange." Nate mumbles. He reaches for his phone that's on a little stand on his dashboard. I take the time to finally take a decent breath as I look out the window. I hear the phone ringing and assume he's just calling either Princess Isabella or his lap dog, Tucker. Until I hear John's voice echo throughout the car and almost have a heart attack myself. My head flies towards the phone, and I let out a slight sigh.

"Sorry, I'm too busy either working or fucking. Call back later," John's voicemail says before it beeps for him to leave a message.

"Hey…" Nate begins but I cut him off by talking over him. Just in case the police end up listening I need to keep Nate as far away and as innocent as possible.

"John, it's me. Dunno where you are or why you didn't pick me up but call me back when you get this message"

I hit the button to hang up. "What the fuck do you think you're doing?" I snap.

"I was calling John for you" Nate replies, understandably confused.

"Well don't. I can sort my own shit thanks"

"Okay," Nate says with a scowl. "I was just trying to help."

We continue driving in silence until we get closer to home, "Take me to work," I snap, far more rudely than intended.

"Oh I thought you might wanna shower and stuff first." he questions. "No I'm late already; take me to goddam work, Nate" I huff.

I hear him mumble something along the lines of "You're always late," but I don't reply.

"Oh and don't tell anyone where you picked me up from, or why we were late" I huff as we were pulling down the street here at work.

"Whatever" Nate snaps back, clearly pissed off with me.

We both climb out of his car and make our way towards O'Malley's. Nate heads straight over to a couple of his friends and I hear him apologizing for being late, stating we had car issues, which seems a good enough excuse, and is met with "it happens" and "don't worry about it" from the other guys.

I make my way straight to my office. I finally turn my phone on, having been too scared to risk having it on since Riley called earlier just in case police somehow track it, once people realize John has gone missing.

As it loads I notice two more missed calls and a few texts from Riley. Everything in me is screaming for me to call her. My whole body is desperate for the peace and tranquility that only her presence can bring. But I resist the urge. I need to make a clean break from her. I need to keep her as far away from all my drama and the darkness my life brings. As long as she's away from me she's safe. If I try to hold on though, I'm putting her in danger.

My fears and the conviction of my decision are further confirmed when I sit down at my desk and spot a brown envelope placed on my desk. There's no name on it and no postage so it was obviously left by hand.

I open it and inside is a picture of me and Riley taken at Six Flags. *How the fuck did someone get this? Who had this? And why?* I flip the picture over and see the words,

*I hope that last goodbye was worth it because if we see you together again we'll make sure the next goodbye is permanent!!*

*Marko*! Only he would be this evil and twisted. Needing to dig that knife in one last time for his own sadistic pleasure.

Part of me wants to burn the picture, burn his threat. But as I look at the picture again, I realize this is the last picture I have where we were truly happy. Probably the only picture I will ever have where I'm happy again.

So instead I take it inside and place it in my top drawer, ready to take home with me to sit beside my bed. If I can't ever hold her again, at least she'll get to be my last sight every night.

I head out and begin barking random orders at the guys, telling them to speed up, complaining about the quality of their flawless work, and just generally being an ass, but ensuring I have an alibi and lots of witnesses in case the police come calling.

Next, I head to the hardware store and do the same there, pick an argument with the guy working, complaining they don't have the supplies I didn't order, again making sure I'm seen on camera and remembered to further lay my alibi that I've been at work all day.

Once it reaches 4 p.m. and I've finally managed to piss everyone off, I make my excuses to leave.

"I'm going, I can't be around you useless pricks any longer. I suggest all this is fixed by the time I get back tomorrow" I snap as I make my way toward the exit.

"Wait Gabe," Nate says, calling after me. " You came in with me, let me drive you home."

"I'm going to the pub, I need to unwind." I snap back, not even turning to look at him as I continue walking away.

I head to Saints, ready to drown myself in alcohol, while I wait for everyone else at work to leave so I can sneak back and retrieve my bike from where I stashed it earlier.

# Chapter Two

# Riley

Earlier that morning.

I wake up to the infuriating sound of my alarm. I roll over to turn it off before scooting backward, hoping for a few more minutes nestled in Gabe's arms before I have to get up. Even after scooting my ass back further, I don't reach him. "Gaaabe," I whine, before rolling over. I expect to see him, either sitting up drinking his coffee as usual, or perhaps moving away purposefully just to annoy me, but I'm surprised and disappointed to realize I'm completely alone. *Oh, that sucks. Where is he?* Sitting up with a disappointed scowl I look around the room. I reach for my phone ready to text him and let him know he's in trouble, when I see a message from my sister.

Twinnie

> Really? Guys in our room? I'm sleeping at Izzy's!

I can't help but smirk as I imagine how furious Harper would have been to find us both in bed together. Especially since we share said room. *Oops! Sorry, not sorry!*

*I bet that's why Gabe left. He's such a light sleeper; I bet he woke up when she got home and then left, not wanting to either face her wrath or end up bumping into my parents over breakfast.*

I fire off a quick text.

> Me
> Can't believe you left without saying goodbye. No more sexy time for you today… and I had some great ideas planned. Your loss! Call me when you finish work.

And then I drag myself into the shower. I wash my hair and am just finishing getting dressed when Harper walks through the door.

"Oh, you're awake? Good," Harper says, still clearly annoyed. "And is our new roommate gone now?" She snaps.

"Yes," I groan. "You probably scared him off last night; he was gone by the time I woke up."

"Good." Harper huffs back. "No more late night booty calls, please. Or if you're gonna, at least give me some warning so I don't walk in on anything. I'm just grateful you were both asleep and not otherwise occupied when I got home," Harper says as she shudders.

Deciding now isn't the time to joke about liking the idea of people watching, I keep my mouth shut and continue getting ready.

I check my phone as I'm putting on my makeup, expecting to find a few messages from Gabe. It's about the time he normally would be getting up and ready for work. But nothing.

I finish putting on my make up then head upstairs to make myself a coffee while Harper finishes getting ready. While I'm waiting, I attempt to call Gabe but it just rings and rings. I try again and this time it goes straight to voicemail. *How odd!*

"Are you ready to go?" Harper calls as she makes her way into the kitchen.

"Yup, even had time to make us both coffee," I say as I hand her the little purple travel mug and grab myself the matching red one.

Our grandparents thought it would be funny to buy us matching R and H mugs last year for Christmas. As if we had somehow forgotten we were identical twins.

"Okay so perhaps this makes me a little less mad at you," Harper says as she takes a sip and lets out a satisfied little moan.

"See, I'm a pain in the ass, but I have my uses." I say with a little 'I know you really love me' smirk.

We make our way to Izzy's ready to study and by the time we arrive, Ava is already there armed with energy drinks, candy, and cakes.

"Didn't realize we were planning on camping out all week," I laugh.

"Brain food," Ava says as she taps her head. "Ouch!" she grumbles as she pokes herself in the temple with the wrong end of her pencil.

"Seems like you need to eat more since you clearly left your brain under your pillow this morning."

"Fuck you," she grumbles, while doing exactly what I just said and shoving a piece of brownie into her mouth.

Harper pulls out her study cards and for the next few hours we all study and quiz each other.

A knock at the door finally distracts us as Nana walks in with a plate full of sandwiches. "Thought you girls might be hungry. But it seems like you've been having a little feast up here." Izzy's nana laughs, as she takes in the wrappers and empty boxes sprawled all around us.

"Thanks Mrs. Williams," Harper says politely. "We could do with something substantial rather than just sugar."

"Hey, sugar is good," Ava groans, as she continues to eat her store bought cupcake.

"Is that as good as mine?" Nana asks cheekily.

"Nothing is as good as your baking, Nana," Ava says with a wide smile.

"She's not actually YOUR Nana" I whisper to Ava.

"She's everyone's Nana; ain't that right, Nana?" Ava proclaims loudly.

"Yes dear," Nana says with a proud smile. "I've told you all, you don't have to call me Mrs. Williams. That makes me feel old, Nana will do."

"You are old Nana" Ava teases.

"Oh really? Ava-quaver? I'll remember that next time I'm making my famous cheesecake and don't save you a slice."

"And by old, I mean, not a day over twenty-one." Ava says with an exaggerated grin.

"That's what I thought," Nana says with a smirk before leaving.

"Ava-quaver?" I question once she's finally gone and I can let out my giggle.

"Yeah, Ava was around a couple of weeks ago and Nana was telling me off for throwing a pair of red socks in with her whites, and accidentally dying some of them pink. Anyway, she fully named me. I got the full on Isabella, which I never get unless I'm in trouble. Ava laughed so Nana tried to tell her off and realized that since Ava is literally 3 letters it does not hold the same weight, so Nana decided Ava-quaver was her new, bad girl name."

"Yup... Ava-quaver strikes fear into all those who hear it, right?" Ava laughs.

"Not exactly," I reply with a chuckle.

"Do you not have a middle name or anything?" Harper quizzes and it makes me realize we've been friends for years but never thought to ask.

"Nope, literally just 3 letters." Ava shrugs.

We go back to studying for a few more hours before every one of us has a brain ache and has to stop for the night. "We're gonna head off," Harper yawns.

"See you tomorrow girls," I say as I reach for my bag and phone and head downstairs.

As soon as we get outside I switch my phone on again,

since the girls demanded I switched it off earlier after catching me texting for the third time. When I do though I'm disappointed to realize I still haven't had a reply from Gabe. I call him thinking perhaps he's run out of minutes, but the phone goes straight to voicemail. *Strange! He's usually pretty quick to text back.*

The car pulls into the driveway and I realize I've spent the entire journey thinking about Gabe. *Why hasn't he contacted me today?* I walk through the door, grab myself a soda, and head downstairs to get my pajamas on. I try one last time to call and text him before I decide enough is enough and just go to bed instead.

# Chapter Three

# Gabe

I make my way inside and order a whiskey. "You look like fucking shit," Declan jokes as he brings me my drink but the look I fire back lets him know to leave me the fuck alone as I'm in no mood to banter and joke with him. Not today.

"Anything I can get you? An ice pack? Some painkillers?" Declan questions with concern in his voice.

"You can do your mother fucking job and get me a drink." I snap back in response

I'm on my fourth whiskey when I spot Marko and the rest of the Sinners walking in. I'm up out of my chair and making my way toward them before my mind even has a chance to consider what I'm doing.

"What the fuck did you do with the body?" I snap.

I see a couple of the guys' eyes widen as they look at me with a mixture of fear, confusion, anger, and shame splashed over their faces. Marko, on the other hand, his face is completely void of emotion. "You look a little rough there Gabe, bad night?"

"Where is the fucking body Marko?" I say through gritted teeth.

"And whose body are we talking about?" Marko says with a sadistic smile.

"You know exactly whose body I'm talking about." I step closer, getting into Marko's face, and see the way the rest of his gang of misfits step in closer, ready to throw hands and protect their goddam leader.

"Hmm, maybe you need to refresh my memory. Do you mean John's or that of your little whore?"

My mind fills with panic for a moment. Panic that must be evident on my face as I see another sadistic smile, this one wider than the last, form on Marko's face.

*She's alive. She's been blowing up your phone all day.* My mind thankfully reminds me.

"Go get the drinks, slave, and maybe I'll tell you," Marko says, loving every single moment of his newfound power. Everything in me is begging for me to beat his ass. *Heck, the way I feel right now I could happily murder him.* But knowing that I have to control myself, be smart, and bide my time, I keep my mouth shut and turn back towards the bar.

"Fuck, he didn't even argue," I hear Deeno say in disbelief.

"Got the cunt right where I want him," Marko says proudly.

*You keep thinking that asshole. I'll get my revenge, don't you worry! And I'll take great pleasure in watching each and every one of you get what's coming to you.*

I head to the bar, order everyone's usual drinks, and then instruct Declan to put them all on my tab.

"So who's drink am I poisoning today?" Declan laughs.

I want to smile, knowing full well he's not joking. He's added laxatives to their drinks a few times. Heck, once he even spat in one and we both looked on with an internal grin as they drank the whole thing up.

"No one. Just pour the drinks and shut the fuck up," I reply sharply.

"Fuck dude, keep talking to me like that and maybe I'll poison yours instead," he huffs.

I make my way to the bathroom, feeling kind of guilty. Declan is a good guy. He's been sort of a friend to me the last few years; he doesn't deserve the shit I'm gonna have to put him through. But like everyone else I care for, I'm gonna have to keep him at arm's length to keep him safe. Any weakness the Sinners find, they will manipulate, and I refuse to stand back and allow anyone else to become collateral damage in the war between me and Marko.

When I return the drinks are all on a tray waiting for me at the bar. "I poured you a glass of a new whiskey, just got it shipped over from Ireland, think you'll enjoy it," Declan says with a kind smile.

I take a sip and he's right, it tastes great - has a hint of sweetness, *perhaps honey?* Declan stares at me expectantly and despite the fact I want to praise him for his choice, especially since I know he doesn't even drink whiskey, I just give him a shrug, "It's okay I guess." I see his face drop slightly, but I just grab the tray and take it outside.

For the next half hour, I slowly sip my sweet drink, one that gets better and better with every taste, as I pretend that I'm interested in whatever they're saying. But in reality, I'm fantasizing about all the ways I'd like to torture each and every one of these assholes.

Contrary to what I know people probably say about me, I've never been one who gets pleasure out of hurting and harming others. Sure, fighting fist on fist with someone can sometimes be calming, and yeah I'm no stranger to that, but unlike these assholes, I don't get sadistic pleasure from hurting and often leaving people damaged beyond repair. Violence has always been purely a means to an end for me. One that is often unavoidable. But I've never intentionally taken anyone's life or left someone bleeding out in a gutter, straddling the line between life and death. It's why I refuse to carry a weapon. But for these cunt's, I would be willing to make an exception. Nothing would please me more than standing over Marko's body while I watch the life drain from it.

Declan comes over to take our order again, and the sound of his voice breaks me from my devious thoughts. I clear my throat trying to get his attention but he doesn't even look at me. When he comes out a few moments later I take my drink and realize instead of the sweet honey flavored delight I was previously enjoying, it's some shitty, cheap, and nasty blend that tastes more like floor cleaner. I look up at Declan and am met with the fakest smile I've ever seen as he politely asks, "Nice?"

I lean back in my chair and tip my glass into a nearby plant pot. "I'll take a beer instead," I grumble at Declan.

"Coming right up," he replies with that fake smile again. I hear him chuckling under his breath as he walks away.

My shitty beer is almost empty when I spot Deeno heading to the bathroom. I give it a few seconds then head in after him. Knowing that of them all. Deeno will be the easiest to scare.

Deeno is just exiting the stall as I make my way inside, his eyes widen when he sees me enter and he takes a step backward. I don't say a word, instead I turn and lock the door behind me. The sound of the lock clicking echoes in the silence. When I turn back, Deeno is looking at me like the terrified little kid he is. *I almost feel guilty, almost!*

"Erm.. Gabe .. err," he stutters while looking like he's about to piss his pants at any moment.

"I think you and I need a little chat." I say menacingly as I close the gap between us

"I was just following orders… I didn't know what they were gonna do… I, uh, I thought we were just gonna scare you a little, pull you back into the fold." He stammers, clearly unable to decide what it is he wants to say.

"And the girl? Where does she fit into all this?" I snarl as I lunge forward and grab him by the throat.

"She…she…she . . ." Deeno says through gasped breaths.

I release my grasp but continue to stand in his space, pinning him against the wall and glaring at him menacingly.

"She what?"

"How did you know it was me?" he asks slowly.

"I fucking heard you." I sneer right into his face.

"Oh," he mumbles. "She wasn't supposed to get hurt…Marko promised we were just gonna scare her…scare her to scare you.

That's all, I promise. I stopped it when it got out of hand though, I made Logan drop the knife."

*Logan, So that's who had the knife? Good to know!* That's now two names added to my mental hit list.

"I know, and that's the only reason you're not gasping for your last breath right about now, because if you had hurt her, not even the devil himself would have been able to save you from my wrath. You got that?" I say as I give the side of his face two small slaps.

"Ye...yes Gabe. Can I... Can I go now?" he whimpers.

"For now. But tell anyone about our conversation and the next time I see you, I won't be so forgiving." I say as I take a step back.

Deeno scurries towards the door but just as he's about to unlock it I speak again. "Oh and Deeno, from now on you're MY eyes and ears. I wanna know EVERYTHING they do and say. You got it kiddo?"

"Y..yes!" he replies, fear lacing his voice, as he bolts out the door.

I make my way to the bar to order a real drink, "I'll take a whiskey, a decent one this time."

"Sorry, decent whiskey is reserved for decent guys," Declan replies. Before turning his back on me. *Damn, he's really fucking pissed off. Let's just add it to a long list of people who either hate me or are about to.*

I accept the shitty drink Declan shoves in front of me, then make my way back outside to the Sinners.

"So what did you do with John's body? Police are gonna come looking soon." I try asking again. I see a few confused faces around the group as they all look towards Marko. *So they obvious-*

*ly weren't included in whatever cover up Marko planned. I don't know if that's a good or bad thing...*

"None of your fucking business! That's for me to know, and you to find out," Marko sneers.

"I'm out of here," I grumble, realizing I'm never going to get a straight answer, not while Marko is around. I lean forward to place my glass on the table and attempt to stand but Marko stands quicker.

"You'll sit your ass down until I tell you that you are allowed to leave. You'll do as you're told and play the little bitch boy you now are. I own you and unless you want me to bury another body right beside John, you will do as I say!" Marko threatens.

Despite the anger forming in my whole body, I know this is anything but an idle threat, so I sit my ass back down. Knowing the only way to keep those I love safe is by playing my part, luring Marko into a false sense of security. *I'll make him think he has me where he wants me and then strike when he least expects it.*

I sit there, still nursing the same drink for another hour before the guys start leaving one by one. Until it's just me, Marko, and Phoenix left.

"You can fuck off now!" Phoenix smirks as he waves his hand, shooing me away. "The big boys wanna talk, run along minion," Marko adds with a smirk.

I leave like a dog with its tail between his legs, but as I'm walking out the door Declan calls my name. I turn around and make my way over to him, silently grateful he's finally talking to me and desperate for just an ounce of friendship right now. But like the cruel bitch life is, instead of friendship he hands me a piece of paper.

"What's this?" I ask as I open it.

"Your bill," Declan says nonchalantly.

I look at it and realize it's close to $400. "What is this? The drinks in no way added up to that." I say as I screw up my face in confusion.

"It's your tab. I want it paid in full before you leave." Declan says, sounding far more authoritative than usual. *Where's my playful friend gone?*

I reach into my wallet and realize I only have about $150 in cash, and I rarely add money to my bank account, not really trusting the government with my money. "I'll drop it around another day," I say, before turning to leave.

"No, I said I want it paid before you leave. Which part of your dumb brain didn't understand that?" Declan snaps.

"Seriously? I've had a tab here for years. You know that I have the money, you know I do. I'll pay it tomorrow, I can drop the money off first thing." I reply, perplexed by the sudden icyness radiating off him.

"Tabs are for friends, and if you're a Sinner now, a true Sinner, you're anything but a friend. So pay the fuck up now!" Declan demands, his tone as sharp as a knife.

"I. Don't. Have. It!" I snarl as I empty my pockets proving all I have is my keys and some gum before opening my wallet as proof that all I have is a few bills inside.

"You can have these back when you pay your tab," he says as he swipes my bike keys off the bar.

"Fucking really Dec? You're gonna hold my baby hostage over a goddamn $400 tab?" I say with a frown.

"You fuck with my baby," he says motioning around to his family's bar, "and I fuck with yours."

"Fuck this!" I shout out and I spin on my feet to leave this fucking place.

I walk outside, my head pounding. *How did this become my life? Just as I was starting to feel comfortable in my own skin... just as I was starting to experience happiness.* I stop my train of thought. This isn't helping me. I look around and luckily see the familiar banner of a taxi on the horizon. I walk to the road and manage to hail it. When I get home, I find the door locked and Nate nowhere to be found. *For fuck sake!!* I make a makeshift bed on the deck chair in the garden and fall asleep.

# Chapter Four

## Nate

I leave Bella's house and drive home after what can only be described as the most uncomfortable night of my life. I went to see Bella after work hoping to blow off some steam after putting up with Gabe's attitude all day, but when I got there, she was with Riley, Ava, and Harper.

I could barely look Riley in the face when she asked me if I'd seen Gabe today, especially after Ava informed me that he'd basically abandoned her in the middle of the night. I pray that what Gabe said about John calling him for an emergency job was the truth because if I find out that he left Riley to go sleep with another girl I will be so pissed at him. To add insult to injury I know Riley's been trying to call him all day, and he's been ignoring her, which pushes me more towards believing he was lying earlier. *Add that to the fact he's been in a vile mood all day. It just screams guilty conscience!*

I pull up outside my house and am just walking towards the door when I spot Gabe asleep in the garden. My first thought is to wake him and tell him to go to bed inside, but he probably got drunk and passed out, so maybe he deserves to spend the night out here. Rolling my eyes at him, I walk straight past where he's sleeping, not so quietly, and go into the house. I consider locking the door behind me to really teach him a lesson, but I'm not that cruel, so I leave it unlocked so he can come in and go to bed when he does finally wake up.

When I leave for my 6 a.m. run, I find him still in the same spot in the garden. "Gabe, wake up," I say as I shake him. "Either go to bed or get up for work," I add as I shake him again.

"What? Where? What?" Gabe mumbles as he rubs his eyes.

"You passed out in the garden Gabe. Come inside, you must be freezing," I say, feeling like the worst brother ever for intentionally leaving him outside to freeze, purely because I was frustrated and disappointed in him.

"Shit." Gabe mumbles as he stands, stretching out his probably achy limbs.

"Are you going into work today?" I question.

"What time is it? What day is it?" he groans.

"It's quarter past six, and it's Monday." I laugh while shaking my head. *Seriously, how much did he drink last night?*

"Err yeah, let me go get in the shower," he says wearily as he awkwardly walks back inside, even though it's clear his legs are still half asleep.

I head off on my run, doing my usual lap and when I return an hour later, Gabe is dressed but still looks as half dead as he did when I woke him. *He's never been the most conscious of his looks. He's definitely not a pretty boy by any stretch of the imagination and the messy rogue look works for him. But right now he's looking even less lovable, more rough, and is bordering on owning the homeless bum look.*

"Are you okay Gabe?" I ask, a hint of concern lacing my voice. "We've got plenty of time if you want to brush your hair, or wash your face or something."

"I'm fine. Are we leaving or what?" he snaps. *Seriously, what's eating him now?*

"Dude, let me just shower first. I'll be ready in about thirty minutes. Unless you wanna take your bike and I'll meet you at work." I offer.

"Ain't got my bike." Gabe mumbles.

"What? Where is it then? Has it been stolen? Have you reported it?" I ask as I fire question after question at him. *He loves that bike. Is that why he's been in such a vile mood all weekend?*

"Nah, I just.. Erm.. misplaced the keys, but I've got the spare ones. I just need to go grab it from work," he replies.

*He's clearly hiding something.* I always know when he's lying because he twitches his nose, something he has done since we were kids. But it's clear whatever he's hiding, he's in no mood to share so I just nod along and make my way towards the bathroom.

Twenty minutes later, I'm showered, dressed, and ready for work. "You ready Gabe?" I call out as I leave my room. But I don't get a response. "Gabe?" I call out again as I make my way through the house and out towards the garden.

"Really?" I question when I spot him sitting in his chair in the garden, beer bottle in hand. *He promised at our last therapy session that he was gonna cut down on the day drinking and look into his alcohol dependency.*

"Shut the fuck up and drive," Gabe growls as he walks towards my ride.

The whole journey is done in silence. I don't really know what I've done to Gabe, apart from perhaps leaving him outside, but he's acting like a complete dick today, even more so than usual.

"Are you not coming inside?" I ask as we exit the car and I make my way inside and he walks in the opposite direction.

"Nah, got shit to do," I hear him respond, as he continues to walk away from me.

*What a dickhead! I agreed to work today to help him since I have a free study day and this is how the asshole repays me. By dumping me here to do his work while he fucks off doing god knows what?*

I make my way inside, stopping only briefly to talk to Davis and then I start on the work, since I already know today is going to be chaotic.

Two hours later we're absolutely swamped. There are only about five of us here but we're trying to do the job of at least eight guys. "You think your friend would wanna pull an extra shift?" Davis pants, as he throws down another sack of cement at my feet.

"I could ask him, I guess." I reply pulling out my phone.

"Hey Tuck, wanna earn some cash? I'm totally using the best friend card here. Get your ass down here please, we need you. I'll owe you big time," I say, laying it on thick.

"Course dude, what do ya need? Where are you?" Tucker asks.

"Any chance you could come to O'Malley's and pull an extra shift?" Tucker lets out a little undecided grumble, so I add, "Please, I know you only work weekends usually, but Gabe roped me into helping him today, and then the bastard fucked off and left me."

"What a dick! What did John say? Is he okay with me coming in?"

"Erm," I say as I put him on a loudspeaker.

"Will John be okay with this?" I whisper to Davis.

"Hey Tucker, it's Davis. Look, John's been AWOL since yesterday and isn't answering his phone. But I know he'd rather have extra bodies in and work out the payment later than have us struggling or not completing jobs over a couple of hours of wages. I'm happy to take the blame if he says anything, but I know he won't. Just come in and we'll sort the rest out later."

"Oh okay, I can be there in an hour if that works?" Tucker asks.

"Sure, an hour is fine. Swing by Maccies on the way and grab us a few burgers as well. I'll place the order and pay now. You will just have to pick 'em up." Davis says before handing the phone back to me.

"You got it." Tucker chuckles.

"Thanks Tuck, you really are a lifesaver," I say before hanging up.

# GABE

## 3 HOURS EARLIER

I head towards the shower, hoping to wash the last 24 hours off my skin, desperately praying it was all a bad dream but knowing it wasn't.

I stand, allowing the hot water to cascade over my body, taking some twisted delight in the feeling of the pain and burn as the water hits against all my cuts and bruises. At least this way I get to replace some of the unbearable, internal pain I'm suffering with actual physical pain. Physical pain I can handle, heck, I've become a master at managing physical pain. The clearly broken ribs I have is nothing compared to the pain I feel in my chest. Emotional pain. That type of pain I'm completely ill equipped to handle. So instead I focus on the physical.

I climb out and wrap a towel around myself. As I walk into my room I catch sight of my reflection in the cracked mirror. I cringe seeing that I have a split lip, swollen and bruised eye, and bruises all up my sides and back. *I look like a complete mess!*

I contemplate throwing on my jeans and jacket like usual, but just can't be bothered so instead I throw on some old joggers and a hoodie that I find sprawled over the end of my bed. *Fuck it, this will do.*

I bend down, trying not to wince, and retrieve my phone from my jeans pocket. But it's dead. *Of course it is!* I plug it into the charger beside my bed, then carefully lift my mattress and retrieve the stash of cash I keep under there for emergencies. I grab the $400 I need to get my bike back from Declan, throw it into my wallet, and then stash the rest back where I got it from.

Next, I head out and am rummaging through the kitchen drawers for an envelope when Nate gets home. "Are you okay, Gabe?"

he asks as he eyes me up and down. "We've got plenty of time if you want to brush your hair, or wash your face or something."

*Oh fuck off. Yes I know I look like shit, Mr. Perfect. No need to make me feel shittier than I already do, though.*

"I'm fine, are we leaving or what?" I snap, wanting to head out, grab my bike, and disappear as quickly as possible.

Nate tells me he needs to get ready and that he won't be long, even suggesting I make my way there myself. "Ain't got my bike." I reply as I feel the frustration building. Nate replies by bombarding me with questions about whether or not it was stolen, but I'm in no mood to explain.

Once he leaves, I carefully slide the money into an envelope, grab a beer, and make my way outside to wait for Nate to be ready to leave. As soon as he comes out he takes one look at my bottle and gives me a disappointed look, "Really?" he says in that condescending tone of his.

*Yep, that's me Nate, your loser brother. It surprises me that I still surprise you by disappointing you. I wonder when that will stop and you won't expect more of me. God knows I'm just a loser, always disappointing people. Look, I had to break Riley's heart because of how toxic I am. Bad shit is my shadow. Nothing good survives around me.*

I am drawn out of my thoughts only to endure more of Nate's disappointment and commentary about my day drinking.

*Yeah Mr. High and Mighty, if you were dealing with half the shit I was, you'd need a goddamn beer too. It's easy looking down on me when your standing on a mother fucking pedestal!*

I let out an agitated sigh and turn my back on him. I make my way to his car, continuing to drink the last of my bottle as I walk.

When I get to his car, I turn around and down the last bit. Just as I see him opening up his mouth to say more shit to me, I force out the loudest, longest belch I can. Then I turn around, open the door, and sit in the car. I don't even look at him when he gets into the vehicle.

The whole journey I can feel the waves of disappointment radiating off him as he looks at me out of the corner of his eye and grips his steering wheel tighter. By the time we arrive at work, I'm about ready to kick his ass, yet I'm trying so hard to keep my mouth shut and not say anything. *I've already lost Riley, John is dead, Declan fucking hates me, and he's the last person I have left.*

As we pull up I see Davis making his way over, and not having the social battery to deal with yet another asshole who thinks the world is all sunshine and motherfucking rainbows, talking about how god all mighty blessed him with his precious daughter, I turn and walk in the opposite direction. *What's so great about babies anyway? All they do is cry and shit all day.*

"Are you not coming inside?" Nate questions as he lets out a frustrated huff.

"Nah, got shit to do," I snap back as I walked away, desperately willing myself not to verbally attack him.

I hear him muttering something under his breath but continue walking away. I make my way over to Saints and bang on the door. "What?" Declan shouts out of what I assume is his bedroom window above the bar.

"I got your money," I shout up at him.

"Give me five," he says before slamming the window closed again.

A few minutes later the bar door flies open and I see Declan standing in just a pair of superhero pajama bottoms, "Hey man, can I come in?" I say as I attempt to walk in but Declan holds the door blocking my entrance.

"Depends?" he snaps. "Are you back to your senses or are you still part of that band of fuckwits?"

"Let me in and I'll explain, you see…" I begin but Declan cuts me off.

"Simple question Gabe."

"It's not that simple…" I begin but again he talks over me.

"I've got my answer!" he snaps before trying to close the door in my face, but I put my foot in the doorway stopping him.

"So what? I'm no longer welcome here? Is that it?" I snap, feeling the anger and frustration that I've been desperately trying to hold in, bubbling up.

"During working hours I have no goddamn choice but to let you in, do I? Your new besties made sure of that! Until my father's debts are paid off, his legacy is nothing but a home base for those fuckers. But mark my words Gabe, everything else, the middle of the night visits, the free drinks, tabs, heck even the letting you crash on my sofa, that all ends here!" Declan's nostrils flare as he speaks. *He's absolutely fuming.*

"I have your money. Here," I say, taking a step back so I can get the envelope out of my pocket, hoping that will in some way pacify him.

Declan snatches the envelope out of my hand without a word then slams the door in my face.

"My bike keys!" I scream as I bang on the door. A couple of seconds later the door flies open again. I hold out my hand, ready for him to hand me my keys. But the bastard looks me square in the eyes, drops the keys right past my hand, and lets them land at my feet, before slamming the door again.

"You fucking asshole, go screw yourself you jumped up little shit. Just you wait!" I scream as I punch and kick at the door. After a few minutes of unleashing my frustration on the sturdy door that refuses to budge, I bend down, retrieve my keys then walk away.

I walk towards where I stashed my bike, mentally reliving the argument in my mind, thinking of all the nasty and vile things I could have said to him. I reach my bike, hop on, and drive home. As soon as I get home, I grab a whole pack of beer out of the fridge and head to my bedroom. Opening and downing the first one, still reliving my fight with Declan. The look of hatred, anger, and disappointment on his face. *Fucking asshole, who the fuck does he think he is?*

I grab a second beer, then rummage around in the back of my drawer, grateful when I find an old pot of weed and roll myself a joint. Desperately needing something more than beer to take the edge off.

# Chapter Five

# Riley

Harper wakes me up, not so nicely, and demands that I get up and ready so we can head into town to grab coffee with the girls before making our way to the library for Study Hall.

A few hours later, while Izzy and Harper are quizzing each other on geography, I pull out my phone yet again. *Still nothing. It's been two days and I've not heard a word from Gabe.*

I know we don't meet up much during the week, what with me studying for my finals, and him working all the time. Plus, I can tell Gabe is still a little hesitant to be my 'boyfriend' in public, especially here in town. But we never go this long without talking. Even if it's just a flirty text here or there we talk every day.

I fire off yet another text message.

Me

> Hey Gabe, are you mad at me for something? I miss speaking to you. Is everything okay? Maybe we could meet up later, go for a drive or something?

"Earth to Riley," brings me out of my thoughts just seconds before a chip hits me in the chest.

"Really? Was that necessary?" I laugh as I remove the chip now making its way down my cleavage.

"You were ignoring me, you rude bitch," Ava whines as she continues to eat her chips.

"Sorry, I was just thinking I've not heard from Gabe in like two days. I hope everything is okay."

"He's a big boy; he'll be fine." Ava shrugs, but something in my gut tells me that I should be worried.

"Hey Izzy, have you spoken to Nate today?"

"Not as much as usual." Izzy shrugs. "Nate has been rushed off his feet. Gabe didn't show up for work today so he ended up having to drag Tucker in to help him finish some big job."

"Gabe just didn't turn up for work? That's odd right?" I question, as that little knot in my stomach gets bigger. *What's going on? This is not the Gabe I know. He's always responsible when it comes to work. I know something is going on, but what could it be?*

"I guess, sometimes Gabe does just ditch work, but usually he lets Nate know beforehand. But this time Nate has no idea where he is." Izzy admits, her face mirroring concern and realization that something isn't quite right now that she's saying the words out loud and piecing the puzzle together.

"Any chance you could call Nate? See if he's heard from him?" I ask. *Although beg is probably a better description since even I can hear the desperation in my own voice.*

"'Course." Izzy says before making her way out of the library to call.

Izzy returns around ten minutes later and informs us all that Gabe is basically MIA. Nate has texted him a bunch of times, I've texted him a bunch of times, but nobody has seen or heard from him.

"Something really isn't right. I'm gonna go see if I can find him." I say as I stand to leave.

"Wait," Harper says as she grabs my arm. "One more hour, let us just finish this subject and we'll all come with you, right girls?"

"Of course." Izzy says, Ava nods in agreement.

I send one more message letting Gabe know I'm worried and then go back to studying, even though my mind isn't really in it.

True to their word, an hour later we're all in Ava's car driving towards O'Malley's ready to go and speak to Nate directly.

# Gabe

By the time I finally wake up, it's almost mid afternoon. I reach for my phone, turn it on, and find it bombarded with calls and texts from today and yesterday.

Yesterday

8:20

Smoking Hot Cock Tease

> Can't believe you left without saying goodbye. No more sexy time for you today... and I had some great ideas planned. Your loss! Call me when you finish work.

9:00

Smoking Hot Cock Tease

> Hey babe, tried calling you but can't get through. Where are you? I was really sad when I woke and realized you'd left. Never mind, I get it I guess. You probably didn't wanna risk running into the family haha.

9:45

Nate

> Gabe, where are you? I've called you twice but your phone is going to voicemail.

9:50

Nate

> I think I'm lost. I followed the ping you sent, but this is a really shitty ass neighborhood, call me back.

10:15

Smoking Hot Cock Tease

> Me, and the rest of the girls are all having a study session at Izzy's. Gotta pass this biology exam so I'm turning my phone off.

> We all are, so we're not distracted by Insta or TikTok haha.

16:30

*Smoking Hot Cock Tease*

> Hey, I've finished with the girls now. I'm a bit sad you haven't replied. I was hoping to have some sexy 'lil messages to brighten my day, but oh well. Call or text me when you can.

A smile forms on my face as I imagine the stubborn little pout on my little Spitfire's face as she sent that message.

I continue scrolling through and spot another message from my girl.

21:00

*Smoking Hot Cock Tease*

> Okay, now I'm seriously pissed, you've ignored me all day. I had to ask Nate about you like some needy little bitch, and he told me you weren't feeling well. I guess I understand, but still, you've not had two seconds to send a little message just to let me know you're alive? That's pretty shitty Gabe. That's not what boyfriends do.

*Boyfriend! That word has so much power and importance in nine little letters.* My heart hurts even more at the thought that I'd finally overcome all my fears. Finally tore my walls down and stepped up enough to feel worthy of those nine letters only to have it all come crashing down at my feet. All because of my own stupidity and one power hungry son of a bitch.

Reaching over I light another joint and smoke it in bed while I wallow in my own self-pity. As if the pain I'm already feeling isn't bad enough, I decide to torture myself a little more by reading the rest of my messages, the ones from today.

8:00

Smoking Hot Cock Tease

> Morning Hot Stuff! You pulled your head out of your ass yet? Hopefully you're ready to actually talk to your girlfriend today? I expect flowers, chocolates, or orgasms as an apology!

My mouth forms into a smirk, and my dick stirs as I imagine fucking that attitude and brattish behavior right out of her. But like an arrow straight to my dick I feel nothing but pain as I'm reminded I will never again get to experience that sassy mouth first hand.

8:30

Nate

> Where the fuck did you go? John hasn't turned up for work either. We could really do with some help, call me when you get this.

9:00

Nate

> Seriously Gabe, we are drowning. Jack has called in sick, Scott is away on vacation and it's pretty much just me, Davis, and a couple of the others trying to hold down

the fort. I dunno what's up with you today but get your ass to work. Please!

9:30

Nate

Still can't get hold of John but I managed to get Tucker to join me. So wherever you are, don't worry about rushing in. But if you want to, we'd be really grateful for the extra hand. Either way, you owe us one.

11:15

Smoking Hot Cocktease

Just spoke to Izzy. Nate says you haven't turned up for work, is everything okay? Call me please.

12:30

Smoking Hot Cocktease

Okay, I've tried calling you and so has Nate; we're all really worried. What's up? Is this because of your nightmare? I vaguely remember you having one. Or have I done something to piss you off? Either way, the silent treatment is ridiculous! Talk to me please. I'm here for you always.

12:50

Nate

Gabe, call me back please. I dunno where you are or what you're doing but Riley is

> freaking out and I'll be honest, so am I. Call me.

13:15

Nate

> We are swamped at work but Izzy and Riley are going to see if you're at home. I don't care if you don't like it; they're on their way now.

*Fuck!* I look at my watch; it's close to 2pm, and girls will be here any second since it's around an hour's drive. I throw on the discarded joggers and a shirt sneak out my bedroom window, and run through the woods. I know Izzy sort of knows the area but she's still pretty unsure so I should be able to make it through the trees without her spotting me, since she tends to stick to the open paths, even though it takes longer to get from her cabin to ours. I've barely made it in twenty steps when the sound of a car breaks the silence around me. I duck down and hide in the nearby woodland knowing that if I try to make it to where I parked my bike they'll hear its engine roaring to life.

I hear the sound of talking as what sounds like the whole group descends out of the car.

"Gabe? Gabe?" I hear the sound of loud knocking echoing through the air.

I feel my phone vibrating in my pocket so I quickly hit the silence button and stare at the face of an angel as my girl's beautiful face lights up my screen.

I can hear talking and multiple voices but I'm too far away to hear what's actually being said. I stay hidden like the mother fucking coward I am until I hear the sound of an engine revving before driving off into the distance.

Once I'm sure they've gone, I exit my hiding space and walk back to the house, climbing back through the same window to my bedroom.

I sneak through the house, just in case the girls come back, grab myself a beer, and then head back to my bedroom. I'm just rolling up the last of my weed when my phone rings again. Everything in me is fighting, my head desperately wanting me to ignore it, pushing her away like I know I need to. But my heart desperately wants to hear her voice even if only one more time. The ringing ends and seconds later another text pings through letting me know I have a new voice message.

Smoking Hot Cock Tease

> Where are you Gabe? I'm really worried, we all are. Nate has no idea where you are; I have no fucking idea where you are, please if I've done something I apologize. If you don't want to talk to me that's fine but at least text one of us to let us know you're safe.

My whole body aches for her. Finally, I've found a girl who seems to truly care about me, worries about my safety, and goes out of her way to come find me. Yet it's all too late. Fate is a cruel mistress who wants nothing more than to watch me suffer.

I light my joint, enjoying the feeling of some much needed calmness washing over me. I curl up in a tight ball replaying Riley's message over and over again until I pass out.

## Chapter Six

## Riley

### Four Hours Earlier

"Hey girls," Nate greets as he opens the door for Izzy and then gives her a little kiss.

"Look, I really wish I could stay and chat but Bella tells me you wanna talk about Gabe, and honestly we are really busy with a tight timeline so I gotta run. I'm sorry."

"Please, just five minutes then we'll leave. Please?" I eventually beg.

"Okay, what do you wanna know?"

I fire question after question at him: When did he last see Gabe? How did he seem? Has he spoken to Gabe at all? Is it like Gabe to just disappear and go radio silent?

Nate answers the best he can but his answers don't really do much to ease the ever growing fear in the pit of my stomach.

*What the fuck is going on? I thought we were doing so well. Was he just playing me? Am I not good enough for him?*

Tucker comes running over when he spots us and goes to give Ava a big squeeze. "Don't even think about it," Ava warns as she takes in his dirty, sweaty, appearance.

"Sorry, babe," Tucker says as he carefully bends his head to kiss her cheek, careful not to get any of his dirt on her white summer dress.

"You really have no idea where he could be?" I ask, turning my attention back to Nate.

"Not really. I guess you could try the pub? It's still early, so it probably won't be open, but no harm in trying, I guess." Nate says with a small shrug.

"Either that or the local fight club," Tucker says with a laugh.

"Fight club?" I practically shriek, the unease in my stomach getting worse and I can feel bile rising up my esophagus.

"Yeah, Nate said he was covered in bruises. Didn't ya Nate?" Tucker says. *What?!? Bruises?!? What is going on? Is he hurt? Does he need help?*

I don't miss the side eye Nate gives him. "What are you hiding, Nate?" I snap, poking my finger into his chest. I have no patience left for half truths and spared feelings. "You need to tell me everything you know. Right. Now."

Sighing deeply he starts, "When I saw Gabe yesterday his face was all bruised. I suspect he got into a fight but when I asked him, he said he'd been jumped by a few guys who had stolen his wallet. He seems fine though and he was okay this morning." Nate adds.

"You said he was in a vile mood, really rude and snappy." Tucker interrupts. And again I see Nate give him a 'stop talking now.' kind of look.

"Nate seriously, cut the bullshit!" I yell right into his face. *Why won't he just tell me! Doesn't he understand how much I care for his ass of a brother? And why isn't Izzy helping me?* "I know he's your brother and you're trying to protect him, I get it, but he could be lying in a ditch somewhere with internal bleeding or some shit so just tell me what you know."

"Relax Riley, he's trying to help," Izzy says but I'm in no mood to listen.

"Well he isn't really, is he?" I snap, "He's giving me half truths and hiding shit."

"Riley, it's his brother; you're asking him to betray his own brother here." Izzy snaps, a hint of frustration and anger to her voice, that I very rarely hear.

"I'm sorry, okay, I'm just worried and stressed," I admit, giving her an apologetic smile. *After all, I can't be mad at her for trying to protect her man, not when I'd do the same and so much more to protect mine.*

"Fine. But don't shoot the messenger." Nate says, letting out a big sigh. "I don't know much though. Yesterday he called me to pick him up from the middle of nowhere. Apparently, he and John went to some early job and then John just fucked off and left him, which to me, doesn't seem like something John would do. Then he said as he was trying to get home, he was jumped by a couple of thugs looking to steal his wallet. And then he ended up in a pub in the middle of literally the roughest neighborhood I've ever seen and called me for a ride." Nate explains.

"When I picked him up, I saw the bruises and offered to take him to the emergency room, but like the stubborn ass he is, he demanded to come straight here. Where he was a complete and utter dick all day to me before he left and went to the pub. He then had me drive him into work this morning but didn't even make it as far as the gates before he walked off in the opposite direction and I've not seen or heard a word from him since."

"Which way did he go?" I demand.

"That way I think," Nate says as he points towards town.

"I think I know where he could be," I say before I thank Nate and we drive off.

I direct Ava to drive to Saints Bar, praying to find him there. The doors are locked but I bang on it anyway, knowing that since it's his local hangout and that he's kind of friends with the bartender, he may have just persuaded Declan to let him inside.

I keep banging on the door and Declan finally opens it. "What?" he snaps, before his angry face morphs into a friendlier one.

"Sorry Blondie, I thought you were someone else, what can I do for you?"

"Hey, you probably have no idea who I am but.."

"Gabe's girl right?" he interrupts.

"Yeah." I say, grateful I don't have to try and explain who I am. "I'm actually looking for him; I don't suppose he's inside, is he?"

"Nah blondie, sorry," he says with a sympathetic smile.

"You sure? If this is some, don't tell the missus I'm here, kind of deal that's fine. Just blink if he's alive" I say, trying to make a joke.

"Honestly if he was here I'd tell you, but he's not."

"Can I ask that if you see him, you tell him to call me?" I ask, hating how desperate and needy I sound.

"I won't be seeing him, haven't seen him, don't wanna see him. Sorry." Declan says before he shuts the door slowly.

*Well there goes my bright idea!*

We drive around for a bit longer, hit some other local bars, and then drive to a few local bike garages, thanks to the help of Google, and even call the local jails and hospitals as a last resort. But he's absolutely nowhere to be seen.

I try again and again to call and text but I'm met by continued silence.

"Izzy, do you know where he and Nate live?" I ask.

"Erm..." Izzy replies seemingly unsure or nervous about answering. "Kind of, but we can't go there," Izzy adds.

"Izzy, please. You have to take us."

"I don't know, Gabe would absolutely hate it," Izzy adds.

"I don't give a fuck what Gabe would or wouldn't like; I need to find him Iz," I say, as my voice cracks slightly from desperately trying to hold in my emotions so I don't burst into tears.

"Let me just call Nate," Izzy says before she pulls out her phone and begins dialing.

"What? Why? Why can't you just take me, Izzy? What if this was Nate who was missing and I had information I was keeping from you? What if I told you I had to ask Gabe? Why can't you be my friend first?" But my pleas fall on deaf ears because Izzy is already on her phone to Nate. All I can do now is pray he agrees.

I wait with bated breath, " Yes... okay.... I won't... okay... I promise." Izzy says but without being able to hear Nate I have no idea what any of those words mean.

"Okay," Izzy says as she finally gets off the phone. "Nate says we can go. BUT we cannot go inside. He made me promise I wouldn't let any of you inside. But we can go and see, bang on the door, hope he's there and that he answers," she replies.

"Thank you," I say, as I practically drag her into a hug, full of gratitude. "I'm sorry for losing it on you."

"Swap seats with me; it's kind of hard to find, " Izzy says as she climbs into the passenger's seat and I climb in the back seat.

An hour later we pulled up to some run down house surrounded by woodlands. "Do they live here?" I ask, feeling confused.

I know Izzy says they live in their family's old house and the dad was a waste of space, but Gabe has shit loads of money. I see how full his wallet is whenever we're together, and while money and materialistic things mean very little to me, I would have thought he'd have spent some on fixing up his home. From the outside, it looks like the sort of abandoned house you'd find in some true crime drama.

"Yeah. Don't judge though. Now you see why they don't let people here," Izzy says as she gives me a sad, almost hurt look.

We stop the car and head towards the door where I bang and bang as loudly as I can while shouting his name, and when that gets no response I walk around, banging on other doors and windows hoping to get some sort of response. It soon becomes obvious no one is inside, and if they are, they are happy to pretend they're not.

"Come on, let's go." I say to the girls as the feeling of hopelessness washes over me. We all make our way to the car desperately trying to think about where else to go.

"Does he have any friends?" Harper asks as she throws her arm around my shoulders as we walk towards the car. Clearly deciding her love for her sister is stronger than her dislike for Gabe.

"No. Not that I know of. Declan, the guy from the bar, is literally the only other person I've ever heard him speak about."

"What about places he may go? Somewhere he goes to think, heck, even somewhere the two of you sneak off to fuck?" Ava adds, trying to make a joke.

"No, nowhere. I mean we could try the beach I guess, we've driven there a few times, but I don't think it's anywhere special to him."

"It's worth a try though, right?" Izzy adds.

So yet again we all pile into Ava's little car and head off aimlessly hoping to find him. *I swear to god, once I find out he's safe and alive, I'm going to kill him just for putting me through all this.*

# Chapter Seven

## Gabe

I'm fighting through my nightmares. The ones from my childhood, but instead of me or Nate being hurt, the images are replaced with those of Riley being stabbed repeatedly as I'm forced to watch, unable to help. My phone buzzing on the nightstand drags me out of my subconscious and forces me awake. I reach for it and see that this time it's a call from Nate.

"Hello?" I say groggily.

"Gabe?!? Thank fuck! Where are you? Where have you been? We've all been so worried? The girls have spent the whole day driving around looking for your dumb ass. Sorry I didn't mean that, I'm just so glad you're alive. You have no idea what thoughts have been running through my mind." Nate says, speaking far too quickly and clearly in a panic.

"I'm fine; I'm alive," I say, trying to calm him down.

I hear him take a deep breath before he speaks again. "Seriously, what the fuck Gabe?" This time his panicked voice has been replaced by an annoyed one. "You need to call Riley right now,

I don't care what is going on with you, that girl has been beside herself all day. You owe it to her to at least let her know you're alive."

"But. . ." I begin, however, Nate cuts me off.

"No I don't care what you're gonna say; I don't care what argument you two are clearly having. I'm putting this phone down right now and you're gonna call that poor girl back." Nate says hanging up before I even get a chance to reply.

It's then I spot two more messages from Riley.

3:00

Smoking Hot Cock Tease

> Okay, so now I'm just pissed. Where are you? Why are you shutting me out? Me and the girls have been to your house and either you're not home or you're ignoring me, as we banged and banged on the door. We've even been to Saints but Declan says he hasn't seen you. Heck, we've even been to the local bike shops in case you were there. Where the fuck are you Gabe?

4:15

Smoking Hot Cock Tease

> Now I'm way past worried and pissed off and in full panic mode. Nate let it slip the last time he saw you, you were battered and bruised, so we've even been to all the local hospitals in case you got in a bike crash. I don't know what I've done or

> said but I'm sorry. Please just let me know you're alive at least.

I noticed then that I have a phone full of missed calls and a bunch of voice messages so I decided that since I can't talk to her, I'd at least get to listen to her voice. There are a few from Nate that I pretty much skip straight away but most of them are from Riley wanting to know where I am. The panic and fear in her voice, especially in the last few, make my heart break even more.

I told myself I should cut all contact. That it would be easier for her if I walked away; and let her hate me. It is better to break her heart so she can move on, but I hate to see my little firefly so worried about and scared for me. She deserves to at least know I'm alive and okay. Even if I feel anything but okay at this moment.

I dial her number, and my heart fractures even more when I hear her voice. It's hoarse from either shouting or crying. "Gabe? Is that you? Thank fuck! Where have you been? I've been so worried? Are you okay? Where are you? I'll come right over?"

When I don't reply quick enough, she starts again. "Hello, can you hear me? Gabe? Hello? Fuck! Are you there?"

"I'm here," I mumble. *Man, hearing her voice is making this even harder.*

"Thank fuck! Where the hell have you been? We've all been in a panic searching for you. I'm glad you're alive but I could just kill you right now," she huffs, as the fear subsides and the anger takes over.

"That doesn't matter; I'm alive so you can stop worrying."

"Stop worrying?" she snaps. "You've been MIA all fucking day, you disappear from my bed in the middle of the night then ignore me all day yesterday. And today. . . today you fucking vanished! Nobody has seen or heard from you since first thing this morning when you walked away covered in bruises and no explanation on how you got them," she fumes. "Now to fucking top it all off you're just gonna brush it all off like I mean nothing to you. Well fuck you Gabe! You owe me more than that! Tell me where you are right now and I'll come over. I want to see you in person. Now!"

"I don't want to see you," I lie. Even though every single fiber in my body wants nothing more than to see her, hold her, and run away with her. *But I know that I have to be strong, it's for her safety.*

"Don't want to see me?" She screams. "I don't care what you fucking want. I'm your girlfriend and you scared the shit out of me today. So now you WILL see me, and you will explain to me what the fuck happened. Or so help me Gabe, I'll leave your ass and won't ever come back!"

"Good, because I want you to go. We're done. Move on; find someone else." I push out and even as the words leave my mouth I want to take them back. I don't want her to leave. I don't want her to ever find someone else. *I love her. Wait, I love her? I do! I fucking love her! I'm in love with her. I think I've been in love with her for a long time. Yet, still, I have no choice but to leave her.*

"Someone else?" she gasps. "What do you mean someone else? I don't want anyone else. I want you, I lo.." she says before she stops herself mid sentence. *Wait, was she going to say she loves me? Surely not! I'm unloveable. Nobody could ever love a broken asshole like me.*

"Please Gabe," she says quietly, I can hear the quiver of her lip as she speaks, "don't do this; don't push me away. Whatever you've done, I can forgive you. Just tell me and we can work on it."

"I can't, just . . ." Escapes my lips in a whisper before I can stop myself.

The sound of her begging and crying on the phone destroys me. Even after all the shit I've said or done to her in the past. All the times I've fucked up, this is the most heartbroken she's ever sounded. All I want to do is crawl through this phone, drop to my knees, and beg for her forgiveness; tell her this was all a mistake and that together we can overcome anything. But life isn't like that. My life isn't like that. No, this isn't one of those movies where love conquers all and everyone gets to live happily ever after. This is real life where the villain always gets what's coming to him in the end. My darkness has finally put out the only light in my life. And now I'm destined to spend the rest of my life alone wandering in the shadows.

## Riley

"Please," I sob when he doesn't answer me.

"Goodbye, Firefly." Gabe whispers before the line goes dead. I try to call him back but his phone is now turned off.

"Ri-ley?" Harper says nervously. I look at her and open my mouth to speak, but the words don't come out instead all that comes out is a whimper.

"What did he say?" Izzy questions cautiously.

"It's.. it's over." I say and the whimper turns into full on sobs.

"What do you mean it's over?" Harper asks, sounding defensive as she takes my hand and guides me over to the bed, encouraging me to sit down.

"It's...just over." I repeat, shell shocked and unsure what else to say or do.

"I'm sure whatever it is will blow over, you know Gabe, he messes up then you fix things. It'll be okay, Rilez," Izzy tries to soothe. *But I know this time is different. It feels different. So final somehow. And the worst part is I have no idea what happened. What did he mean he can't?*

"Izzy, go get some ice cream from the freezer; forget the crappy half fat one at the top, there's some cookie dough at the very back. Grab it" Harper orders.

Izzy scurries out of the room and up the stairs but I don't even have the strength to speak. My mind whirls with possibilities for what could have caused this. *Did I do something? Did he do something? Did he find someone else?*

We had a great time when we went to Six Flags; no issues there. We met up the next day for a ride and that went great. We even talked about him coming to prom with me and that he'd have to buy a suit.

*Wait. Is that it? Did I push him too far? Did I make it too couple-y? Was it too much pressure on him? Maybe that's too much of a boyfriend/girlfriend thing for him, I know the whole relationship thing is brand new. Maybe I freaked him out...*

It's possible but that doesn't make sense either because he seemed fine when we spoke later that night. And he seemed more than happy when he came over last night.

*It didn't feel any different when we were having sex. It didn't feel like it was a last fuck or anything. Everything seemed fine.*

So what the fuck happened between us having sex, him staying over with me, having a nightmare, and now?? *It's gotta be the dream! That's the only thing that makes sense. But why?*

I've been there when he's had nightmares before, and if anything, it brought us closer as it made him open up. *So why is this time any different?*

Izzy returns with the ice cream and hands it to me sympathetically. "I just don't understand," I say as I scoop a spoonful into my mouth. *Fuck me that tastes good.*

"Mmm," I moan as the taste hits my tongue.

"See, bet you're glad I saved a tub now," Harper says with a sad smile.

The whole family has been on a low fat diet for months, what with prom coming up and my parents getting ready to celebrate their twenty year anniversary with a belated honeymoon cruise, everyone has been on a diet. *But thank fuck for Harper and her sweet tooth.*

"Tell us everything." Ava demands as she bursts through the door. *Where the fuck did she come from?*

"I thought you were on your way home?" Harper asks, clearly as confused as I am at Ava's sudden reappearance.

"Shh," she says, waving her hand in the air. "Izzy called me. Now tell me, am I here to offer you consolation or an alibi? Because either one I'm more than happy to do."

As much as I don't want to, I can't help but smile at Ava. The crazy bitch would one hundred percent provide me with an alibi for murder if I needed one, and I've seen her acting skills, the cops would believe her too. "Both?" I reply with a shrug.

"So what the fuck did he do? Izzy didn't tell me much other than that he made you cry and I needed to get my ass back here." Ava says side-eying her best friend.

"It wasn't my place to say," Izzy replies timidly as she begs for Ava's forgiveness with a nervous smile.

All of us girls are close, but she and Ava, and me and Harper each form our own little inseparable duo. Which is nice since Izzy definitely needs a protective big sister in her life and it's nice for Ava to not be an accidental third wheel the way she has for most of our friendship. My sister and I never intend to leave her out, but I know it's hard breaking through our twin bond.

"So come on then Riley, on a scale of - give him dirty looks whenever we see him, to stick his dick in a food blender - how mad are we at him?" Ava questions.

"Stick his dick in a food blender... and make him drink it" I reply with a forced half smile.

"Damn girl that's savage, even for me. What the fuck did he do?"

"He made me fall in love with him. Made me think I was special, worth changing and growing for, only to throw me away like I meant nothing" I reply honestly, as the tears begin to fall again.

"Oh Riley, I'm sure he didn't mean it. Things will get better, you can get through this." Izzy tries to soothe but her sweeter than sweet attitude just adds fuel to the fire burning inside. I don't even realize what I'm doing till the words fly out of my mouth. "Oh grow the fuck up Izzy, the world isn't all sunshine and goddamn rainbows you know."

I see the surprised and hurt look on her face as she tries to speak but it comes out more of a stutter. " I... I know, I just meant..."

"Look I'm sorry Izzy, I didn't mean to take it out on you," I apologize but it's too late, I can see her whole demeanor has changed. Gone is the playful girl we've all come to love, and in her place is the shy, nervous, insecure people pleaser we met last year.

"It's fine," she replies with a timid smile that doesn't reach her eyes.

"It's not, you didn't deserve the way I just spoke to you, I was taking my feelings out on you. You're one of my best friends Izzy, I'm sorry" I say as I reach out to hug her, but she doesn't hug back. Instead, she makes her excuses, saying she needs the bathroom.

"I know you're hurting Rilez, but that was just wrong. Izzy is only trying to be helpful and you squashed her like a fucking bug!!" Ava snaps as she chases after her best friend.

"I agree, that was uncalled for Rilez, but I get that it just slipped out." Harper says as she shakes her head at me, before grabbing me by the shoulders and forcing my head onto her shoulder, while she hugs me.

"I know, I fucking know. I couldn't help it. Sometimes I just attack when I feel vulnerable; you know that." I whisper. "I don't mean it though."

"I know." Harper replies softly.

"I'm going to apologize, again," I say standing and making my way towards the bathroom.

"Can I have a minute?" I ask Ava as I walk in and see her consoling Izzy. Ava fires me a murderous look before nodding her head and releasing her friend.

"Izzy," I say softly as I drop to my knees in front of Izzy who is perched on the side of my bathtub staring down at the ground. "Izzy please look at me," I whisper as I bend my head so that I can try to get some sort of eye contact.

Izzy lifts her head ever so slightly and I see her mascara streaked cheeks. I loop my arms around her legs since it's easier than trying to stand and place my head on her lap.

"Izzy, I'm so fucking sorry; I didn't mean to take my pain out on you. My world came crumbling down but that doesn't give me the right to bring you down with me," I say.

"It's fine, I deserved it…"

"No Izzy you didn't deserve it, you didn't deserve it in the slightest. You deserve a friend who treats you like the absolute ray of sunshine you are, not a bitch like me who uses your own sunshine and goodness against you." I say frustrated at myself.

"You're not a bitch," Izzy says as a tiny smile forms on her lips. One that I know is partly there because she just cursed.

"I am a bitch, a total bitch, the biggest bitch of all the bitches in the whole world." I see the smile getting a little bigger on Izzy's face so I stand up and continue my silly rant. "I Riley Foster am the queen of the bitches" I proclaim. "No bitch is as big of a bitch as I am," I say.

"Now, can you Isabella Williams ever forgive this bitch for being such a bitchy bitch?" I say reaching out my hand and looking directly into her face, happy to see that a real smile is finally staring back at me.

"Fine, if you promise to stop saying bitch," she giggles and I have to laugh at the fact that even though I proudly said it like one hundred times she still felt the need to whisper the word bitch.

"Come on then", I say as I help her to her feet. "I best get you back to Ava, because damn, I may be a super bitch, but she's the one who taught this bitch, how to be a bitch," I laugh.

As soon as we make it to my bedroom I push open the door and am met with a furious Ava glaring in my direction. "See, the master bitch," I whisper to Izzy which causes her to not only laugh but snort.

"Glad to see you two have made up," Ava says as her scowl turns into a smile.

"Yeah, all friends again, no need to throw a bitch fit," I remark, which causes Izzy to laugh and snort even louder.

"Here, Princess Snorts A Lot" I joke, as I snatch the ice cream off Harper's lap and present it to Izzy like some sort of treasure.

"Why thank you miss B.I.T.C.H," she replies with a naughty smirk. *Honestly, only Izzy could think she was being naughty by simply spelling the word.*

"Good. Now that I don't have to kick your ass anymore, when are we kicking Gabe's?" Ava asks and I feel that instant arrow to my heart at the mention of his name.

"Another time," I say softly. Thankfully Ava doesn't push it any further and instead we spend the next couple of hours eating junk food, and watching The Notebook since we all decided a good cry was in order.

# Chapter Eight

## Gabe

Hanging up on Riley destroyed me; knowing that I broke her heart and hearing her sobbing crushed me. In anger, I turn my phone off and then throw it across the room. "Fuck!!" I shout as it connects with my wardrobe door. I walk across the room to retrieve it, noticing it now has a huge crack across the screen.

Knowing this is a pain that not even alcohol can numb, I make the first of what I assume will be many terrible decisions. I get on my bike and ride to a place I've not been to in years, the drug den run by the same men that murdered my father.

*Sure the official report stated that it was an accident caused by a bar fight. What isn't in the report though, the stuff that John and his men paid to be kept out, is that my sperm donor was killed in a targeted hit.* My father stole money and drugs from the wrong people, slept with the wrong women, and eventually paid for that with his life.

Even to this day John still refuses to confirm exactly what his role was in the whole ordeal, but he's said enough to let me know he was involved somehow.

*John! I still can't believe he's gone. He's been a part of my life, good or bad, for as long as I can remember. He may not have been the best role model in the world but he was someone who was always there.*

I push my way through, stepping over junkie after junkie, as I make my way toward someone who can get me what I need. Not much has changed in the years since I was last here, so hopefully I'm going in the right direction.

I spot J, a local drug dealer I know. I've scored from him in the past and know he has decent shit so I head over to where he is sitting getting blown by some chick likely only doing it to get her own score. As soon as he spots me he looks confused, but he pushes the crackhead off his lap and pushes his dick back into his jeans before reaching out to fist bump me anyway. I look down at his dirty fist in disgust until he pulls it back. "Same old Gabe," he mutters under his breath, as he places his hand back into his grubby black jeans and adjusts himself. *What the fuck am I doing here with this vile cretin. But fuck, the only choices and options I have now are bad ones, so I might as well go all in.*

"What are you doing around my parts? John send ya?"

"No, just looking to score. Same as everyone else around here."

He opens his mouth to say something, before stopping himself and simply shrugs his shoulders in response. *He clearly wants me here about as much as I want to be here.* "Follow me," he says as he leads me into a side room.

"So we got Shrooms, Blow, E, Weed, or Oxy; pick your poison." J says as he points to a collection of drugs, some of which even I don't know.

"Which of these will make me forget I'm living in this fucked up life of mine but won't actually kill me, hopefully, or maybe it will?"

*Death may be better than this. Hopefully when I get to hell my torture won't be that of Riley's sobs. But I can't die. Then it would be open season for those bastards to hurt Nate and Riley!*

"What's your budget?" he questions as he eyes me suspiciously and shakes me from my thoughts.

"Whatever it fucking takes," I reply honestly. *I don't care what it costs me or what it is, I just wanna escape reality for a bit.*

"Great answer," J says as he rubs his hands together. "I'll make you a cocktail."

A few minutes and almost $500 later I'm leaving with a selection of drugs from weed to cocaine. Pretty much the only thing I refused was heroin.

I ride back home and as one final last ditch attempt to save myself from the darkest of dark sides, I knock on my brother's door. I wait for a moment, unsure if I'm praying for him to be inside, or praying for him not to be. But when I don't get a response I push the door open. But his room is empty. I look at my watch, it's almost eight o'clock at night, where could he be? *With her, with his princess, living his own little fantasy.* My bitter and jealous mind reminds me.

Realizing yet again I'm all alone in my own despair, I grab all the alcohol I can find, then head to my bedroom. I line up the baggies of drugs on the top shelf of my bedside table, take a few random pills, and then wait for the numbness to set in.

I'm unsure how much time passes, but soon the sound of a door slamming breaks me out of my daydream.

"Gabe? Gabe?" A male voice shouts and I make my way towards it.

"There you are," the blurry face says.

"Gabe?" The face says again, I step closer, fists clenched at my sides. But my concern subsides when I realize that the blurry face belongs to my brother.

"What the fuck Gabe?" Nate says as he gives me a small shove, making me realize I am almost nose to nose with him.

"How much have you had to drink?" Nate asks.

"Not enough!" I say cheerfully.

"Seems like too much," Nate huffs as he drags me somewhere by my wrist.

As I'm being dragged along, I feel my legs bumping into random items, items I can barely even make out. "Sit here!" Nate snaps as he pushes me onto a seat.

I hear the tap running, but can only make out the shape of a figure the rest is just blurry. "Here drink this," Nate says as he takes my hand and thrusts something into it.

I attempt to bring the cup to my mouth but it slips out of my hands and I hear it smash against the floor. "Fuck sake, Gabe," Nate huffs as I hear the tap run again.

This time he takes both my hands and guides me to holding a different cup. *This one feels cold and metallic in my palm.*

This time I carefully bring it to my lips, opening my mouth to swallow, but nothing happened. *Wait? Why is my shirt getting wet?*

"Fucking hell, Gabe," Nate snaps, as he snatches the metallic mug from my hand and runs the tap yet again.

I reach out my hands ready to grab the cup for the third time, but am shocked when I feel someone grab the back of my head and pull it back. "Damn, if you wanted to get kinky all you had to do was ask," I say, before giggling at my own joke.

"Shut the fuck up Gabe!" Nate snaps, as he pulls my head again and tries to god damn waterboard me.

"Swallow," he snaps as the water fills my mouth and dribbles down the side.

"I said swallow," he snaps again. *Damn is that what I sound like when I'm ramming my dick down some whore's throat?*

"What was that?" I splutter, once I can finally breathe again.

"Water. Now drink another," Nate demands seconds before he's forcing another cup full down my throat.

"What have you taken Gabe? This isn't just alcohol. What have you done?" Nate asks, a mixture of fear and anger in his tone.

"Something... something... but nothing compares to the blue and yellow purple pills," I sing loudly.

"Pills? Gabe? Are you telling me you took pills?" Nate quizzes.

"Your face is so funny" I laugh as I reach out and stroke his fuzzy little face. He pulls away and then begins patting me down before thrusting his hands into my jeans.

"Woah bro... I'm not about that incest is best lifestyle," I laugh while trying to squirm away from his imposing hands.

"Shut the fuck up Gabe, I'm looking for whatever you've taken," he says as he continues rummaging in all my pockets.

"What have you taken Gabe?" Nate snaps again. *I think he's mad at me. Doesn't he know? Doesn't he know he should just let me be; that I'm just ruined and ruin everything and everyone that I touch? He's ruining my buzz!*

"I told ya... Blue and yellow purple pills," I sing again. *God I'm hysterical. Why isn't he laughing? I should be on fucking stage I'm that funny.*

"Grr, you're infuriating," he huffs before he grabs me and whips me off my chair, drags me down the corridor, and virtually throws me into the shower.

"Woah dude, I like it rough as much as the next guy, but damn you're rough. Poor princess, you must have destroyed her little pussy if this is how rough you like it."

I feel a strong thump hit me on my chest before I feel Nate's strong arms shaking me. "Say anything like that again and I'll fucking kill you long before these pills get the chance to." Nate snaps and I can hear from the furious tone in his voice that it was said through gritted teeth.

"I was just kidding," I replied. *Why is he being such a killjoy?*

"Well fucking don't!" he snaps again.

I feel water pouring down on my face from above, stopping me before I get the chance to reply with an amazing witty comeback.

I stand, letting the warm water run down through my hair and soak my face. *I wonder why water is so wet? It doesn't feel wet when I'm naked, yet if you wear clothes, it's very wet.*

"Google says it should be cold" Nate grumbles before the warm water that I'm currently enjoying, despite the fact I'm fully clothed, turns into what can only be described as hell freezing over.

"Fuck that!" I squeal as I try to get away, but a strong arm pushes me back.

"Fuck... that's cold," I cry out as the ice water continues to attack me.

"It's for your own good," Nate groans as he desperately tries to push me back under the torture stream.

I grab hold of him, wrapping my arms around him like a cat trying to avoid a bath. "Let me out. Please!" I bellow as I continue trying to clamber out, while Nate uses all his force to push me back in.

Nate finally overpowers me as I lose my footing and stumble backward, but this time, since I'm wrapped so tightly around my brother I end up dragging him in with me.

"Fuck!" he cries out and we both end up in a huddle all arms and legs at the bottom of the shower as the ice water attacks us both.

"This. Is. For. Your. Own. Good!" Nate says with chattering teeth and he pins me down.

"I....fucking.... hate... you," I reply, as I fight to get the words out too.

"Hating...me... means... you're... still...alive.."

"I...don't...wanna...be...alive!" I admit, as a strange sound erupts causing my voice to wobble. *Wait? Am I fucking crying? No, can't be.*

"Gabe?" Nate says, concern, confusion, and even surprise evident in his tone. "What did you say?"

"I wish I was dead!" I confess. "Life would be better for everyone if I didn't fucking exist" I snap, the sound of sobs bursting from my throat as my defenses come crashing down and my vulnerability shines through.

"You can't believe…" Nate begins, as he tries to reassure me but I'm in no mood for him sugar coating shit.

"It's true. I'm a waste of space, a waste of air. Everyone would be better if I just stopped breathing. You'd be better off without me, Riley would be better off without me, everyone would be better without me. Just let me die!!!"

I feel arms squeeze me tighter, I assume he's gonna put me out of my misery but soon realize rather than trying to crush me, he's hugging me. And way too tightly.

"But...I... need..you.. alive." he says against my ear.

I try to buck him off but I have no strength or coordination left so I just stop. Stop moving, stop wiggling, stop fighting, just stop and lay silently while Nate crushes me with a hug.

Eventually, the ice water gets warmer, either that or my body becomes accustomed to it. I feel Nate finally releases me and he disappears somewhere but I continue lying slumped here, not even having the energy or desire to move.

"Here," Nate finally says as he thrusts something soft and warm towards me.

I reach out and realize it's a towel. "You need to remove your clothes," Nate says, his voice softer than before.

I attempt to remove my top but it is like trying to wrestle a bloody octopus - I suddenly seem to have eight arms and no arm holes.

"Come here," Nate says as I feel him drag the t-shirt over my head.

"Jeans next," he sighs but again I seem to have completely lost the ability to lift one leg and balance on the other.

"Fuck sake," Nate grumbles. "Cover your dick," Nate says as he thrusts another towel in my direction.

"The ladies have told me it's pretty huge, so the towel may not cover it," I laugh, trying to lighten some of the tension in the air.

"If it covers your whole body it's big enough to cover your micro penis," Nate huffs as he pushes the towel towards me again. I do as instructed and scrunch the towel into a bundle and then cover my dick, just as my brother guides me out of my trousers and into some dry ones like I'm a mother fucking invalid.

Once dressed he walks me into my room and tucks me in like I'm a fucking child. I hear him walk away and assume he's gonna finally leave me, but the screeching sound of the chair lets me know he intends to sit down instead.

"What are you doing?" I grumble as I attempt to sit up.

"I'm gonna sit here and make sure you don't choke on your own vomit," Nate says as he walks over to me, pushes me back down and tucks me back in.

I hear him sit back down, and that's the last thing I remember before my eyes are flying open as the overwhelming urge to throw up flashes through me.

"Here you go," Nate says, moments before I'm puking into a bucket.

"Feel better now?" Nate asks once I've thrown up until there's nothing but bile left in my stomach.

"Not really." I grumble. "Can I.." I go to ask before Nate answers my prayers by handing me a cold bottle of water.

"Wow, I needed that," I groan as the cool feeling eases my throat.

"Any more water and you'll turn into a goddamn fish," Nate teases.

I look past him to my nightstand that's full of what must be ten different types of mugs, cups, and sports bottles. Basically everything we own.

"How are you feeling?" he probes gently as he takes a seat on the edge of my bed.

"Like the Devil himself came for me, and then I went twelve rounds with the Grim Reaper" I admit as a pain and aching, one that makes me hurt from the root of my hair all the way to the tip of my toes, washes over me in angry waves.

"Had I not been here that could very well have been a reality," Nate replies.

"Huh?"

"You took something Gabe, I dunno what it was but you were fucked, beyond fucked. You could barely move, kept stroking my face and fucking flirting with me. I swear if I wasn't already in therapy I'd need it, just to discuss the fact that my own brother kept making sexual comments towards me." Nate says as he screws his face up in disgust and shakes his head.

"Oh my god, was I that bad?" I laugh.

"You were worse.. At one point you were basically telling me how you liked it rough and telling me how kinky you are." Nate groans as he covers his eyes as if that will stop the memories.

"Well..." I smirk. "I'm sure it didn't come as that much of a surprise..."

"A surprise no, not really, but when you're butt naked with your dick inches from my face and I'm having to force you to cover it with a towel while you gloat about how many girls have complimented you on your size... it's pretty fucking nauseating." Nate says with an awkward laugh.

"Wow. that's, ahhh.." I reply unsure what else to do other than laugh while I rub my hand down my face.

*How the fuck could I let him see me like that? This is a new low, even for me. For sure now he is going to move out and be with his princess, just to be able to escape from me.*

"Yup... I know I've always said I wanted us to be closer, but damn I guess there is such a thing as too close," Nate laughs. "Honestly, what Riley sees in you, I do not know," Nate teases, but the mention of her name hits my already aching body like a mother fucking steam train.

## NATE

As soon as I said it, I saw Gabe's face screw up in pain as if he'd been hit by a tidal wave of emotions. Izzy told me last night that he and Riley had gotten into some big argument. In fact, that's why I was so angry when I came home. I was fully ready to rip him a new one for hurting Riley, especially if it was for that other woman like I suspect it was. But once I saw him and how out of it he was, it was clear to see he didn't need a scolding, he needed saving.

I don't know what the fuck he took last night or why, but it was the scariest shit I've ever seen. He was as high as a goddamn kite; he couldn't even hold a cup and bring it to his own mouth without tipping it all over himself. I threw him in the shower, hoping it would shock him back to reality, but even that was a disaster.

I stand up and stretch out my own achy muscles, muscles that are screaming at me after spending the whole night sitting in that goddamn chair watching my idiot brother sleep. Bringing him wet cloth after wet cloth to try and counteract the sweats and shakes. Basically anything to try and help him recover as quickly as possible.

I make my way to the kitchen and put on the coffee pot before realizing every mug we own is in Gabe's room. I was too terrified to leave him long enough to wash up in case he choked on his own vomit or had a goddamn seizure or something.

I turn around and head back into Gabe's room to find him curled in a ball as he stares into space. Thankfully, even though he's in his own world, it's obviously a different world from what he was in all night. So I grab the cups and carry as many as I can back to the kitchen, giving Gabe a moment alone with whatever internal demons he's currently battling.

I wash up everything from last night and leave it to dry on the draining board, then make me and Gabe a coffee and take them into his room.

"Here Gabe," I say as I carefully hand him his mug.

"Thanks," Gabe says, so softly I barely hear him.

"Do you wanna talk about it?" I ask after we sit in silence for almost twenty minutes.

"Do you know?" Gabe asks, sounding unnaturally small and timid.

"Know what?" I ask.

"About Riley?"

"Erm, kind of, I think. I don't know much. Izzy kind of told me you'd broken up. But didn't really say much more," I admit honestly, because it's the truth. "I tried asking Izzy what happened, but all she'd said was that you had called up Riley and ended it for no reason."

"Oh."

"Well, do you want to tell me what happened?"

"Not really," he admits before turning his back on me and rolling back over in bed.

I sit for a few minutes more, but it's apparent he's not gonna suddenly spill his guts to me so I leave, pulling the door closed behind me.

I'm loading the washing machine with all the towels and soaked clothes from last night when my phone rings.

"Hey, Tuck."

"Hey bro, I missed you at school. Mr. Robinson was pissed you missed the study group, but I told him you'd had a big family emergency and that you'll be back tomorrow.... You will be back tomorrow, right? We've got finals coming up. This is super important."

"I know Tucker, believe me, I know. I'll be back tomorrow, I just gotta deal with a few things at home first."

"Okay bro, speak to you tomorrow."

I fire off a quick text to Izzy updating her on the situation. I haven't said much partly because I don't want to worry her, but also because I don't really want her to judge Gabe either. But she knows that I came home last night and found Gabe in a state and that I'd spent the night keeping an eye on him which is why I couldn't take her to school today. She's been really caring and supportive but it's an awkward situation. She's torn between her love for Riley and wanting to be there for her, and I'm torn between my love for my brother and wanting to be here for him.

Me

> I'll meet you bright and early tomorrow, I'll even bring that coffee you like. Love you, Bella.

> My Bella
>
> **Love you more than all the stars in the sky.**

I pour another coffee and take it to my brother. "Here, thought you could do with another," I say as I flash him a sympathetic smile.

"Thanks Nate, I appreciate it, but do me a favor, yeah?"

"Sure. What do you need?" I ask, with a wider smile.

"Fuck off and leave me alone, will ya. I just can't stand staring at the stupid puppy dog face a moment longer." he says, his tone void of emotion.

*Well fuck you too! I* think to myself as I walk away.

I go and sit myself down on the sofa and flick on the TV.

*I take the whole day off when I should be studying, studying for an exam in a class I'm already struggling in, for you, and this is the thanks I get.*

I finally settle on a show I like and watch episode after episode all the while I don't hear a single peep from Gabe. Worrying something is wrong, I tiptoe toward his bedroom, but the second I turn the handle to open it I hear, "I said fuck off and leave me alone Nate," Gabe complains in a monotone and emotionless voice.

*Something is definitely wrong with him. It's gotta be more than just a fight with Riley. Heck, right about now I'd love a sarcastic comment or a grumpy tone. But he just sounds numb. Broken perhaps.*

I head back to the sofa and stick on a movie. Halfway through it, I hear Gabe's bedroom door open and him scurry down the hall toward the bathroom. I stand and by the time he comes out, I'm waiting near the door. "Leave me alone Nate," Gabe grumbles as he brushes past me and back into his bedroom.

*Fine. Wallow in your own self pity, see if I care!*

I head back to the sofa and finish my movie before putting on another. I must fall asleep though as the next thing I know I'm waking up and the end credits are rolling. I look at my watch, it's barely even ten o'clock, but either way after last night I'm exhausted. So I make my way to my bedroom, but as I reach Gabe's I decide to peek my head in just in case.

He's sprawled out on his back in bed. Fearing the worst I rush over, but when I see his chest rising and falling I realize he's simply in a deep sleep. So I make my way to bed myself.

"Hey baby, I missed you so much today." I murmur to Bella when I see her sweet face on the phone.

"Aww babe, you look exhausted," Bella says sympathetically.

"How's your day been?" I say with a yawn.

"Go to sleep baby, you're exhausted."

"No it's fine," I say, rubbing my eyes, "I wanna hear about your day."

"I can tell you all about it tomorrow." Bella offers.

"Are you sure? I don't mind listening." I say as another yawn escapes my lips.

"It's fine baby, not much to tell. Me, Ava, and Tucker studied and then grabbed iced coffee at that new little cafe on the corner. That's pretty much it."

"Did Harper and Riley not join you?"

"Nope, the twins stayed home. It was just the three of us."

"Oh," I reply, unsure what else to say. Clearly whatever happened between Gabe and Riley was big, bigger than I even realized.

"See you tomorrow baby, now go get some sleep. I love you," Bella says as she blows little kisses towards the screen.

"Love you too baby." I reply as I blow one back before hanging up and drifting off to sleep myself.

## Gabe

I wake up in the early hours of the morning and make my way to the kitchen looking for a beer but the fridge is empty. *I already drank them all.* So I grab my bike keys and jacket and drive to the all night gas station. I grab as much booze as I can fit on my bike and pay, praying I don't run into any cops on my way home.

As I'm riding home, my heart seems to take command of my body because instead of turning in the direction of home, I find myself veering off course toward Riley's house. I slow down as I turn on her street and I park my bike a couple of houses down. I make my way towards Riley's on foot. *It's bad enough I'm here, but I don't want the sound of my bike alerting her to the fact that I'm here.* Looking at my watch I realize it's barely five a.m. and the rest of the world is sleeping so when I spot her bedroom window, I make my way towards it and peer in.

*Does that make me a total creep? Probably. But do I care? Absolutely not.*

I carefully try to slide the window open, feeling equally relieved and pissed off when I realize it's locked. I turn the flashlight on my phone on and shine it into the room, desperate to get a glimpse of my little Firefly. Needing to see with my own eyes that she's okay. I shine the light in and see not one, but two sets of feet poking out the bottom of the quilt. *Wtf? She's with someone else already?* I feel a mixture of rage and devastation forming in the pit of my stomach. Without thinking I bang on the window and see one of the bodies move. I quickly cover my light, and move out of sight. I wait a few minutes and then light up my flashlight again and point it in the direction of her bed, hoping to get a better look at exactly which dude I will be kicking the shit out of later.

I spot two heads of blond hair, curled up together, and as the light hits their faces the one at the back turns and it becomes obvious that either I'm seeing double still, or the two people in the bed are Riley and her twin sister.

One of the girls turns again and rubs her eyes, clearly bothered by my light, and instantly I realize the one at the back must be Harpy. My girl takes a lot more than a simple light to wake her up.

A sense of relief washes over me when I am finally convinced she's not cheating on me. *Although technically is it even cheating if we're no longer together? Yes, yes it is, because together or not she's still my girl.* I leave, not wanting to risk her sister catching me staring through their window like a motherfucking peeping tom.

I walk back to where I parked my bike and make my way home. When I get there I take all the alcohol straight to my bedroom, close the door and demolish one after another while I roll up another joint, not risking whatever fucking pills J gave me.

## Chapter Nine

## Riley

Yesterday was nothing more than a blur. I spent the whole day either crying or sleeping and the hours ticked by like I was in the Twilight Zone. On one hand, I felt like the day was over in just a few hours; yet on the other, I felt like I was trapped in an endless sea of doom.

I vaguely remember the girls coming to see me, but couldn't tell you how long they stayed or what they spoke about; all I feel is numbness. I spend the whole day in bed sobbing, and sobbing, and fucking sobbing. How anyone can even cry that much is beyond me but somehow I did. I sit up and reach for where my phone should be, but it's nowhere to be seen. That's when the memory of Harper physically confiscating it pops into my mind.

I roll over in bed and notice an extra pillow beside me. *Why's that here?"*

"Morning," Harper says softly as she walks over and hands me a hot chocolate complete with whipped cream and marshmallows. *I hate that she feels sorry for me. I can see it in her eyes. I'm not this* weak, pathetic person that she thinks she sees in front of her right now. I need to get up, hold my head high, and say a big 'fuck you' to life and Gabe right now. Urgh, but I can't move yet.

"Did you sleep here last night?" I ask as I motion my eyes to her pillow.

"Yup, we had a bit of a little threesome," Harper says with a soft yet playful tone.

"A threesome?" I question. *Who else was here?*

"Yup. you, me and.... Sir Hops A Lot," Harper adds as she bends down and retrieves my childhood stuffed rabbit from the floor.

"I slept with Sir Hops A Lot..." I say with what should have been a laugh but comes out more like a hoarse throat croak.

"Yeah, you held him and hugged him most of the night, I've never seen you like that. Do you remember anything from yesterday?" Harper asks as she shuffles closer, takes my now empty mug, and hands me her half full one.

"Not really; it's all a blur," I admit honestly.

"Riley, you were like a zombie, all you did was cry or stare into space. Ava and Izzy came around in the afternoon and even brought Chinese since you'd refused to eat all day, but you didn't say a word to either of them. Instead, you just sat staring at your food like you expected it to jump into your mouth all on its own. I ended up having to give you one of mom's sleeping pills just to give your mind a chance to rest."

"Heck, was I that bad?" I gasp.

"You were worse. Seriously. I was beyond terrified. I must have laid there holding you all night, as every time I tried to move you would grab me and pull me closer. I had to give you the bunny to hold just so I could go for a pee."

*Fuck. I know when I was a child I used to crawl into Harper's bed if I got scared or had a nightmare as she made me feel safe, but I've not done that since I was about five.*

"What about school, did you go to school at least?"

"No, I couldn't risk leaving you so I stayed here all day. The girls brought me study notes though, so I at least got some work done." Harper says as she motions to the colorful post it notes stuck all over our wall

"I'm so sorry, Harper." I say as I look down.

*Fuck, now I'm screwing things up for Harper too! I need to snap out of this. NOW!*

"You've got nothing to be sorry for. Gabe on the other hand, that boy I could easily murder with my bare hands for what he's putting you through." My already fractured and damaged heart breaks all over again at the mention of his name.

*How could he just decide we're done, and throw me away like this? Did I mean nothing at all to him? I gave him every single piece of me, and yet he clearly couldn't care less. Once a womanizing player, always a womanizing player I guess.*

"Do you want to go out? It can either be just the two of us or I can call the girls?" Harper asks sweetly.

"I really don't, sorry, but I just can't face the world yet." I admit.

"That's fine, then I'll stay here with you. But Rilez... maybe you should have a shower at least? It might make you feel better."

I give my pajamas a little sniff and almost knock myself out, clearly not showering for two days, and crying non-stop, has led to me smelling like last week's trash.

"Good idea." I laugh as I scrunch my nose up as my own stench invades my nostrils.

I jump in the shower, wash my body twice for good measure, and then apply a hair mask, wanting to at least feel pampered on the outside even if I feel like shit on the inside.

I come out, throw on some clean pajamas then climb back into bed. "So shall we watch a movie?" Harper asks as she comes over and sits beside me.

"Or we could watch Vampire Diaries or The Originals; heck, I'll even let you watch Sons of Anarchy if you really want." Harper offers, even though I know she hates Sons. She's not really a fan of violence, or drugs, or bikers- *basically the polar opposite to me.*

"I just can't deal with any of that shit today. I don't wanna deal with hot guys, red flags, or fucking motorbikes." I huff.

"What about a nice romcom?" Harper offers.

"What, girls falling in love with the man of their dreams, and living goddamn happily ever after?" I huff.

"Okay, what about a comedy then?"

"Don't feel like laughing." I huff again while pouting. This only makes my heart hurt more as I imagine the way Gabe would be calling me a brat right about now and telling me he would fuck the attitude out of me.

"Fine then," Harper says with an exaggerated sigh, "horror it is."

So for the rest of the day we watch people being murdered, having their limbs chopped off, and running away from masked men intent on causing them harm. *At least that feels realistic!*

# Riley

The next three days go by pretty much the same. I wake up, shower, climb back into bed, and watch people being tortured and murdered.

I can't remember the last time I even ate. Harper and the girls have been around a few times, brought me all types of food and drinks, even goddamn meal replacement protein shakes that they probably stole from Tucker. But the thought of eating anything just doesn't appeal to me. I'm basically surviving off water, a few cans of Coke, and an occasional bag of gummy worms.

Ava storms into my room, not even bothering with knocking anymore. *I guess after being told to fuck off or leave me alone so many times, she's had enough of asking for permission.*

"What the fuck?" I snap.

"I'm done with this, I've been nice, I've been caring, I've been understanding and supportive. But now it's time for some tough love." Ava says as she walks over, snatches the remote, and turns the TV off.

"Come on get up," she calls as she rips the quilt right off my body.

"Fuck off Ava, I'm not going anywhere." I snap as I try to scramble for my discarded bedding.

"Nope!" she snaps, as she picks up my quilt and throws it across the room. "Enough moping, you're coming out into the real world," she adds as she pulls my legs so they are no longer on the bed and are now in a better position to stand.

"Fuck you Ava!" I shout. As I try to move my legs again.

"Either you get yourself up, or I fucking drag you up." Ava quirks her brow in a challenge while using that stern, authoritative voice of hers.

Knowing that I'm not going to win I reluctantly shuffle out of bed. "I fucking hate you, you know," I grumble.

"I don't give a fuck, you can hate me all you like, but hate me outside, hate me in the sunshine, hate me over goddamn coffee for all I care." Ava says as she begins rummaging in my closet to find clothes for me to wear.

She begins throwing random items in my direction - a pair of jeans, a t-shirt, and even goddamn underwear. She then sits herself down on Harper's bed with her arms folded. "Well, come on," she huffs when I still haven't started getting dressed a few minutes later.

"Some privacy perhaps?" I snap.

"Oh shut up, I'm the cheer captain of a squad of cheerleaders, you think yours is the first set of tits and ass I've ever seen?" she says with raised eyebrows. "Just get dressed already!"

Reluctantly I do as I'm told, physically not having the energy to argue. I throw on my clothes, not missing the way my normally snug jeans now hang off my hips. Ava notices too as she grabs one of Harper's belts from the jeans hanging on her wardrobe door and hands it to me.

Next I attempt to style my hair, but having not been brushed in close to a week, it's more like a bird's nest. Lots of gel, and strategically placed headband later, my hair is in a semi acceptable messy bun.

I throw on a little foundation, concealer, and mascara then finally head out the door. "Where are the others?" I ask as I climb into Ava's car.

"Harper is at work so we're meeting her there; Izzy is on her way to meet us too."

The whole drive, my eyes virtually burn as the sun beams down on us. I *guess a week locked in a bedroom will do that to you.*

We finally pull up outside the little family run cafe Harper works at and head inside. " You owe me twenty dollars," Ava says with an accomplished smirk as soon as we spot Harper walking past, with a tray of empty mugs.

"Twenty dollars, well earned," Harper smiles as places the tray down on a nearby table, reaches into her apron, and hands her a folded up bill.

"What was that for?" I ask as Harper walks away and me and Ava find a table.

"We had a bet on whether or not I could drag you back to the land of the living."

"Really? You bet on your own sister?" I say with a disapproving stare when Harper returns a few minutes later with our usual drinks order. Harper just shrugs and gives a little nod in response.

The three of us have barely touched our drinks when Izzy storms in, throws her purse on the table, and slams herself down on the chair.

"Everything okay?" Harper asks, looking shocked at Izzy's uncharacteristically high level of frustration.

"No," she huffs. "That man is a real pain... no scrap that, he's an ass," Izzy snaps.

All three of our eyes widen and our mouths fly open in shock. Izzy never curses. Like ever. Occasionally she'll whisper or mouth the odd curse word but never just full on shouts them.

"Who?" Ava gasps.

Izzy looks over and spots me beside Ava and her whole face changes, "Erm, no one," she says timidly.

*Gabe ... of course it was Gabe. Who else could be such a mother fucking asshole that he'd literally make a nun want to cuss.*

"What did Gabe do?" I ask with a deep sigh.

"Nothing, forget about it. It's nothing." Izzy says with a forced smile, her face flushing as she tries and fails to lie.

"He clearly did something, so you might as well just tell us." I add as I internally roll my eyes.

"No it's fine, let's talk about something else, " Izzy offers.

"Seriously it's fine, you can say his name Iz." I say even though inside I'm begging she doesn't. "Harper hates him, Ava definitely hates him, I want to hate him, so you might as well tell us why you hate him as well," I sigh.

"Fine soo…" Izzy begins, her voice clearly agitated and desperate to share. "I went to see Nate as I always do and… You know who… was there, which was fine, whatever. Then from nowhere, he literally began screaming at me telling me I'm not welcome there anymore. Nate tried to argue with him and he just began screaming at Nate as well. It was really goddam scary. I froze. Then to top it off, Ga.. you know who, picked me up, threw me over his shoulder, and dropped me on the sidewalk, pulling and locking the gate behind me so I couldn't get back in. It was so damn mean and uncalled for. I know you love him Riley, and honestly, I try to see the best in him, you know I do, but sometimes I could just… just kick him!" she snaps.

I know I shouldn't laugh, Izzy is clearly upset and what Gabe did was completely uncalled for but part of me desperately wishes I could have been a fly on the wall to watch it as it sounds hysterical. More so the way Izzy tells it, her sweet face morphing into so much anger and frustration she kind of looks like a toddler having a tantrum.

"Don't laugh," Izzy huffs, as I clearly do a terrible job of holding in my smirk.

"I'm sorry Iz, I really am. Gabe sounded like a complete and utter dick, and he was totally out of order treating you like that. But something about seeing little Miss Sunshine and Rainbows all angry, frustrated, and saying cuss words, is just kind of comical. I'm sorry. I know that makes me a terrible friend. I've just never seen this side of you before. Who knew the cute little kitty had claws."

A smile forms on Izzy's face for a moment, although I'm not sure why. "That's what Gabe said too" she says with a little smile.

"What is?"

"The whole, who knew the sweet kitty had claws, thing. That's what Gabe said the first time I lost my temper at him too."

*Seems we're even more alike than I realized.*

# Chapter Ten

## Gabe

### One Hour Earlier

I've had no choice but to throw myself into work to keep my mind occupied and to stop me from turning up at Riley's in a drunken state begging for her forgiveness. Plus with John still missing and police sniffing around, I can't risk doing or saying anything that makes me appear suspicious.

I'm in my office going through some paperwork when my phone begins ringing. The theme to The Omen bouncing off the walls, lets me know it's mother fucking Marko calling. That man has been blowing up my phone all week. Having me run around like his personal little errand boy. Picking him up from parties, collecting weed and cocaine for him, and just generally doing whatever he asks for. *And I've hated every fucking moment of it! Literally, the only thing that's got me through is booze, weed and occasionally even coke to cope.*

I answer the phone reluctantly. "What?" I snap.

"Now is that any way to speak to a buddy?" he says, tone dripping with false sincerity.

"We're not buddies. Now what do you want?"

"None of us have been paid since John did his little disappearing act," he states innocently as if he doesn't know exactly why John hasn't been around.

"Disappearing act, of course," I reply, full of contempt and sarcasm.

"Anyway, I suggest you get us our money, today, unless you think you need a little more motivation of course?" he sneers.

*That word, motivation! The threat he's been using to get his own way and keep me under his thumb all week.*

"I'll have it for you by the end of the day," I say in my calmest tone, while seething silently.

"We're on our way now, have it ready in thirty minutes!" he snaps before hanging up.

I scurry and try to find the 2k he needs as quickly as I can. Thankfully we had a down payment for a shipment that came in late last night so we got around $1500 sitting in the safe, waiting to go to the bank. I empty the safe and count out every dollar we have but it still only makes $1800. Pulling out my own wallet and managed to scrape together the remaining $200 and slide it into the envelope.

I'm just making my way out when I spot Isabella, talking to Nate. *Fuck, what is she doing here?*

I march over to them. "Nate, you're needed over with Davis, stop slacking off and go help. NOW!" I snap in my most authoritative tone.

"Yeah, yeah give me five min.."

"No. Now!" I snap. "Get the fuck out of my sight!"

"Gotta go Princess," I say, turning to Isabella and giving her a gentle spin to make her turn away. *I need to get her the fuck out of here before those assholes show up and she gets put on their radar too!*

"Don't fucking.." Nate begins but I cut him off

"Shut the fuck up Nate; I'll do what the fuck I like. Now either you get her to leave or I make her," I snap, the fear further rising as I know Marko is due here any moment, and if he spots Izzy and thinks she's someone else he can manipulate, he won't think twice about it.

"Sorry baby," Nate says, giving her a small kiss on the cheek, "I'll call you later."

Isabella smiles and walks off meanwhile Nate fires me a furious look. "You're a real asshole, you know that right." he snaps before walking away.

I think the coast is clear just as I hear a loud car horn beep, letting me know Marko is here and is wanting his money.

I walk out and am just making my way to meet him when out of the corner of my eye I spot Izzy talking to Tucker. *No. no. no! Fuck!!*

Not wanting to risk Marko seeing her and putting two and two together, I storm over there.

"I told you to fuck off," I snap, as I grip her arm and try to escort her away.

"No!" Izzy snaps as she yanks her hand out of my grip. "I can walk on my own. Thank you very much," she huffs and I see that fire burning in her. The same, frustrated, defiant frown she had that night she bailed me out of jail. *This isn't gonna end well!*

I spot Marko and his crew exiting their car and making their way towards mine and John's office so I have to act fast.

"For fuck sake," I huff before I grab Isabella and throw her over my shoulder. I feel her go stiff and rigid in my arms, and part of me feels bad that I've obviously scared or traumatized her by doing so.

"Can't you see I'm trying to protect you? If you think I'm an asshole, you really don't want to meet someone who is the Devil incarnate." I mumble under my breath before I realize I had said that out loud. *Fuck sake, I hope she didn't hear me. It's better if she just hates me and stays away from me. It's safer that way for her and for Nate.*

Unlike the times when I've done this to Riley and she's either giggled or kicked out in anger, Izzy is as stiff as a board. The same way I go whenever people touch me without permission. I know I should release her, apologize, and make everything better. But I can't. I need her gone as soon as possible. So for now, my touch is the lesser of two evils. *Rather it is me grabbing her than Marko.*

I walk her as quickly as I can and carefully place her back down on the sidewalk. She looks at me with so much confusion and shock I don't know what to do or say, or how to make it up to her. So instead I simply pull the gate shut so I don't have to look at her puppy eyes a moment longer.

"What the fuck Gabe?" Tucker says as he stares at me looking equally as surprised, but also pissed off.

"Get back to work," I snap before heading to my office where Marko is waiting for me.

"What the fuck was that all about?" Marko adds as I unlock the door and let him in.

"Nothing, just some random slut, trying to stake her claim on one of the guys, can't be bothered with her whiney presence," I lie. Trying my best to sound nonchalant.

"She looked familiar," Marko says as he scratches his head.

*Fuck, how does Marko recognize her? Has he been watching her and Nate too?*

"Dunno," I shrug. " probably had her on her knees at some point."

"Yeah maybe," Phoenix adds. "She did kind of look like a bathroom bunny"

"Nice ass, wouldn't mind tapping that," Marko adds. While everything in me wants to rip his throat out for talking about Nate's girl like that, I keep my cool and just nod along. The less important they think she is, the safer she will be.

## RILEY

We're just finishing up our coffee when the talk gets onto the prom. "Shit, we were supposed to be going into the city tomorrow for prom dresses weren't we?" I gasp as the reality dawns on me.

*The last thing I want to be doing after just having my heart blown to pieces is shopping for prom dresses; a prom I'm not even sure I want to attend anymore, not now that I'm single.*

"Don't worry, I told my parents we'd visit next month instead." Izzy says as she gives my hand a reassuring tap.

"And they were okay with that?" I question, knowing how strict and grumpy her parents are.

"Nope they were furious, but let's face it it's not like they've never canceled on me, plus, they'll probably ignore me anyway," Izzy shrugs.

"We thought you might need a little more time," Harper interjects.

"Thanks girls, you three could have still gone though," I offer

"Nah it's fine; we all go or none of us goes." Izzy says with a smile.

"God, I love you all."

"Oh good, so you don't hate me anymore then?" Ava smirks, as she finishes the last of her drink.

"I only hate you a little bit," I say before poking my tongue out at her playfully.

We say our goodbyes to Harper and then drive to Izzy's where we spend the rest of the evening studying. Harper comes over after work and between the three of them, they try to catch me up with everything I've missed the last week.

We've got less than a month until we have to take our finals, and if we don't pass we can't graduate.

"Enough! I give up, my head is going to explode" I say as I throw myself down on the bed.

"Yeah me too." Izzy admits with a yawn.

"Fine. How about we all meet up tomorrow? We'll get the boys together and make a day of it - pack a picnic, head to the beach and just blow off some steam?" Ava suggests.

As much as I don't want to go anywhere and do anything, the idea of a day at the beach does sound appealing. All three girls look at me expectantly, waiting for my response.

"Fine." I say throwing my hands in the air, "Beach day it is!"

A round of "yay" and small claps echo around the room.

"I'll tell Nate." Izzy says excitedly, before running off to call him.

"You gonna be okay with the boys joining us?" Harper whispers as we begin collecting up our things.

I give her a little nod in response. After all, just because Gabe broke my heart doesn't mean Nate and Izzy deserve to be punished too.

# NATE

I'm sitting playing video games with Gabe when my phone rings.

"Hey Princess, how's your day been?" I say excitedly. *Damn, I feel like I've barely seen her this week.*

*What with me trying to be here for Gabe and her trying to take care of Riley, we've barely had any time together. I finally saw her briefly today, until fucking Gabe demanded she leave. A demand that had us arguing and snapping at each other for the rest of the day.*

"It's been okay, thanks. Did Tucker say anything to you about me today?" she questions.

"No. Why? Should he have said something?" I question. *Tucker didn't say a word about Izzy, I didn't even know they spoke earlier.*

"Oh no, it's nothing, I just told Tucker to tell you I'd call you after I met up with Riley for coffee, nothing important."

"Oh great, so Riley finally left the house then?" I ask. *Happy to see that Riley is clearly doing better.*

*I wanted to reach out to her myself, but what am I supposed to say? Sorry my brother is a complete asshole who broke your heart; by the way are we still friends?*

"Riley?" Gabe says from beside me before placing his head closer to me to try and listen to my call.

I tut in response and push him away.

"Yeah she's okay, still not herself, but she joined us for coffee and came over here. Oh, and she agreed to a day out. That's why I'm calling actually, do you and Tucker want to join us tomorrow at the beach for a sun, sand, sandwiches, and some fun in the sea, kind of day?"

"Sure baby, a beach day sounds amazing. Is Riley fine with you inviting me?" I question, again not wanting to make anything even more awkward than it already is for the group.

"What about Riley?" Gabe interrupts once again.

I wave my hand in annoyance before getting up and walking to the kitchen to finish my call in peace. Once we've finished and finalized all the plans for tomorrow, I say goodbye and hang up. I grab a can of coke for both me and Gabe and head back into the living room.

He looks at the can like it's poison, probably wishing it was beer, but just shrugs and opens it anyway.

"So what were you saying about Riley?" Gabe asks trying too hard to be nonchalant about his question.

"Nothing."

"You were, don't lie, I heard you mention her name, twice." Gabe says, his voice coming out unusually whiney.

"I'm not trying to be an ass Gabe, but anything to do with Riley has fuck all to do with you anymore; you've made your bed. Now you gotta sleep in it." I say, not wanting to get pulled into the drama and end up like some double agent passing information to both sides.

"It has everything to do with me." he snaps, sounding more like his usual asshole self. "Everything my girl says or does is my business."

*His girl. HIS GIRL? What the heck is he talking about? Izzy has told me how callously he broke her heart, with no warning. And now he wants to make out like he still has some claim on her?*

I take a deep breath and will myself to calm down before I do something I know I will regret.

"But she's not YOUR girl anymore, is she Gabe? You fucked that shit up. You lost her now you've got to either fight to get her back or move on and let her heal."

"She will always be MY girl," Gabe snaps as he crushes his coke can in his hand, spraying soda all over the both of us.

I get up to grab something to clean up the mess and Gabe marches past me, grabs a whole pack of beer from the fridge before storming into his bedroom, and slams the door. *I swear to god I'm living with a moody teenager these days.*

## Chapter Eleven

## Riley

We arrived at the beach a couple of hours ago and while I tried to enjoy myself - I joined the others for a little game of beach ball, went for a dip in the sea, and even ate some rather sandy sandwiches - my heart is just not in it. My mind keeps thinking about the last time I was here, just a couple of months ago. Coincidently that was after Gabe fucked up too. It was after I gave him my virginity and then I found out he'd slept with Kelly the night before.

*I should have known then this relationship was doomed to fail. Why couldn't I have just walked away? Found myself a nice guy like Tucker and Nate, who would have treated me like a queen?*

*Because you're not into the sweet guys, you don't want to be someone's pampered princess, you want to be their dirty whore.* My annoying brain reminds me.

Either way, we'd barely been on one date at that point and yet he still chased me, begging for another chance. Yet now nothing. Two weeks ago I was his girlfriend and we were planning our futures together and now, I clearly mean nothing to him. My eyes keep darting to the pier, part of me desperately wishing to see him bounding down it.

"Come on Rilez, we're gonna hire a paddle boat. You coming?" Tucker says as he shakes his wet hair over me like a goddamn dog.

"Nah, I'm fine." I say but he's already tugging me up.

"It'll be fun," he begs.

"Fine, fine." I finally agree.

We go towards where the pedalos are but spot a sign for a boat tour leaving in about fifteen minutes.

"Come on, it'll be so much fun, let's do that instead." Ava cheers as she practically bounces up and down in excitement.

We all agree, pay, and make our way to the harbor ready to board. When we get there we notice the boats are full of other people, most of which seem about our age or early twenties. *Perhaps this will be fun after all.*

The boat sets sail and before long we're sitting on the deck with two other groups; five guys who are here for one last crazy weekend before heading back to college, and another group of three, all girls.

We get chatting, and the drinks begin flowing since the older guys keep supplying us with beers from a cooler they brought with them.

Two of the boys keep flirting with me and as much as I have zero interest in either of them, I have to admit, it feels nice to feel wanted again.

One of them kind of reminds me of Gabe, dark hair, tattoos, a few piercings, and although he seems nice and is super friendly, his larger stature gives off a kind of don't fuck with me vibe.

"So what's a girl like you doing here alone? No boyfriend ready to kick my ass for talking to his woman?" the wannabe Gabe asks. And I almost laugh out loud at the thought. *Damn, if Gabe was here right now he'd be damn near murderous.* I'm about to reply, but Izzy beats me to it, with possibly the worst thing she could have said.

"No, they just broke up actually."

"Aww that's awful, are you okay?" The three girls all say sympathetically, but the look they're all giving me, like I'm some poor defenseless broken bird, just ignites a stubborn fire deep within me.

"Yeah, his loss really, I couldn't give a fuck." I lie, even as the words leave my mouth I want to take them back but it's as if my rational side has completely disappeared and instead my brain and body are being controlled by the worst sides of me.

"Oh, in that case," fake Gabe says before he pulls me down and forces me to sit beside him.

I see the rest of the gang eyeing me with pure confusion. But thankfully nobody says anything. The next few hours are fun. I manage to distance myself from Fake Gabe and turn my attention to his friends as we all play rounds of Truth or Dare. We challenge each other to do things like steal alcohol, jump off the now docked boat, or just general harmless fun.

That is until it's my turn. "Dare!" I decide.

"I dare you to kiss me," Fake Gabe purrs.

"Err.." my mind goes completely blank.

"Or not!" he laughs when I clearly spend too long staring at him like a deer in headlights.

"New dare, go find a stranger to swap tops with you." one of the girls suggests.

I scurry off like a little bug, out of sight, and hide out below deck. Eventually, Harper finds me. "What the fuck was that?" Harper asks.

"I don't know; I just panicked." I say as I wipe away a single tear.

"Then why the heck have you been flirting with him all day?" Harper questions.

Shrugging, "I guess it felt good to be wanted; felt good to know some other guy wants me, even if Gabe doesn't." I admit.

"It's no coincidence that, out of all the guys, you went for the Gabe look alike. Is it?" Harper laughs.

"You saw that too?" I smile.

"Yeah, Dummy, I have eyes too - tall, dark, and tattooed - basically Gabe 2.0. You clearly have a type," Harper laughs as she pulls me up to my feet, "Come on, let's head back," she suggests as she throws her arms around my shoulders.

We finish the rest of the boat journey pretty uneventfully. But as we disembark, fake Gabe hands me a napkin. I open it and see his name 'Zander' followed by his cell number.

"Give me a call if you ever wanna hang out," he offers before he runs ahead to catch up with his friend.

Unsure what to do with the napkin, whether to keep it or throw it out I simply slide it into my shorts pocket.

# Chapter Twelve

# Gabe

Nate is back at school, cramming for some stupid exams, but at least it means he's not around work anymore. The police have been sniffing around for weeks. Thankfully, as of thirty minutes ago, they concluded it was an accidental drowning after John's car somehow ended up in a lake almost four hours away.

Thankfully, other than his daughter, who lives in Australia, and his granddaughter, who lives with her mother, John had no other living relatives. His eldest son, the little girl's father, died years ago while stationed overseas while serving a tour with the army.

Unfortunately though, now that John's death has been ruled as an accident, and despite the fact there is no body recovered to officially bury, his daughter Rebecca is flying back to collect some of his belongings.

We've shared quite a few phone conversations over the last couple of weeks since John 'disappeared.' At first, she called looking for her dad because he had missed several of their scheduled calls. Apparently unbeknown to even me, every Wednesday and Saturday he called her like clockwork. He had done this since she moved back to Australia to live with her grandparents.

My phone buzzes in my pocket and without looking I know it's going to be Rebecca. If I know nothing else about Rebecca, I know she's punctual. Perhaps it's growing up with a father, brother, and grandfather who were all army men. Or maybe it's just her personality in general, but when she says she will call at eleven, she means eleven. Not five to eleven or five past eleven. But eleven o'clock on the dot.

"Hello?"

"Hello, Gabe. My plane has landed on time and I should be at the hotel around noon. I would appreciate it if you could meet me there to take me to my fathers around one o'clock please"

I can't help but roll my eyes at the formality of her request "Yeah, no worries, I've already packed up a few of his belongings from work. So I'll pick you up on my bike and take you straight to your dads."

"A bike?" she practically gasps. "No, that won't be necessary, I've rented a car. So I will meet you at the hotel and we can either go together or I can follow you," she says, matter of factly.

Not wanting to be stuck in a car with a woman I don't know, especially when it's my fault her dad's dead, I tell her I will meet her there and she can follow me as I have stuff to do after.

Two hours later, I am waiting outside the Four Seasons Hotel, feeling like an absolute idiot. People are walking past, eyeing me up and down as I just stand there smoking. *Clearly, I'm not the type of clientele they're expecting for this place.*

"Gabe?" a feminine voice questions.

I look over at the tiny little mouse of a girl. I knew from our conversations she was around my age, but from her strict and formal tone over the phone, I was expecting an uptight, rough, and tough kind of person. But she looks like a meek and mild little field mouse.

Clearing my throat, "Hi, I'm guessing you're Rebecca?"

"Yes, I am. Nice to meet you, in person," she says as she reaches out her hand for me to shake.

I look at her hand for a moment, having zero desire to shake it. But, it's my fault her dad is dead, or should I say missing, so the least I can do is pretend I'm a semi-civilized person I guess.

"Nice to meet you, shame it's not under better circumstances." I reply, trying my best to be polite. "So you ready to go then?" I ask as I throw my cigarette butt on the road ready to head towards my bike.

"Would it be okay if I dropped my bags off first?" she laughs, only now do I register she had a huge suitcase and a shoulder knapsack slumped over her tiny shoulders. *Seriously, this bag looks like it weighs more than she does.*

"Give that here," I say as I practically pull the huge bag off her shoulder.

She politely declines, but I just give her a 'shut up and do as you're told' scowl.

She leads the way, quickly checking into the hotel, and grabbing her room key, all the while I lug her suitcases up to her room.

"I'll meet you down in the bar when you're done." I say as I drop her bags in her room and walk away, giving her time to freshen up from her long flight.

I order myself a beer, half expecting, like most girls, she'll take ages changing, fixing her makeup, unpacking her clothes, or just doing random shit I will never understand. But I'm barely halfway through my beer when I feel a little tap on my shoulder.

"Are you ready to go? I'd like to get on with things if that's okay," she says softly.

Her eyes dart to the beer in my hand as she adds. "I'm assuming you'll leave your bike here and I will drive?"

Quickly lifting my beer and downing the remaining half as quickly as possible I add, "Not a chance," before wiping my mouth with the sleeve of my leather jacket.

I see a mixture of fear and confusion flash across her face, she opens and closes her mouth like she's about to say something but decides against it.

I put my empty bottle back on the bar and make my way outside, smirking as I hear the sound of quick footsteps behind me as Rebecca struggles to keep up.

I get on my bike and wait for her to start up her car before leading her toward her dad's house. Once there, I take the keys out of my pocket. Thankfully I remembered to grab the spare ones John kept at work. I give her a quick tour of his house and explain the basics of it to her, not that it needs much explaining. It's a very simple and minimalist two bedroom house. The place shows its wear and tear, but it's not filthy, more so in need of a woman's touch. Much like mine and Nate's house. I open some doors and windows, letting in some air to ease some of the mustiness that has settled in the place since no one's been here in weeks, and then I turn to leave.

"Wait!" Rebecca calls. "Are you just leaving?"

*Well, that was my plan.* Yet the desperation and pleading tone forces me to reconsider. *Seriously, when the fuck did I become some sort of white knight? Probably around the same time Riley made you realize you had a heart, buried under years of ice!*

My mind flies back to Riley, and all the times she had that same insecure, desperate look in her eyes. The way she virtually pleaded for my help and my broken heart pounds. *If she was here now she'd want me to help. So that's what I will do.*

"I guess I could stay for a bit if you want," I shrug.

"Thank you so much Gabe, I have no idea what I'm doing," she replies with a grateful half smile and watery eyes.

For the next few hours, I help her sort through the house, using garbage bags to separate the items that need to be thrown out from what she thinks can be kept or donated. There is also a small box of personal effects Rebecca wants to keep.

"We're all out of bags," Rebecca sighs as she rummages around under the sink.

"No problem, I can head out and get some." I say as I stretch my achy legs and stand.

"Can you see if you can get some cardboard boxes as well, please? There's money in my purse if you hand me my bag," she offers.

"I can afford a box of garbage bags and some boxes. I may look like a bum, but I'm doing fine." I reply defensively, as I can't help but notice her fine and fancy looking clothes.

"Oh no, that's not what I meant at all," she answers, sounding horrified by my accusation.

"I'm just fucking with ya," I smirk. I'll be back in about half an hour. I say as I grab my bike keys and head out the door.

Once outside I light up a smoke and take a moment to let the whole situation sink in. John is officially gone and soon so will any memory of him. Before I get too wrapped up in the crapfest that my life has become, I jump on my bike and head out to the store.

Over an hour later, I finally arrived back at John's with all the items we need to finish this gut wrenching task.

"There you are, you're late," Rebecca says as I walk through the door.

"Yeah, I don't really stick to a timetable. I do shit when I do shit," I shrug.

"I gathered that." Rebecca mumbles, barely loud enough to hear.

"Okay, these can all go in the trash, I think," she says, biting her lip and pointing to a pile of random items. "The stuff on the bed I would like to keep, those items seem good enough to donate," she says this time pointing to a few items of clothing folded neatly in the corner of the room. "But this box here, I'm not sure what to do with. Dad obviously kept them for sentimental reasons, so I don't want to throw them away, but they also don't really mean anything to me." she says as she picks up a small wooden box and places it on the bed.

"What is it?" I ask as I step closer to look inside.

"I don't know, I found it at the bottom of his wardrobe, I'm guessing things Ollie and I made for him, growing up.

I sit down on the bed and begin rummaging through the items. I see handmade drawings, some pictures of a little boy and a girl, and some other knick knacks that were obviously made by his kids. A few family photos of a much younger, and much slimmer John holding a baby in the hospital, again clearly his kids. I spot a stupid 'World Best Grandpa' teddy from his granddaughter. *Clearly these are all just mementos of his family.*

I am just about to put the lid back on when something catches my eye. It's a small wooden bear. You can barely make out that it's a bear, but I know that it is because I'm the one who made it. I carefully remove the bear from the box and study it. *Why the fuck does he still have this?* My mind transports me back to the day I made this.

## Flashback- Age 8

Dad is passed out on the sofa again, beer bottles and his white powder covering the table.

"I'm hungry," Nathaniel whines from beside me.

"Go and play outside, I will try and make you something." I say as I usher my brother outside so he won't have to witness the state my father is in yet again. He's barely even six but already knows he has to be quiet and avoid our dad whenever possible. Especially since Mommy left us earlier this year.

Nathaniel sneaks past the living room, quietly opens the door, careful not to push it all the way to the point it makes that annoying squeak and heads outside. I head to the kitchen desperately looking for some food, but surprise surprise there is none. I rummage around and manage to find a box of mac and cheese at the very back. I check the date and it's only a couple of weeks out of date, so deciding I'd rather have a full tummy, that might make me sick, than go to bed with an empty tummy that's guaranteed to make me feel sick. I begin making it. We have no milk so I use water instead. Hoping it will still work. I taste a little bit while it's cooking and although it's not made right, it still tastes pretty good so I pour it into two bowls. There's barely enough here for one bowl though so I tip half of mine into Nate's bowl just leaving myself enough to curb off the sick empty feeling.

"Here you go kiddo," I say as I hand Nate the fullest bowl, he begins shoveling it into his face and then stops.

"Why did you only get a little bit Gabe?" He questions, and knowing if I tell the truth, Nate, being the huge hearted angel he is, will demand I share his, I lie.

"I already ate mine, while I was cooking yours, this is just a little bit I've got left."

"Oh okay then," he says with a smile before continuing to shovel the sticky yellow substance into his mouth.

I hear a car pulling up and fearing trouble, I force Nate to put his bowl down and drag him with me to hide in the bushes.

"Be quiet," I whisper as we hear a car door slam. "Don't move" I whisper forcefully as the footsteps get closer and closer.

"Uncle Johnny," Nathaniel squeals as he runs out of our hiding spot.

"Hey Rugrat, where's your dad?" John questions as he reaches into his pocket and hands Nate a small chocolate bar.

"Where he always is, passed out; has been all day." I huff as I walk over.

"Your old man make you dinner?" John questions.

"Gabriel did, look it's yummy," Nate says as he picks up his bowl and begins eating again.

John peers into Nate's bowl and shakes his head, "How about I treat you to a burger instead"

"Really?" Nate chimes as he bounces from foot to foot excitedly.

"We're fine, we don't need goddamn charity," I snap.

"It ain't fucking charity kiddo, I just don't wanna eat alone." John snaps back.

"Ok, whatever."

We follow John to his car and he drives us to the nearest McDonalds. He gets Nate a burger Happy Meal and some chicken nuggets, and me a super sized Big Mac meal, even after my protests and lies about not being hungry.

"Well eat it then, before it gets cold," he instructs when neither of us dare eat it in the car, despite the fact our mouths are salivating from the smell alone. I can't even remember the last time we had a fresh and hot meal. We've been living on leftovers, things out of a can or box, or just things we find lying around the house that Dad has dropped while drunk.

"Wanna come home with me, there's a fight on TV tonight I think you'll both enjoy," John says, turning his attention to me.

"Oh yeah and when Dad wakes up and realizes we're gone he'll beat our ass for a month," I say as I roll my eyes.

"Fine I'll drop you back home now then," John offers. I hear Nathaniel whine in the backseat, but I know a whine and grumble is better than a beating so I don't even acknowledge it.

John drives us back home, but rather than dropping us off and leaving like I expect him to do, he follows us up the path carrying a now sleeping Nate in his arms. He helps me take him to bed and I throw the blanket over him and then we both head back outside, not daring to risk waking my dad.

I'm sitting outside silently as John takes out a knife from his pocket and begins to widdle on a piece of firewood.

"What ya doing?" I ask as I move closer, curiosity getting the better of me.

"Just passing the time," he says as he holds up the piece of wood that vaguely resembles a dog. "Want me to teach you?" he asks

When I don't answer, he bends down to retrieve another piece of wood and takes out a second knife. It's a small pen knife from his belt and begins teaching me. "Be careful with the blade.... Watch your fingers..... Make small scratches," he instructs as he shows me bit by bit how to turn the wood into a recognizable shape.

"What the fuck is going on out here?" my father slurs as he stumbles over.

"'Bout time your lazy ass woke up." John laughs. "Been here for hours, go get us a beer already."

My father mumbles something in response before walking back inside.

"Here," I say, handing the wood and knife back to John.

"Keep it and keep practicing," he says as he gives my hair a little ruffle, before heading inside to see my dad.

## Now

I continue looking at the bear, running my finger over the rough edges, as I remember how excited I was to show this to him. I spent weeks trying and trying to get it perfect, carving firewood when everyone else was asleep until it finally resembled an animal. John was so proud when I gave it to him. *I can't believe he still has it all these years later though. I'd assumed he'd just thrown it away after I left.*

"What have you got?" Rebecca asks as she comes over and reaches for the wooden bear.

"Nothing, just something I made years ago," I say.

"Well you should keep it then since it clearly means more to you than it does me," she says with a kind smile.

"Nah, it must have somehow got mixed up with all the family stuff. John probably found it and assumed one of his kids made it."

"One of his kids did." Rebecca mumbles as she turns away.

"What did you say?" I question.

"I said one of his kids did make it," she repeats louder.

*Is this girl stupid? I just told her I made it.*

"You really are as stubborn and pigheaded as my father said, aren't you?" she laughs.

"What the fuck you talking about?" I snap. *Who is she to call me stubborn and pigheaded? She doesn't even know me. And what the fuck has John been saying behind my back?*

"You do know that you were my dad's favorite son right?" she says as she sits down beside me and gives me a strange look.

"You telling me John was fucking my mother or some shit?" I snap again. *How dare she tarnish my mother's memory!*

"No, god no. At least I don't think so," Rebecca adds with a frown. "But my dad thought of you as a son, nonetheless. All I ever heard was Gabe this, Gabe that. I'll be honest, as a teenager I was a little jealous. He sent me away to live with my grandparents, yet you worked with him day in and day out."

*My mind feels like it's going to explode. Because in a way she's right. John was the one who brought me my first beer, even if I was way too young. He was the one who regularly made sure food was on the table when I was growing up. He taught me to drive, in a way he trusted me with his whole empire. All those things are what Dads should do. And I guess he was the only man I ever had to look up to growing up. So maybe he was the closest thing I had to a father after all.*

"I need a smoke." I announce before heading outside, unable to deal with feeling so vulnerable in front of a complete stranger.

# Chapter Thirteen

# Riley

"Get up sloth, we've gotta leave soon," Harper grumbles as she yanks the quilt off me. I've been awake since eight, but while Harper has been flapping, trying to make sure her hair is perfect and that she's wearing the right underwear for trying on different styles of dresses, I've just been sitting with my coffee watching her.

I kind of feel bad, prom dress shopping should be exciting, and I get why her and the girls are acting like this is their goddamn wedding rehearsal, but I just feel meh, about the whole thing.

"So help me god Riley Mae, if you don't get your ass up, I'm having Ava drag you out by your bloody hair," Harper huffs.

"Fine!" I snap back, throwing the quilt off of me, and stomping towards the shower, slamming the door behind me.

I manage to shower, shove my hair into a semi neat updo, and even throw on a little makeup in less than half an hour. But I'm still standing in my underwear, about to stick on a cool summer dress when my door flies open.

"Well fucking good morning to you too," I fire as I throw the dress over my head before glaring at Ava.

"Oh good, you're awake. I had visions of having to drag you out of the house kicking and screaming in your pajamas," Ava laughs back as she plops herself down on my bed.

"Told you," Harper mumbles under her breath, which just makes me smirk.

"Where the fuck are my...."

"Shoes?" Harper finishes. I look up and she's holding my favorite Converse out for me.

"Thanks." I say reaching for them. I then make my way to Ava's car so we can pick Izzy up.

As soon as we pull up outside her house Ava honks the horn twice and Izzy comes running. I see Pops follow behind and the two of them stop for a little chat before Izzy jumps in the car.

Izzy's grandfather waves us off, even giving Izzy some extra cash to treat us all to lunch. *He really is the cutest little old guy ever. He's the sort of grandpa you see in Christmas movies.*

We make our way into the city since Izzy is supposed to be meeting her rich and super pompous parents, and then after we're all going prom dress shopping. But as soon as we arrive, to no shock to anyone, *well apart from Izzy who naively still holds out hope they will one day become the parents she deserves,* they cancel on her.

We then walk from one end of the city to the other looking in more shops than I can count. We even visit a few high-end stores, and while there are a few nice dresses here and there, there's nothing that really makes any of us say WOW.

"My feet are killing me, can we go home? Maybe we can find something online?" I suggest.

"No! There has to be somewhere else. We're going to find the perfect dresses, I just know it!" Ava fires back. Her tone is a mixture of stubborn determination, and the slightest hint of sadness.

"Maybe we could speak to Mom. Perhaps the lady who made her dresses for the cruise could make us something?" Harper suggests.

"Ooo, a one of a kind dress? That could work, better than anything Becky frigging Miller would wear, that's for sure." Ava chimes back.

*I can't help but internally roll my eyes, she's had it out for Becky ever since she joined the cheer squad. To be fair Becky is a bitch, her parents are rich as fuck, so she thinks that means the world should bow at her feet.*

"What do you think Izzy? Shall we speak..." Ava turns towards Izzy who is no longer beside her. "Izzy?" Ava calls looking behind her.

We all spot Izzy a few paces behind us staring into a shop window. We make our way over to her, but Izzy doesn't even look up or acknowledge us.

"Whatya doing?" Ava sings songs as she playfully bumps her shoulder.

"Got a secret you wanna share?" I add as I notice Izzy is staring into the window of a bridal shop, her nose practically pressed up against the glass.

"No. Don't be silly," Izzy laughs, her cheeks blushing. "I was just thinking."

"Just thinking of getting married? And I wonder who the lucky groom could be?" Harper teases.

"Come on, you've got about ten more years till you even need to consider that yet." I laugh as I link my arm through hers and prepare to walk us away.

"Wait, I see a red dress on the mannequin inside. Let's go in and see if they have any other dresses." Ava suddenly calls out disappearing inside before any of us have a chance to protest; so we have no choice but to follow her.

"Excuse me, this may sound like a strange question, but do you only sell white wedding dresses?" I hear Ava ask one of the ladies inside.

"We sell white, cream, and ivory wedding dresses, and we also have quinceañera, bridesmaid, and prom dresses upstairs." Ava, Harper, and Izzy practically bounce with excitement at that.

"If you want to try on one of our dresses, you'll need to schedule an appointment because you'll need a store representative to put them on for you." She must see the girls' faces sink as she quickly adds, "I can't promise anything, but our manager is in the back. I can see if she can squeeze you in."

"I hope she can fit us in," Izzy says.

"These dresses are perfect," Harper adds.

"They're perfect; I need one," Ava adds as she looks around, her smile getting wider and wider by the second.

And while I don't want to be here, I have to agree that everywhere I look are stunning dresses. I spot a sexy, sleek skin tight dress on one of the mannequins, and even I can't help but imagine myself in it.

An older, but still elegant woman comes down over to us and she just has an aura of importance about her.

"Hello, ma'am, my name is Isabella. We're looking for some dresses for our prom next month, and after seeing some of the beautiful gowns you stock, we were hoping you could help us."

"As you may have heard, usually we like our customers to make reservations in advance to try on the dresses. Here in *Beautiful Boutiques*, we like to sell not only dresses but also experiences," the woman begins.

"But actually, today you may be in luck because I've had a bit of a disaster myself. I'm supposed to showcase my latest collection of dresses at a wedding fair tomorrow. But two of my models have come down with the flu. I noticed that you're all beautiful girls. If you'd be willing to help me out and model for me tomorrow, I'll gladly repay you by allowing each of you to choose a dress from either our bridesmaid or other collection at a discounted price."

"We would love to!" All four of us cheer excitedly at the same time.

We spend almost three hours trying on dress after dress, while the ladies in the room make us stand in front of the mirror, so they can poke and prod at us. They make us turn this way and all the while they take little pins and mark them to make sure they fit us perfectly for tomorrow. But as amazing as the experience is, we're all exhausted by the time we are done. The manager, Louisa, orders some food, and then finally we get the chance to choose a prom dress.

She leads into a back room filled with dresses of all shapes, styles, and colors. We see dresses that are simple and elegant, as well as others that are extravagant and over the top. Each of us searches for a while, pointing out the ones we want to try on before returning to our dressing room.

First I try on a shorter red dress, it falls to just above my knee and is made from a shimmery, almost glitter like fabric. But I look fucking ridiculous, like a five year old playing dress up, so I quickly remove that.

Next, I try on a dark purple dress, this one is much nicer. It's floor length but has a split that goes up to my thigh, and while classy, still has that sexy, dangerous vibe to it. I'd easily give it an eight out of ten.

Finally I try on the final one, this one is black and floor length with a deep V at the front. I don't hold out much hope though as unlike the others that had a bit of a flowing material, one that will flatter over any little lumps and bumps I may have, this one is practically lycra. So I'm sure I'll look like Princess Fiona in it.

I turn away from the mirror and slide the dress on. *It doesn't feel tight.* I take a deep breath before turning around because even from the parts I can see looking down I already know I love it. *Please let this look as good as it feels.*

I slowly turn around and my eyes widen in shock. *Is that really me? I look hot as fuck! Gabe wouldn't be able to resist me in this, that's for sure. If only Gabe was taking me. It was supposed to be a special night for the two of us. Our coming out, so to say. Now, it's just a night I'm dreading with every fiber of my being.*

My hands glide down the material, it clings to every curve perfectly. *I feel like Jessica Rabbit in this.* The deep V makes my boobs look amazing yet still cover enough that I don't feel like

I'm going to fall out of it. I do a couple of little jumps just to make sure, but nope. Boobs stay put. I turn around and even my ass looks amazing. It has small silver buttons that seem to accentuate it. *I look like I've borrowed Kim K's ass for the night.*

There's no doubt in my mind, this is the dress. The only fucking dress. I could die right now and I'd ask to be buried in this dress.

I slide out from behind the curtain and see the other girls waiting. Ava looks amazing in a long red dress, looking like she's about to step out on the red carpet which is no shock. Ava could wear a trash bag and still look like a million dollars.

I let out a little gasp when I spot Harper. She looks amazing in a pale yellow dress that has a thin band of sheer fabric around her waist, so it looks like she's wearing a top and skirt. The top is full of lace and details, and the skirt is cut to look almost like a mermaid silhouette.

"Wow Harp, you look stunning!" I say, all three of the girls turn to look at me and I can see their eyes widen in shock as they look at me too.

"Holy shit, Riley! You look hot enough to turn even me lesbian, and you know I like me some man meat," Ava jokes while gawking at me.

"Daaamn girl, you look like a hot badass," Izzy exclaims before I see her cheeks redden as she realizes she swore out loud.

"You need to buy that, sis," Harper encourages as she takes my hand and spins me around, so she can see the back of the dress again.

I look over at Izzy now, but for some reason, she's the only one of us not wearing a beautiful dress.

Izzy breaks down when I question her about it, admitting none of them felt right. Ava teases her, trying to lighten the mood, but saying it's because she was too busy looking at the wedding dresses.

That's when Louisa drops a bomb on us and helps Izzy find the perfect dress. One that was practically made and sent to her by a goddamn guardian angel. And one that so happens to be a wedding dress, even if instead of being your standard white, it's the lightest shade of blue you've ever seen.

*I can't wait to see Nate's face when he sees her in it, he's going to lose his shit. I can half imagine him whisking her away from prom and to the nearest wedding chapel then and there.*

I head back to the changing room reluctantly removing my beautiful dress and putting on my summer dress. The one that an hour ago I loved, yet now it feels like a burlap sack.

I carefully place my gown back onto the hanger and that's when my world comes crashing down. *$1100!* I pick up the price tag, praying I read it wrong somehow; but nope, it's as clear as black and white this dress is $1100 even with the discounts Louisa offered us I know this is way out of my budget.

I pull out my phone and check my banking app, just in case I forgot I was secretly a millionaire. But nope, I have $762 in my account and that includes the $300 my father gave us both this week.

I mentally calculate what I could possibly do, or who would lend me money.

*My Nan said she wanted her fence and deck painted, perhaps if I offered to do that, she'd give me some money? And Mrs Banks is always looking for babysitters for her devil spawn triplets. Maybe I could ask Louisa to hold it for me and come back in a few weeks?*

*It doesn't matter what I think or do, I know in my heart this dress will never be mine. I'll just find another dress, a simple online deal; it's fine. I don't even have a date, who the fuck am I trying to look good for anyway? Plus spending over $1000 on a dress I'll only wear once is ridiculous.*

Reluctantly, I hand my dress back to one of the women to put back, mentally saying goodbye to my dream dress, and head back downstairs. Ava and Harper already have their dresses and a huge smile on their faces. But Izzy is nowhere to be seen.

"Did you get the dress?" Harper questions when she sees my empty hands.

"Nah, it just wasn't quite right, it was a bit too tight." I lie.

"We can wait, maybe there's another dress you'll like more?" Ava says kindly.

"Nah, I'm tired, I just wanna go to bed. Maybe I'll come back another day."

Izzy comes down and pays but as soon as she looks at me a deep frown forms on her face. "Where's your dress?"

"I didn't get it; I changed my mind," I mumble.

"You loved the dress! What changed?" She asks, but before I have the chance to respond, she adds, "The truth, please."

"Fine! The dress was too expensive; even with the discount it's still over my budget by almost one hundred and fifty dollars." I admit, unable to keep the disappointment from my tone

"I'll give you the money. I had it saved for my dress anyway, which I've not used. Plus, that dress was made for you. I'd gladly pay the money just so no one else can ever wear it," she declares.

"It's fine you don't have to do that." I smile.

"Riley, you're getting that dress; don't even argue. You love it. And it looks amazing on you. Go and grab it now. I'm not taking no for an answer," she adds. And it's clear from the unusual amount of bossiness to her tone she's sure.

I rush off to get the dress back. *I could practically kiss her. She is such a wonderful friend and has a heart of gold.*

"Thank you, thank you, thank you!" I sing, as I take the dress up to the counter and add the money Izzy has just given me to the money on my card.

"I'll pay you back, I promise."

"Don't bother, it's mostly my parents' guilt money anyway, they ain't gonna miss it and I don't need it." Izzy says as she hugs me.

*I don't know how rich her parents are, but from little bits I've seen or heard from them I'm guessing it's very rich. Yet not once has Izzy ever acted stuck up or made any of us feel below her in any way.*

Since it's so late and we're all so exhausted, we decide to stay overnight at a nearby Holiday Inn for the night since we've still got to do the show tomorrow morning like we promised. But the whole drive there I can't help but imagine what Gabe's face would be like if he could see me in this dress.

*Perhaps I should send him a picture of me in it, to show him what he's missing?*

# Chapter Fourteen

# Riley

I can't believe that I let Harper rope me into helping her decorate the ballroom for prom, especially since I'm still kinda dreading even going. To make matters worse, I've been left to do most of it alone since she's too busy to be here herself. I've got the amazing job of measuring the goddamn wall for the ridiculously large backdrop she and the drama club are designing for the prom.

My shoulders are aching from lugging around all the crap she thinks we need for this 'special day.' All I wanna be doing is sitting in a garden somewhere with a cold drink, soaking up the sun.

*I mean come on, the last thing I want to be doing on a Saturday morning is this shit. Especially when, for once, I've got nothing planned.*

But I guess, after how hard she fought to break me out of my funk and how much effort she put into helping me catch up with my schooling again, often missing out on clubs and studying by herself, I guess I owe her. *This is the least I can do.*

Wiping the sweat off my brow, I get a whiff of odor from my pits. *Yuck, I smell worse than Tucker after a football game.*

I head over to my bag, grateful when I spot a roll-on deodorant and some perfume.

Next, I make my way out of the hall, down the corridor in search of a bathroom or something. When I don't see one in the near vicinity, I head down the corridor, past the reception area, and towards the guest lobby. I'm just coming out when I feel the hairs on the back of my neck stand on edge. I turn my head and spot a gorgeous and very familiar face down the hall. One that makes both my heart beat faster and my stomach turn. *Fuck, fuck, fuck!!*

I see him enter the elevator and without even worrying about being caught I follow him. I watch as the little dial above the door tells me he exits on the first floor. Desperately I push the button again and again, praying it will somehow send it down quicker. *But of course it doesn't.* Eventually, the doors open for me and I take it up to the first floor, but by the time I get there, Gabe is nowhere to be seen.

*Did I imagine him? Was it someone else perhaps? Why would he even be here?* My mind flashes through question after question as I pace from one side of the corridor to the other looking for him. After about ten minutes of searching, I decided enough is enough.

*This is clearly some sort of mirage, where instead of imagining a body of water when dying of thirst, you imagine the ex who broke your heart and crushed it to a million pieces, just as you're finally beginning to rebuild your life.*

I'm almost back to the elevator ready to leave when yet again god, or whoever else is looking down and laughing at me, decides to torture me further. I watch it happen almost like a movie, Gabe's just a few feet ahead of me coming out of a hotel room. I speed up, desperate to finally talk to him after far too long of radio silence, but as well as his beautiful raspy tone I hear a second voice.

The voice is soft, feminine, and one that I don't recognize. I duck behind a pillar and when I peep around it I see Gabe and this woman chatting. He's smiling and looking down at her almost like how he used to look at me when we were together.

"Thanks for being such a sweet and helpful person, Gabe."

*I'm going to be sick. This can't be happening. Is SHE why he left me?* I peek around one more time and catch what looks to be the tail end of an embrace and I sink down to the floor with my head on my knees.

*I can't believe he's moved on so quickly; it's been a month and he's already at hotels with other women, fancy, expensive ones at that. He obviously cares about her. Especially to be so close to home.*

I peer out again, desperate to see what he's doing and who my replacement is, but he's gone. My legs begin moving, quicker than my mind can process what I'm about to do. Without thinking I bring my hand up and knock on the now closed door.

"What did you forget Ga..." the woman calls out before the door flies open.

"Oh you're not Gabe," the woman laughs. I take a moment to take in her appearance, she's beautiful. Gorgeous long brown locks, that cascade over her shoulders, a tiny waist, and a figure that makes me look like a goddamn elephant.

"Err...wrong room" I call out as I run away, back down the stairs and towards the bathroom. I lock the door and break down in tears.

I sit alone crying in the bathroom until I hear the door open and a couple of voices walk in. I stop crying, not wanting to be another cliche girl, crying in a bathroom over her ex. I wipe away my tears and once I hear them exit again I go out to wash my hands. I look at my reflection in the mirror and realize I am an absolute mess. I wash my face, removing all the makeup, since no makeup looks better than mascara all down my cheeks. And then with my head held as high as I can muster I walk out, and am almost out of the door when I hear that familiar voice again

"Riley?"

## Gabe

### Thirty minutes earlier.

"Well thanks for bringing these Gabe, it means alot." Rebecca says as she holds up the photo album I brought.

I felt bad for not being able to help John when he needed me, so since Rebecca came back into town last weekend, I've been doing my best to help her. Together we've bagged up John's clothes, donating most of them to Goodwill, and sorted through the rest of his house trying to decide what to put in storage till she can arrange for a shipping container and what can just go to the scrap yard. I found this photo album, the one containing pictures of Rebecca, her brother, John, and his first wife, her mother, before she passed away.

"I would have been heartbroken to lose these pictures," Rebecca says as she clutches the album close to her chest.

"Do you want a coffee or anything?" she offers. And I don't miss the hopeful little sparkle in her eyes. One that, although I'm being nice for John's sake, I have no desire to explore further.

Sure, she's a good looking girl I guess, kind of looks too breakable though, like one good fuck and she'd end up with a broken back, kind of skinny.

"Nah, I gotta get back to work, I only swung by to drop this off," I say as I stand up to leave.

"Thanks again," she says as she comes to see me out.

I'm just walking down the stairs when I get a strange sense, like I need to go back. *Weird! I* check my pockets quickly, wondering if perhaps I left my phone, but nope it's firmly in my pocket where it always is.

I walk downstairs but rather than leaving right away, I stop for a quick drink in the hotel bar. I'm just paying my tab when I see a familiar looking blond rushing through the lobby, I assume it must be Harper since it kind of looks like Riley but also doesn't. My girl struts. Every time I've ever seen her she's walked into the room like she fucking owns it. And her beautiful curves make sure that if her presence doesn't, her body makes sure every eye in the room is on her.

This girl though is meek and mild. Head down looking at the floor, clothes hanging off her body, making her look like the clothes are wearing her, rather than her wearing the clothes. I take a moment to watch, praying that if Harper is here, Riley may be too. But my expression goes from inquisitive to damn well shocked as the girl gets closer and I realize that this little mouse is none other than my very own firecracker.

"Riley?!" I called out in surprise.

The little mouse turns back and locks eyes with me, confirming all my fears.

"What happened to you?" I ask as my hand instinctively comes up and caresses her face. Riley leans into my hand for a mere second, before she pulls her face away.

"Hi Gabe," she says as her beautiful eyes dart back down to the floor. *What's wrong with her? Was this me? Did I do this?*

"Baby, look at me." I beg but when she doesn't respond I place my finger under her chin and lift her head myself. "Look at me, please my little Wild Fire."

Her eyes slowly find mine, but instead of the usual fire behind them, all I see is nothingness. As if any light she once had has been extinguished. Not even the embers remain.

I throw my arms around her, needing to feel her body against mine. I hear a breath escape her lips, before a barely audible, "Gabe get off me," can be heard. I don't listen, instead holding her tighter until I feel her hands pushing me away. But even that is subdued. She's pushed me before when she's been mad, and it was a full on forceful shove; this feels more like a grazed touch. Barely enough to even register it's there.

"Please Gabe, get off me." she says, a little more intentional, and this time I release her. *What a reversal, a few months ago I did anything to avoid being hugged, yet now, my arms ache to be filled again.*

She turns to leave, but I reach out and grab her wrist, desperate to stop her. Unsure what to do now that I have her, my eyes dart around the hall until I spot what looks like an empty conference room, and drag her into it with me. I guide us both towards it, only releasing her when we are safely inside. As soon as we were in I flick the lock on the door, not even thinking about how creepy that probably seems, just desperate to stop her from leaving again.

"What are you doing?" she questions.

I turn around scoop her into my arms, hating how light and fragile she feels, and gently sit her down on one of the large conference room tables.

"Baby, talk to me?" I beg as I step closer, nothing but her knees keeping me from being as close as I want.

Unsure what to do or say to break her out of this quiet state, I do the only thing I can think of, and let our bodies do the talking. I grip the side of her cheek as I place a soft kiss on her lips. My kiss gets more needy, until her lips finally part, allowing me access, her arms wrap around my neck, and her knees widen, allowing me entrance as I use my free hand to wrap around her back and pull her closer.

Our bodies take on a mind of their own as they slowly fall back into their natural rhythm, her hands find their way into my hair and begin tugging and my fingers dip into the skin of her hip as my other hand grips her jaw.

I release her face and place both hands around her waist so I can lift her off the table and place her on the floor. I hover over her, kissing her harder and harder as I push my body against hers.

I don't even try to hide how hard I am for her. A small moan escapes her lips, letting me know she is enjoying this, and can probably feel my erection pushing against her. My hand is just about to slide under her shirt when suddenly, someone attempts to open the door, the handle rattling against the lock.

And just like that, the moment is gone. Riley shuffles from under me looking at me with so much regret that it shocks me for a moment. I can see the moment of realization she gets about what almost happened and her switch to panic mode. She unlocks the door and runs away like I was fucking attacking her or something.

I lock eyes with a very confused looking woman, and then exit the room myself. I try looking for Riley but she's vanished.

I rush to my bike and start driving it around, desperate to find her and…. Apologize? *No that can't be right because I never want to have to apologize for trying to be close to my girl. But if she doesn't want it then does that mean I should apologize? I'm so confused.*

## Riley

The door rattles and just like that, a tidal wave of reality hits. *What the fuck am I doing?*

I was so caught off guard when I saw Gabe. Gabe, the boy my heart still beats for, the boy I would lay my life down for, the boy who I wanted to spend my future with. but yet again, one look into his beautiful green eyes was all it took for my self respect to disappear, as I followed him into my own destruction. Yet again I let him lead me away, have his fun with me, heck had whomever that was not disturbed us, yet again I would have given him another part of me.

*And for what? For him to just discard me again after? What the fuck is wrong with me? I literally just saw him coming out of another girl's hotel room. He was probably fucking someone else just moments ago, and here I am yet again spreading my goddamn legs for him. I'm a disaster!*

I make the most of the moment of distraction and run out of that room as fast as my legs will carry me. I run straight out the door, out of the hotel, and duck down between two parked cars. I hear Gabe a few seconds later rush out shouting my name but I stay put, I hear the sound of his bike start as he drives off but still, I stay hidden. Once I'm finally sure the coast is clear I scurry out from my hiding spot. I walk back into the hotel, with my tail between my legs, grab my handbag, jacket, and phone then take off again. I text Harper asking her to come pick up the rest of her things, and then rather than wait around I decide to clear my head with a walk.

As I'm walking, reliving the whole saga in my mind I imagine what I should have said and done. *I should have told him to fuck off. Should have refused to kiss him, pulled away when he tried to cradle my face so softly. I should have slapped him! How dare he!*

I begin kicking rocks and random soda cans as I continue having a one sided argument. *Who the fuck does he think he is? While I've been going through hell since our break up, he's clearly been fine. Fine enough to move on to someone else. What a dickhead!*

My anger at myself, at him, at the whole fucked up situation, continues bubbling. And like any bubbling pot it eventually boils over.

By the time Harper finally calls me back, I practically have steam coming out of my ears.

"Hey, Rilez, is everything okay?" Harper asks as I answer the phone.

"Yep," I say angrily.

"You sure? You sound pissed. Did something happen?" she asks again, sounding concerned.

"Nope," I say in a clipped tone. "But I left your shit at the hotel, it's all in a box in the ballroom. You might wanna get one of the guys to pick it up for you."

"Oh, okay. Do you need a ride home? I bet Ava or Nate would be happy to swing by and grab you," she offers.

"No, I'm fine, I got shit to do, bye," I say, not even giving her a chance to speak before I hang up.

*Sure, the smart thing to do would be to go home, talk to the girls first, make a plan, or at least let them talk me out of my current one. But no. I'm not in the mood for talking, I'm in the mood for taking action. And that's exactly what I intend to do!*

## Chapter Fifteen

## Gabe

I search everywhere I can think of before I finally give up. As I pull back up to work I see Marko's shitbox of a truck parked outside. *What the fuck is he doing here?*

I park my bike and make my way inside and find him sitting in my fucking chair, feet up on my motherfucking desk.

"Nice of you to join us," he sneers as he looks at Michael and another guy, one I don't recognize sitting on the sofa that's against the back wall.

"What the fuck do you want Marko? You can't just keep turning up here, you know John's fucking rules… the two businesses stay separate," I seethe.

"Yeah, well good thing John is fucking dead and nothing more than maggot food then, ain't it!" he snaps back, as he pulls himself upright and slams his fist against my desk.

"Fuck you Marko. You sick son of a bitch, I'll get my revenge one of these days. Mark my fucking words," I snap.

It's then I suddenly feel my legs buckle from under me as a sharp kick lands against the back of my knees causing me to fall forward. I manage to put my hands out just in time to catch myself from headbutting the floor.

"That's it Gabe, goddamn kneel for me!" Marko practically squeals, voice full of sadistic delight.

I pull myself up and stand, fury in my face, ready to throw punches. That is until I see Riley's picture sitting on top of my desk. A goddamn knife poking out the top of it.

"Oh, this?" Marko says when he catches me staring. Found this in one of your drawers." he laughs. *Fuck! I meant to take that home with me, instead, I've been staring at it every day as if it's a goddamn beacon of hope.*

"Keep her out of this" I shout.

"Now that all depends on you doesn't it? Are you gonna step up and fall in fucking line like a good little soldier or do I have to pay your little whore another visit; this time myself? Will that drive the message home for you?"

The blood pumping in my ears and the sound of my heart beating in my chest is too loud for me to hear anything else being said. Fear after fear flies through my mind at a trillion miles an hour. "What..do..you..need?" I managed to get out through gritted teeth.

"Saints. One hour. Don't be late," Marko snaps as he removes the knife sticking into my desk and places it back in his waistband. I watch with thunderous eyes as his two cronies follow behind like he's a mother fucking king or some shit.

*Just you wait. I'll make each and every one of you regret fucking with me. Just a few more months and Riley will move away to college...Then I'm coming for you all!*

I carefully pick up Riley's picture, reminding myself exactly why I'm putting up with Marko's shit, and place it in the safe. The only good thing is, other than me, the only other people who know the combination for the safe are John and his most trusted friend Mike.

*Come to think of it, I'm surprised that I haven't seen him around more. I would have thought he'd have offered to help with the businesses.*

I lock up my office, do my rounds quickly to make sure the guys are on track and all know what they're doing for the rest of the day, and then I make my way to Saints.

As soon as I walk in, I spot Declan. He gives me a small nod of recognition, and I start to walk over. I really need to clear the air, since it's been weeks since I've been here. And the last time I was, he practically threw me out.

"Gabe, we're outside." Deeno calls out across the bar as he makes his way towards the bathroom. I look back to Declan and the smile on his face has morphed into fury. So instead of heading to the bar to grab a much needed drink, I make my way out back to where Marko and his guys are waiting. I take a seat and listen along, chiming in every now and again, while Marko talks about his pathetic ideas for expansion and how he's in talks with another guy for some sort of huge fifty/fifty split of some shipment due to come in soon.

I know full well it isn't going to work. The other gang; The Dragons, he's talking about doing runs out of the South side. Their boss and John go way back. Definitely wouldn't call them friends, more like friendly enemies. They have mutual respect and don't cross each other's turf. Compared to Cruz, John was a pussycat. Sure we dealt in drugs, money laundering, and the odd shakedown, but Cruz is more big time. He deals in guns and prostitution mainly. So while I know that this partnership is destined to end in disaster, I keep my mouth shut and let some ideas form.

"I need to piss," I announce when I finally get sick of nodding along and agreeing in the right fucking places.

I head inside and am just taking care of business when I hear Declan's voice behind me.

"What the fuck are you doing Gabe? You really are one of those fuckers now?" he snaps. "I thought you were better than that," he added in a disappointed tone.

Looking around to ensure no one is around and listening I add, "It's not like that; I hate them as much as you do, but sometimes shit just happens."

"Shit happens? Tell that to my dad, Gabe. Because pretty sure if you truly hated them as much as I did you wouldn't be playing nice like you are."

"Maybe we could have this discussion when I'm not standing with my dick in my hands," I add, trying to make a joke but it falls on deaf ears.

"You're a fucking joke Gabe Scott, a mother fucking joke. You make out like you hate them just as much as I do and then you become their fucking puppet. You make me sick." Declan seethes, panting heavily as the anger rolls off of him in waves.

I attempt to turn, then almost end up pissing on my own shoe. *Seriously when the fuck is this piss gonna end? It's like goddamn Niagara Falls.*

Finally I finish, shake and shove my dick back in my jeans. Ready to continue my argument. *But seriously, who the fuck picks a fight with a guy who has his dick out?*

"You just don't get it.." I begin but Declan cuts me off.

"You're right I don't fucking get it because those cunts are the same ones who beat my father half to death over a couple thousand dollars. That man was in a coma Gabe, doctors still don't know if he'll ever regain his memory, and for what? For some shitty loan, to keep this bar, my grandfather's bar, up and running. You know this. You know the shit those assholes are capable of and STILL you go running to them, join their little crew and let Marko, mother fucking Marko of all people, take the lead. That sadistic son of a bitch is the devil incarnate. Do you know that bastard has not just doubled, but fucking tripled my monthly interest amount? I'm barely making ends meet as it is here, hardly anyone comes anymore because of your guys, and now what? After everything I've done to keep this bar, after my father almost died to keep this bar, I'm gonna lose it anyway. All because some jacked up little pricks got greedy?" Declan spews.

My mind flashes back to the first time I met Declan; I was barely nineteen, had only just taken my place as John's right hand man, still desperate to impress and show my worth, when a young Marko joined. This was my first job where John had allowed me to take the lead. It should have been simple. Collecting money from some old guy from the pub down the street sounds simple right? Wrong! Unbeknownst to me, Marko and another guy, Eli, who thankfully disappeared not long after, came packing. While I was doing the usual, breaking a few bottles, smashing a few windows out back, Eli and Marko were beating the shit out of the owner.

A loud sound ricocheted through the air, a gunshot! I came running out in time to see Eli and Marko running out the door as the owner was bleeding out on the floor. I had been tempted to run myself, terrified, but it was the old guy sputtering for help that stopped me. I called an ambulance, stating I was passing by when I heard the gunshot. They managed to save his life, but barely. Since then, riddled with guilt, I visited him in the hospital every week, which is how I met his son Declan who until then had been working away. I've been trying my best to help where I can since, even paying a few of Dec's monthly installments myself. Since that night though, I've had a very strict no weapons policy for all the guys. Fists only.

I reach out to place my hand on his shoulder but he pulls away. "No Gabe, fuck you and your fake friendship. I was a fool for actually believing you had some decency left. You promised me! You motherfucking promised me, over my father's hospital bed that you would make this shit right. That you would take over whatever stupid thug business you guys have going on, and you would make shit right. You mother fucking swore to me that you would make sure no other family suffered the way we have. You swore that you would be better, but you know what? You're worse! You know the shit they do and yet you allow it to happen. You take your place as a fucking side piece for what?"

"Declan, let me explain." I say but again he cuts me off.

"No! Fuck you Gabe, I hope you fucking get what's coming to you," he snaps before he storms out.

I finally wash my hands and leave, making my way back outside. Thankfully no one seems to have noticed I've been gone so long as they're all so invested in their plans for expansion.

"Where the fuck is that cock sucker with our drinks?" Phoenix complains after realizing it's been ages since we last saw Declan.

"I'll go find out," I say, grateful for the excuse to leave.

I head up to the bar and try to get Declan's attention but despite the fact the bar is virtually empty, there is only one other person anywhere near us, he completely ignores me and focuses all his attention on them.

"Declan, Dec," I call out trying to get his attention.

"What?" he snaps as he finally comes over to me.

"Look, meet me here first thing tomorrow. I'll explain everything okay. Nine o'clock."

"Please." I stress when he just stares at me trying to make a decision.

"I fucking live here so I guess I'll be here anyway," he says with a huff. "But you've got one fucking chance Gabe. One." He says as he holds up one finger to really drive his point home.

I'm just giving Declan our order when out of the corner of my eye I see her. *Fuck! I* leap off my seat and rush over.

"There you fucking are," she snaps. "Should have known I'd find you here," she says as she sits on the edge of a nearby table. And while I want to be happy, happy to see she's found a little piece of her fire again, all that I can feel is fear.

"Shh, Riley, " I try to say as I try to guide her away.

"Shush? Fucking shush? Who the fuck do you think you are?" she shouts, drawing some attention from the few people in the bar.

"Baby, you need to go now," I all but beg.

"Go? Fucking go?" she shouts.

Without thinking I reach out and place my hand over her mouth. I see her eyes widen in surprise.

"Where's our fucking drinks?" I hear in the distance behind me, and knowing that means one of the Sinners is about to catch us. I thicken my hold on Riley's mouth, spin her around, wrap my free arm around her waist and part carry, part run with her, using my feet to kick the bar door open as I lead her away. Not letting go until we are outside and around the corner.

*Do I probably look like a kidnapper? Yes? But do I give a fuck? No!*

"What the actual fuck, Gabe?" Riley coughs when I finally release her.

"Sorry, I just needed you out of there." I panicked.

"Need me out of there?" she questions.

"Yeah...err," I begin, unsure what to say.

"Worried your latest conquest would see me and she wouldn't wanna fuck you again?" she says as she squints her eyes and crosses her arms.

*Latest conquest? Fuck me? What is she talking about?*

"Your little side piece from the hotel, your little model!" she snaps, her tone sarcastic and venomous.

*Hotel? What hotel? Oh wait, does she mean Rebecca? I'm so confused.*

"You know…" she begins. "I really fucking hated Kelly for everything she did, for sleeping with you and then rubbing it in my face. But you know what? I get it now, I'm just like fucking Kelly..."

"You're nothing like her, she's" I try to interject but she cuts me off.

"You're right, I'm worse," she says as she begins pacing back and forth in front of me. "At least she knew you were just casual, she was clever enough to protect her heart, me? I was the dumbass who gave my heart and soul to you, only to let you crush it. I'm the dumb bitch that sees you coming out of some other girl's hotel room and STILL allows you to kiss me afterward. What does that make me?" she says, turning back to face me.

"That makes you, my Little Flame, my Firecracker, my girl," I add, but again she talks over me.

"That makes me a fucking fool! But you know what Gabe? I'm done. I'm done with everything. Fuck you, I don't want to ever see you again." she snaps before storming off.

I race after her, but she turns around and verbally floors me.

"You were nothing but a mistake!!" she screams.

Feeling like the wind has just been knocked out of me I stop dead in my tracks and watch as my whole world disappears right in front of my eyes as she gets further and further away.

## Chapter Sixteen

# Riley

I storm off before I goddamn slap him. *Who does he think he is covering my mouth and marching me out the fucking door? What a complete dick!*

His face was a picture when I mentioned the girl from the hotel, his guilty, shocked, confused face as it dawned on him that I knew all about his latest girl.

*Was he seeing her when he was with me? Is that why he cut ties so suddenly? Realized there was someone better? After all, why the fuck would he want a short, tubby, girl like me when he could have a goddamn supermodel?*

I keep going, with no clear direction in mind. Just needing to be as far away from him as possible.

*Seriously, how could I have been so dumb? I should have known I'd never be good enough for a guy as hot as Gabe; wait, scrap that, he's not good enough for ME. That's right. Sure I may be a little bigger than I'd like to be, but I'm still hot in my own way. I mean heck,* the guys on the boat the other week clearly thought I was alright. Plus, I've often caught guys eyeing me up at school.

Feeling more and more confident with each step, I continue walking. *Screw him! I'm better than this. Why should I stay home, moping and pining after him, when he clearly isn't doing that over me.*

I'm almost on the main street when an idea hits me. *Lexi!* I make my way to her salon praying she's working today. I walk inside and spot her behind the reception almost immediately. "Hey freckles, I didn't have you booked today, did I?" she questions as she looks past me, probably expecting to see the rest of the girls.

"Nope," I said confidently. "But I'm hoping you'll be able to fit me in any way."

"Yeah, sure, come on over," she says a little confused as she guides me over to her station.

"So what can I do for you, nails? Waxing? Fake tan?" she questions.

"Everything!"

"Oh, okay," she replies skeptically.

"I want the whole, new year, new me, package" I reply.

"Freckles, it's June." Lexi jokes.

"Fine, then give me the, 'I just had my heart torn out of my chest and ripped into a million small pieces and now I need a whole new look to make myself feel better' package then." I concede.

"Say no more," another girl says as she comes over carrying a glass of water. "My client just canceled so I've got two hours free, let's go get your hair done," she offers.

"I don't think I've got enough…" I begin.

"Don't worry about the money, it's already paid, my client gave me literally thirty minutes' notice, I'm charging the bitch anyway," she says with a smirk, before leading me to her chair.

"So then," The girl says as she begins placing the cloak around me. "How crazy do you want to go? Do you want just a freshen up, or do you want a whole new you?"

"Erm, I'm not sure, maybe shorten it, add some texture, maybe change the color." I begin before a woman at the next chair pipes up.

"Oh dear, I know it's none of my business, but don't dye your beautiful hair, You look beautiful already, like a little doll," the older lady adds, and although deep down I know it was meant as a compliment, it infuriates me. *A little doll? A cute, innocent little doll. What if I don't wanna be a cute little doll, what if I want to be a sexy little minx instead? Fuck it, go big, or go home.*

"I want a total revamp! I want to look hot, sexy, and desirable." I admit.

"That I can do!" the girl says. "Give me a few minutes, I'll be back with some color samples. I'm Brooke by the way" she adds before disappearing into one of the back rooms.

My phone buzzes in my pocket, and when I pull it out I see Harper's name appear. *Is this a sign from god? Trying to tell me I'm making a mistake, and knowing that if I tell Harper what I'm about to do, she'll talk some sense into me? Probably.* That is why I simply decline the call and text her back telling her I'm hanging out with some friends, before turning my phone on silent.

Brooke returns a few minutes later with a stack of color samples, and hair magazines. "Have a little look through, find something you like, and we'll make it happen," she says, sounding excited.

"You want a coffee, tea, or a soda, while you decide?"

"Don't suppose you have iced coffee do you?" I ask, hopefully.

"Don't think we do," she replies furrowing her brow. "But now you mention it I kinda want one too"

"Lola," she shouts.

A girl about my age comes running over, "Yeah?"

"Do us a favor, take some cash out of my tip jar and go grab me and..."

"Riley"

"...me and Riley an iced coffee from across the road, we've got a serious makeover to do." Brooke says with a mischievous grin. *What the fuck have I got myself into?*

Brooke disappears for a few moments, giving me some time to flick through everything. Before long an idea hits me, and I know exactly what I want.

"Any ideas?" Brooke asks as she comes over carrying our drinks.

"Yes, would it be possible to do this cut, with this color, but...."

I show her pictures and ideas, with no clue if what I'm suggesting will work, or look good. I expect Brooke to make another suggestion, and tell me my idea is crazy; but instead, that mischievous look on her face just gets bigger.

"I love it." she squeals. "Your ex isn't gonna know what hit him when he sees you next"

She guides me over to the wash basin and washes my hair. "So you don't have to share if you don't want to, I can be kind of nosey, but I've also been told I'm a great listener. If you want to vent or tell me what idiot broke your heart, I'm happy to listen."

*Should I? Do I want to share all the details of my heartbreak?*

I start off small, telling her how I met Gabe last year in a bar, and how he turned out to be my friend's older brother.

"Oooh friend's hot older brother, I love that trope" Brooke purrs.

"Yup me too. Didn't expect to be living it though." I laugh. "Did I mention he also rides a motorcycle?"

I then go into more detail, and by the time the color is on my hair and processing I've basically spilled my guts. Poor Brooke has heard about how rocky things were at the start, how I thought he'd started to open up to me, about our date at Six Flags, and all the romantic motorcycle rides we went on, even about my stupid idea to leave clues leading him to my bedroom that last night we spent together. Before he just dropped me and moved on with that supermodel from the hotel.

"Woah, that sounds like a complete whirlwind. No wonder you want to mix it up." Brooke says.

"Frec.." Lexi begins to say as she comes around the corner, but her eyes go big when she takes in my crazy appearance. I basically look like Medusa, my hair an array of different foils and clips. "What are you doing?" she asks as she peers into the multiple pots of different colored hair dyes sitting on the trolley beside me.

"You'll see... it's gonna be fire!" Brooke adds with a giggle.

Brooke sends me over to Lexi with my hair still looking wild to get my nails and toes painted.

"So what happened with you and Gabe?" Lexi questions. "The last time I spoke to you things were going really well."

"It was going well, really well. At least I thought it was but…"

"That lying cheating scumbag!" Lexi huffs, when I tell her about the fact that I ran into him earlier at the hotel, and then he had the audacity to try and kiss me. Then to top it all off, he virtually kicked me out of Saints.

"Are you nearly done?" Brooke asks as she comes over to check on my hair. "Because this looks amazing," she says proudly.

She guides me over to the sink and begins carefully removing the foils. "Ooo" and "ahh" ing ever so often.

"Honestly, I thought this would look good, but this looks even better than I imagined," Brooke beams from behind me.

She finishes washing the color out, wraps my hair in a towel, and then leads me back to the styling chair. I inhale deeply hoping that I didn't make a giant mistake, and just when I think I'm going to see the color, she does something strange, she takes out a second towel and uses it to cover the mirror. *Damn her!* I can't see my hair. I hear her chuckle to herself when she must see my face but she just continues to remove the towel from my head and begins cutting and blow drying. Every so often I see a flash of color as a red or orange strand flies past my face, but not enough for me to have any idea what it looks like. *What have I done? What if it looks ridiculous? Was this a stupid idea?"*

"Lexi, Lexi" Brooke calls.

"Yeah?" Lexi calls back as I see her walking over.

"Come and see!" Brooke calls again, excitement in her voice. *It must look good then if she's excited to show others.*

"Woah Freckles, that.." but before she has a chance to finish her sentence Brooke is shushing her.

"Close your eyes and when I say ready, count to five and open them." Brooke instructs.

I do as I'm told and hear footsteps walking in front of me, probably to remove the towel. " Ready," Brooke calls.

"Five...four..." the two girls shout and I feel my tummy doing nervous belly flips. "three...two ..." they call out and my tummy flips, turning into full on somersaults making me feel like I may actually throw up. "One!" I take a calming breath, and then slowly open my eyes. When I do, I can't help but gasp in shock. *Who is this person staring back at me?* While talking to Brooke earlier I'd mentioned how Gabe always told me I was fiery, and used some variation of that as a pet name, Firefly, Firecracker, Spitfire, you name it he probably used it. But I explained how since he abandoned me, I feel like I'd lost that fire. So she decided to give it back to me. But nothing could have prepared me for how fucking right she was.

"What do you think?" Brooke asks nervously.

"I love it!" I all but cheer.

She hasn't taken too much off the length but underneath the top layer, she's added a mixture of red and orange, and then cut a few layers into my hair so that the color pokes out from beneath the blind. I sway my head from side to side, watching as the 'flames' flash with each sway from the breeze. Brooke spins me around and has me look into a smaller hand mirror so that I can get a better view of the back and when I say it looks beyond amazing, I mean it looks beyond fucking amazing.

"Damn, move aside Katniss Everdeen, we got a new girl on fire," Lexi adds as she bounces on the spot excitedly.

"Do you mind if I get some pictures? Brooke asks.

"No," I laugh, "of course not, it's the least I can do."

"What are you doing tonight?" Lexi asks, a plan clearly forming in her mind if her mischievous smirk is anything to go by.

"Erm nothing really, why?"

"Brooke," Lexi calls, "you think your boyfriend will be okay with us bringing a friend tonight?"

"You really think I'm gonna let a masterpiece like that go to waste sitting at home alone?" she laughs as she comes back over and begins taking pictures of my hair.

"You're coming out with us tonight Freckles. The best way to get over a shitty ex is to find someone better," Lexi says with a smirk.

The word ex, to describe Gabe seems so worthless, so small, so insignificant. It doesn't even begin to describe what he is to me. I'm not yet ready for him to be just a chapter in my story. The idea of finding anyone else feels strange, alien even. But the thought of forgetting everything for a night, having a few drinks, enjoying some dancing maybe, and perhaps having some innocent flirting does sound appealing. *If Gabe can move on, so can I!*

"Go get your things. You can spend the night at mine, and I'll meet you back here in say an hour? How does that sound?" Lexi offers.

"Any chance I can borrow some of your clothes instead? I kind of don't want to go home." I admit, knowing full well if I go home now and see Harper she will try and talk me out of whatever tonight is going to bring. She likes Lexi, we both do, but she thinks Lexi brings out the more rebellious side of me. And I know right now I don't have someone to remind me to be smart or to make good choices. I don't need a guardian; I need someone who will take the reins and let me go crazy instead.

"Yeah sure. Looks like Sophie? No, Stacey! Is making a repeat appearance then," she smirks.

"Stacey?" Brooke questions.

"Stacey is apparently Riley's confident and sexy alter ego, last time she partied with us she bagged the hottest guy in the club." I see Lexi's proud smile turn into an awkward one as she suddenly remembers that the hottie in question is exactly who I'm trying to forget.

"Well then I look forward to meeting her," Brooke chimes.

## Chapter Seventeen

## Riley

I'm really starting to look forward to tonight and am checking myself out as I put one last coat of mascara on my lashes. *Damn! I look good! I can't believe I did this to my hair.* I feel my self confidence returning and then all of a sudden, it's like the floor drops out from beneath me because I hear a familiar voice. One that I had hoped to never hear again.

"Lex, mom said..." comes the voice seconds before the door swings open.

"Who's your friend Lex?"

I turn around just in time to see Justin, checking me out.

"What the fuck?" he says as his eyes scan up my body and finally land on my face.

"Hey Justin, how's Jess?" I ask with nothing but venom in my voice.

"Erm, err, yeah," he mumbles before closing his mouth.

"What am I missing?" Brooke says as she looks from me to Justin and eventually to Lexi.

"Oh, not much, we dated briefly, a lifetime ago," I say as I hold my ground and look directly into Justin's stupid face. *What did I ever see in him?*

"But he's not…" Brooke begins but I cut her off, refusing to let one ex know that another one has dumped me too.

"Nope, he's not my big, bad, biker. He's just some boy. A very distant memory. Someone I dated briefly growing up."

"We were a little more than that Rilez" Justin replies sounding genuinely hurt.

"Were we?" I ask. Before turning back around and reaching for my purse. "I'm ready when you are girlies."

"Yep, let's go then," Lexi replied, her voice clearly having a slight giggle to it.

We walk down the stairs and the whole time I can feel eyes boring into the back of my head. I turn my head slightly and can see that Justin's eyes are focused on my ass. *Hmm, bet you wished you hadn't fucked Jessica now!*

As soon as we get into Lexi's car she bursts out in hysterics, "Oh my god Freckles, that was fucking savage!"

"I want to be you when I grow up," Brooke chimes in. "No wonder your nickname is Fire, because damn, I feel like I've got third degree burns just from watching that."

"Was it that bad?" I ask, starting to feel a little guilty, after all, Justin is still Lexi's brother.

"Yes, but in the best way. About time that little shit got a taste of his own medicine." Lexi adds.

We pull up outside some frat house, one that looks every bit as ridiculous and wild as in the movies. People doing keg stands in the front garden and drunken idiots everywhere.

*You got this. Just have fun, have some drinks, and forget all about Gabe fucking Scott.*

I get out of the car, following Lexi and Brooke inside. The inside is even more wild than the outside. Half naked girls in nothing but shorts and bralettes run past me. The music booms through the house; it's just madness. Exactly what I'd expect for my first college party.

"Stay with me," Lexi instructs as she sees me scanning the room. She takes me by the arm and leads me through the house to the kitchen so we can all get a drink and then towards the so-called dance floor.

"Hey baby," a guy purrs as he begins kissing Brooke, and by kissing I mean, full on kissing. His hands clamp her ass as he virtually swallows her whole face. I begin looking around, scanning the room, suddenly feeling like a total third wheel.

"Baby, this is my new friend Riley," Brooke says as she pushes her boyfriend, *at least I hope it's her boyfriend,* away.

"Hey," the guy replies, giving me a quick nod.

"The guys and I are out back if you wanna join us," the guy adds, before giving Brooke another small kiss on the cheek and walking away.

We continue dancing and are soon joined by a couple more of Lexi and Brooke's friends. The drinks are flowing, but the heat from all the bodies starts to get to me.

"I'm heading out for some fresh air; I feel like I'm gonna pass out from the heat." I say as I try to leave.

"Wait, I'll come with you." Lexi offers.

"No it's fine, I won't be long."

Lexi grabs hold of my arm and pulls me close to her. "Don't go far, Freckles. Come back here when you're done."

"I will," I assure her. *And there she is, my protective babysitter.*

I head outside, loving the feel of the breeze on my face as I close my eyes and finally take some relaxing breaths. The smell of cigarette smoke wafts over me, I look over and see a few guys all smoking just a few feet away. Suddenly, craving the taste of smoke on my tongue I make my way over.

"Hey, don't suppose I could steal a smoke, could I?" I ask the nearest guy.

"Sure," he replies as he hands me one. I don't miss the way his eyes dart to my chest, even though I'm not wearing anything particularly sexy tonight, just jeans and a simple top. My boobs have always liked to be center stage, especially now that I've dropped a dress size, making them look even bigger.

The guy begins patting his pockets before turning to his friends, "Who's got my lighter?" he asks. I throw the cigarette into my mouth, and seconds later someone is leaning over to light it. "Thanks," I say as I look up, and realize that the person lighting it is none other than Zander, the fake Gabe from the boat.

"You're welcome. Love the hair by the way, total firecracker" he smirks.

*Really universe? You're gonna have me face to face with another tattooed hunk? A tattooed hunk that also smokes and calls me a firecracker? You hate me that much, do you God?*

"Did I say something wrong?" Zander asks.

"No, why?" I question.

"Oh, your face kind of dropped."

"Sorry," I blush, "my ex used to call me his Firecracker. Guess it kind of just reminded me of him.." I admit.

"Got it! No more calling you that. Tonight's a party, a happy type of party. We're over here," he says as he waves a couple of his buddies over to us.

I don't know how long the bunch of us spent chatting, but it must have been a while because the next thing I know, Lexi and Brooke are running over to us.

"There you are," Lexi huffs, seeming a bit perturbed.

"Oh sorry, I've been talking," I admit.

"Is this the ex?" Brooke questions as she looks Zander up and down.

"No." I laugh, "Just a new friend."

"Well, I could have been more, but your girl ghosted me after I gave her my number," Zander says as he playfully shoulder bumps me.

"Damn girl. You got men drooling over you left, right, and center." Brooke laughs.

"I'm just not looking for anyone else." I say as I give Zander an awkward smile.

"It's fine, I'm just messing with you. You're not the first, and I'm sure you won't be the last pretty girl to turn me down." he says with a warm smile.

*What a difference in response that was. If that was Gabe when we first met, he'd have called me out for being a bitch, and said something to try and hurt me for fracturing his fragile male ego. Yet Zander just smiled in response.*

"Oh my god! I love this song, come dance," Lexi says as she drags me away and back inside. "Sorry," I mouth to Zander as I'm dragged away. He just smirks back in response as he continues to smoke.

We hit the dance floor and are having a great time when I feel someone virtually grinding up against me. I move away slightly, but moments later I feel the familiar sense of someone invading my space.

"Not interested," I say over my shoulder, before moving away again. Seconds later the creep puts his hands on my hips and I spin around. "Leave me the fuck alone" I snap, the drunken asshole just smiles at me.

"Come on doll, I just want a dance" he slurs as he tries to pull me in closer.

I'm about to snap back when I suddenly hear, "There you are babe, I've been looking everywhere for you," before I feel someone lightly graze my lips.

I pull back furious, until I realize it's Zander.

The drunk guy mutters, "fuck this," and stumbles away.

I look back at Zander who is still standing there looking a bit worried "Sorry," he says, as he looks down guiltily. "You looked like you needed some help, but he's the head of the football team I'm trying to get on so I couldn't exactly fight him." Zander adds with a shrug.

"It's fine." I say with a smile.

*Okay so think first, react second, that's definitely not what I'm used to. Gabe would have floored the guy, threw me over his shoulder, and marched me out of here kicking and screaming.*

"I'll leave you to it," Zander offers as he turns to leave. But something, I don't know what, *probably the alcohol coursing through my veins,* makes me reach out to stop him.

"Well, since you're clearly my boyfriend now, wanna dance?" I ask cheekily.

We continued dancing, chatting, and smoking for most of the night. I finally agreed to exchange numbers. But I make it very clear that all I'm looking for at the moment is friendship, something which he graciously accepts.

"You ready to go? Uber will be here in ten," Lexi informs me.

"Yup." I reply as I climb off the small wall me and Zander are sitting on. "Thanks for tonight; I needed some fun" I add as I give Zander a small hug. Then follow Lexi and Brooke.

"Soo, he seems hot? Anything exciting happen?" Brooke teases once the Uber takes off.

"Nah, it's not like that at all," I admit honestly. "He's just a friend."

"Well, he can be my friend anytime." Brooke laughs.

"Sure he's hot, but don't go jumping into anything serious. A little flirting is fine, but you don't want to jump from one relationship to another. Find yourself first." Lexi advises me.

"Honestly, I swear to god, I'm not looking for a boyfriend. My heart is still too broken and scarred from Gabe to give it to anyone else yet." I say.

"Okay," Lexi says with an accepting nod. "A little harmless fun and a confidence boost never hurt anyone though," she adds with a smile.

*It sure didn't! And maybe that's exactly what I need, a little fun and flirting with a hot guy who is a perfect combination of the tattooed rebel I want, and the nice guy I need.*

## Chapter Eighteen

## Gabe

The last thing I want to be doing at eight o'clock on a Sunday morning is waiting in line at some overpriced coffee house. But if I've got any chance at forgiveness from Declan, I'm gonna have to turn up bearing gifts.

*For Declan, coffee is the way to his forgiveness. I think. The man seems to live for his sweet, girly coffee drinks, just like my firefly does. Maybe though I could really show how sorry I am, by getting him the number of that girl he's been too much of a pussy to ask out? That would show I'm a good friend, right?*

"Hello, welcome to Like You A Latte. What can I get you today?" the overly peppy and annoying barista asks.

"Uhm, I'll take one of those," I say pointing to some sickly looking drink on the menu behind her.

"Okay, that's not what I'd expect from you," the woman says as she eyes me up and down. "I'm usually pretty good at guessing people's orders," she adds with a frown.

"Nah, I don't drink that shit, it's for my buddy Declan." I can't help but notice the little smile that forms on her face, or the way she is suddenly avoiding eye contact.

"From Saints? The bar around the corner?" she asks.

"Yeah, you know him?" I ask even though I already know that Declan has been coming here multiple times a day and the fucker still hasn't mustered up the courage to fuck her yet or even ask her out.

"Yeah, he's a regular. Don't worry, I know exactly what he likes."

*I bet you do.* I think to myself with a smirk.

She disappears for a few moments and comes back with some monstrosity in a clear cup. "What the fuck is that?" I say lifting the cup to glare at it.

"Iced Caramel Macchiato with extra dark caramel sauce and whip cream." she replies proudly like any of those words will mean shit to me. "What about you? You don't strike me as a very exotic drinker, perhaps something simple. Cappuccino, perhaps?" she adds sweetly.

"Just plain coffee, warm and wet will do" I reply as I eye up my watch. *Eight twenty already.*

"Wet and warm? That's not an order I get often." she replies with an awkward laugh. "Okay, do you want it milky? Strong? Sweet? Give me some ideas." she adds.

"I just like it plain, dark, with one sugar." I say blowing out a frustrated breath.

*How the fuck does Declan put up with this shit? I'm ordering a drink not picking a goddamn bike out; how hard is it to pour some coffee into a cup?*

"Okay we're getting somewhere, so you like it strong then? How dark?"

"As dark as my fucking soul. That dark enough for you?" I snap while making eye contact with her.

"Okay, plain black coffee it is." she says, rolling her eyes.

She pours me a drink with way less enthusiasm than she poured Declan's, before practically slamming it down on the counter. "That will be $11 please, unless I can get you anything else."

"Actually, yeah your phone number as well." I see the shock and confusion on her face so quickly add, "Not for me, for Declan. The guy's too much of a pussy to ask you out himself."

I watch her frown disappear as her cheeks begin to blush. She reaches over and retrieves a napkin before scribbling her number down on it and reluctantly passing it to me. I take the napkin, shove it into my pocket, and then throw twenty dollars down on the counter before leaving.

I walk back to Saints, coffee in hand, kicking my foot against the door since both of my hands are full.

"Here Dickhead!" I joke, when Declan finally opens the door, but the scowl he gives me in return lets me know he's still furious at me and in no mood for my assholery. "Peace offering?" I say as I continue to hold out his drink to him.

He snatches the drink from my hand, but offers me no smile or thanks in return.

He walks over to the two soft chairs in the corner of the pub and sits down. I move over to sit in the chair opposite him but he throws his legs onto it blocking my path. *Don't lose your shit. Stay calm.* I remind myself as I pull over a standard wooden chair and sit down.

"So, I suggest you start talking," Declan snaps, his tone cold and distant.

"Chill the fuck out Dec, I came here to explain shit. But keep talking to me like that and we'll be sorting this shit out with our fists." I fire back.

Declan just rolls his eyes and takes a sip of his drink. "Mmm, did Jessie make this?" he questions. His tone is finally less hostile.

"Dunno her name. The girl from that shitty coffee place down the street, the one you've been drooling over for weeks."

"I've not been drooling, just taking my time. She's not the sort of girl you just ask out on the first day, you gotta find the right time…" Declan explains, but I cut him off.

"Funny, it took me literally thirty seconds to get her number." I tease.

"What?" Declan says, his tone oddly pissed off. *I thought he'd be happy, grateful even.*

"You son of a bitch! Please tell me you didn't sleep with her, what sort of person…." Declan rants, and I can't help but smirk, something that clearly pisses him off even more. "You think this is funny?"

"Kinda." I laugh as I retrieve the crumpled napkin from my pocket and throw it at him. "I got her number for you, you fucking jackass."

"Oh." Declan mumbles as he settles back down in his chair, "Sorry, dude."

"It's fine. We both know a year ago I'd have done something like that and not even given it a second thought," I admit.

"How are things with you and Riley?" Declan asks cautiously.

All the air leaves my lungs at the thought of Riley and how badly I've screwed everything up with her. I've spent more nights than I can count recently, drinking or smoking myself into oblivion hoping to forget or get some relief from the constant ache in my chest. "Awful! She hates me. I hate me. The whole fucking world hates me."

"Well maybe if you hadn't lost your goddamn mind and gotten into bed with the motherfucking Sinners, people wouldn't hate you so much." Declan fires back, a hint of disdain and anger in his tone.

"You think I fucking want this shit?" I snap, as I stand with such speed and force it causes my chair to scratch along the floor. "You think I don't wish I could kill each and every one of those cunts? Of course I do, but I gotta bide my time."

"What the fuck are you talking about? You're making no goddamn sense." Declan questions, as he looks up at me with a frown.

"Fine. But you can't breathe a word of this," I say as I point my finger at him. "This is dangerous shit. You can walk away now, knowing I'm handling it, or I can let you in; but if you betray me, I'll gut you like a fucking fish." I threaten as I continue to tower over him.

"Oh, shut the fuck up with the cryptic James Bond shit and just tell me," Declan huffs as he slaps my finger away.

"Fine, but I'm gonna need a goddamn drink first." I say as I make my way to the bar.

"It's barely even breakfast." Declan calls after me.

"Then put in some goddamn toast," I fire back as I grab two whiskeys.

"I'll stick to my coffee thanks." Declan laughs when I sit back down.

"Who said one was for you?" I reply as I down the first glass, the fire burning my throat and almost making me cough as it slides down.

Declan's eyes widen, before he shakes his head and takes another sip of his coffee. *In fact, screw that, that monstrosity can't even be called coffee, it's basically diabetes in a cup.*

"It all started a couple of months ago…" I break down and the whole ordeal comes flying out of my mouth like vomit. I'm thankful to finally have someone to talk to about all this. I tell him about the night they attacked me and took me to the barn. About the threat they made to Riley's life and how I was forced to watch it unfold, unable to save her. But I'm careful to leave out the part about John. I may trust Declan, but I'm still not going to risk admitting my involvement in a possible murder and covering it up. *I've learned in life even your closest friends can be your biggest enemies given the right motivation.*

Declan gasps along, even heading to the bar and returning with the bottle of whiskey and another glass as he listens to all the sordid details of my plan.

"Dude! You gotta go to the police about that shit," Declan practically begs.

"What and risk Riley, Nate, or even Isabella paying for my betrayal? Never. I've gotta end this shit, and keep all of them safe."

"Gabe, you can't take on something like that alone. I know you've done some fucked up shit in the past, god knows, I've seen, and cleaned up after some of your fights in here. But this? This is a whole new level of fucked up dude."

"You think I don't know that?" I snap, slamming my glass down on the table, thankful when it doesn't shatter in my hand.

"Does anyone else know? Your brother? Your girl? Anyone?" Declan asks, concern lacing his tone.

"No, I'm not risking anyone else getting dragged into this shit."

"Is there anything I can do? Like I'm not gonna go all John Wick on their ass, but is there anything else I can do?" Declan says as he places his hand on my shoulder.

"Just keep your nose clean. Keep my secret, and if the time comes, trust me I guess." I reply as I shuffle away from his touch.

"And you're sure it's not worth telling the cops? Maybe they can help," Declan tries to persuade.

"No one can help. This is my hole to climb out of; I'm not dragging anyone else in here with me."

Our conversation goes back and forth for a little while before Declan reluctantly gives in, with a small nod of his head.

"Fine, but be fucking careful man," Declan adds as I turn to leave.

I leave Declan, hop on my bike, and make my way towards O'Malley's. Praying that the distraction of work will help ease the constant dread I have in my gut.

## Chapter Nineteen

# Riley

My head pounds as some incessant sound invades my peace and sleep. I try to hide my head under my pillow, but the sound goes on and on. Every time it stops, it restarts a few seconds later. Finally realizing I'm never gonna get back to sleep I reach for my phone and answer it. "What?" I bark.

"There you are. Where the fuck have you been, Riley? You said you were going to see a friend yesterday afternoon and then I haven't heard from you since. You didn't come home and none of the girls have seen or heard from you. What the fuck?"

"Oh shut up," I snap, as my already sore head hurts more as I'm forced to listen to my sister berating me like a goddamn child. "I went out with Lexi if you must know, went to a frat house and got drunk."

"A frat house, what were you thinking?" Harper gasps. But I'm in no mood for her attitude today.

"I was thinking I needed an escape and that I'm a goddamn adult now so I can do whatever the fuck I want."

"An adult? Really? You sound like a petulant child. Why don't you come back? Me and the girls can meet you for coffee. You sound like you could do some sobering up."

"Sobering up? Really. Go screw yourself, Harper." I snap before hanging up.

*Who does she think she is? Can't she see I'm hurting? I need her support, not her beratement.*

I throw my head back under the pillow and must drift back to sleep as when I wake up a couple of hours later, there are multiple texts and voice messages from Harper apologizing. Telling me it was her worry that made her snap and that she's sorry if I felt like she was trying to control me. Feeling guilty for my part in our argument too, I get dressed and tell her that I will meet her later for lunch.

I call an Uber, head home to shower and change, and then head out to meet her. Of course when I arrive, Ava and Izzy are also there waiting. As soon as I reach the table I see all three of their eyes go straight to my hair.

"Wow! What did you do?" and "You look hot!" can be heard from the girls as they all speak at once.

"Thanks, I needed a change," I admit.

"Well it looks hot!" Ava chimes in again.

"Yeah, so pretty," Izzy agrees.

Ava stands up and begins touching my hair, "Is it supposed to look like flames?" she asks.

"I thought it seemed fitting, I lost my fire, and Brooke and Lexi helped me get it back." I admit.

"It does look nice. Why didn't you tell me you were thinking of changing your hair though?" Harper questions, sounding a little disappointed.

"It wasn't really a plan, what happened was..." I say before going into detail about everything that happened in the last day or so. I tell them all about bumping into Gabe at the hotel, about seeing him coming out of that girl's room, and reluctantly about our kiss.

The story is met by angry faces, shaking heads and open mouthed expressions. I then go on to tell them about what happened when I tried to confront him at Saints, and then how I ended up with Lexi.

Before long the conversation drifts back to prom, where I'm stuck listening to all three of my friends talking about how wonderful it's going to be. How we're gonna hire some big ass limo, rent our hotel rooms, and have 'the best night of our whole lives.'

*The thought of walking into prom alone, wearing the dress I chose because I knew it would drive Gabe wild, and staying in the hotel room I imagined myself and Gabe staying in while celebrating the night we finally took our relationship public and official, is my idea of hell.*

My phone buzzes and when I pull it out of my pocket I'm kind of surprised to see who the text belongs to.

> Zander the Great
>
> Hey Riley or perhaps I should call you Blaze. How's your head feeling today? Mine and Jamie's are throbbing, but we're heading into town for some greasy food and some strong coffee. Wondered if you

> wanted to join us. Maybe catch a movie or something after?

I can't help but smirk at what he saved his name as, but also the idea of blowing off some steam, and getting away from this conversation does sound interesting.

Me

> Zander the Great, yeah? I'll have to see about that. But sure. I'm actually in town now with some friends, but I could meet you in about half an hour if you want.

Zander the Great

> Still at home in bed, so unless your plan is to join me here, perhaps we should make it an hour.

*Hmm a little harmless flirting. Why not!*

Me

> It will take more than the promise of food and coffee to get me into bed Casanova, an hour is fine. Text me when you're on your way.

"What are you smiling at?" Ava quizzes as she snatches the phone from my hand and reads my last message.

"Oooh, new friend?" she quizzes when I snatch it back.

"Yes, just a friend." I say.

"A friend that wants to get you into bed?" Ava asks.

"No. You know I'm not looking for that shit. He's just a friend. Do you remember the guys from the boat?"

"Yeah," Harper says skeptically.

"I bumped into two of them last night and we got to chatting."

"Please tell me it's not the meathead with the tattoos," Harper whines as she shakes her head disapprovingly.

"Maybe," I sing.

"He was hot." Ava says as she pretends to fan herself.

"And does he know you're just looking for friendship? As he seemed kind of into you on the boat." Izzy adds.

"Yeah, I told him all about Gabe …well the fact I had an ex who broke my heart and how I've sworn off men." I explain. "And he's fine with it, it just feels nice to have a guy to do a little flirting with. After all that shit with Gabe, as you know I hit rock bottom, it feels nice to have another guy giving me a little attention for a change." I admit it honestly.

"Please don't jump into another relationship," Harper warns.

"Seriously, why does everyone keep saying that?" I snap.

"I'm allowed friends without wanting to fuck them!"

"I know, I'm just saying." she replies.

"Well don't!" I huff.

"As long as you're happy, we're happy." Izzy says with a smile.

"More like as long as you fill us in if anything spices up, we're happy." Ava says with a cheeky wink.

I finish my coffee and listen to Ava and Izzy chat about their boyfriends for a little longer before my phone buzzes in my pocket.

> **Zander the Great**
> We're just parking now, meet us at the movie theater. There's a great little cafe nearby.

"Anyway, I've got to go. See you all later." I say as I stand to leave.

"Do not stay out late. We're meeting first thing in the morning!" Harper calls out to me in an authoritative and warning tone.

"Yes, mom!" I reply mockingly.

"Forget mom, if you make me late tomorrow I will be your worst nightmare." Ava adds as she points her chocolate cake filled fork at me.

"Yes ma'am," I say as I salute her, before leaving and making my way towards the cinema. I begin feeling a little nervous, as I walk to what I desperately hope isn't a date. Thankfully, as I turn the corner I see Zander and Jamie outside smoking.

"And where's mine?" I joke as I come to stand beside them.

"I have plenty more if you want one." Jamie says as he reaches into his coat pocket.

"Nah, I'm fine thanks, just messing with ya. So where's this amazing cafe? I'm hungry enough to eat a horse."

"Doubt they serve horse, but the burgers are amazing." Zander replies with a smile.

I shake my head at his corny joke and we make our way to the cafe in question, and after the glowing recommendation it received, I order a burger. Thankfully it lives up to the hype. Next, we make our way to the cinema, deciding on a horror movie to watch.

"So you want popcorn, candy, chocolate? What are you craving?" Zander asks.

"Is everything an option?" I laugh.

"A little indecisive are we?" Jamie jokes.

"Sounds like a great plan to me. Each of us picks a different option and then we can mix and match." Zander decides.

"Great plan," I agree.

*See, I knew this guy was perfect. A guy who not only agrees but suggests sharing food. Move over Tucker, I may have just found myself a new boy bestie.*

We each line up in a different line. Zander chooses popcorn and a Coke. Jamie chooses Milk Duds and a Slushy, and I pick Sour Patch Kids, Twizzlers and a Slushy. I even manage to persuade the guy behind the desk to give me an empty popcorn box to tip all my candy into.

Next, we make our way to our allotted seats. Zander sits down first, and I sit beside him. Jamie attempts to walk past me to sit beside his friend but I tap the empty seat beside me.

"Sit here if you want," I offer.

"Aww what's the matter? You need us both to protect you in case the movie gets too scary." Zander teases.

"No," I say, screwing my face up. "My arms aren't long enough to reach over you to steal his food, duh," I say as I flash an exaggerated cheesy grin.

"You're not like most girls." Zander laughs.

"Most girls wish they were as awesome as me. " I reply as I flick the bottom of my hair like I'm in a shampoo commercial.

"I guess you are pretty awesome," Jamie laughs back.

The movie starts and despite a few jump scares it's pretty enjoyable. The three of us settle in like lifelong friends, Jamie happily shares his milk duds, but doesn't really take much else in return. Meanwhile me and Zander are squabbling like siblings as we each try to outdo each other.

He takes a small handful of sweets, so I take a bigger handful of his popcorn. He, in turn, steals a bigger handful of sweets and so on.

"Stop," Zander whispers, laughing, as I rummage around in the almost empty popcorn tub trying to grab as much as possible.

"Nope," I whisper with a smirk. I pull my hand out and am about to put it into my mouth when Zander grabs my hand and guides it to his mouth instead. "Eww you're gross." I wine as he all but licks my hand when I refuse to open it to feed him.

Zander just shrugs and smirks in response.

A few minutes later Zander reaches for my last piece of licorice and to stop him from getting it, I shove it into my mouth. Leaving half of it hanging out as I grin up at him.

Zander leans forward, almost as if he's going to kiss me, but instead bites the Twizzler and pulls away with an accomplished grin.

"That's stealing." I huff.

"Be glad that's all I stole," he replies in a flirty tone.

The movie comes to an end and Jamie heads off saying he has to meet another friend. Meanwhile, me and Zander decide to take a walk around town. Making the most of the sunshine.

"So, do you wanna meet up tomorrow? A few of us are thinking of heading to the beach again."

"I can't." I admit as I roll my eyes "Gotta go to prom."

"Wait prom? As in high school prom? How old are you?" Zander questions.

"Eighteen. I'm one of the oldest in our class, had me and Harper been born just two weeks earlier we would have finished school last year and I wouldn't be forced to go now."

"Oh thank god for that, for a minute I thought I'd spent my day flirting with jailbait." He chuckles a little uneasily.

"Oh that was flirting, was it? I didn't realize. Perhaps you need to step up your game Casanova," I tease.

"You little…" Zander says in mock annoyance as he pokes me in the ribs playfully. "You don't sound too excited about prom though," Zander points out.

"If I'm honest, I don't really want to go." *I'm not going to cry. I'm not going to cry.*

"Why not? Back when I was at school the girls made it seem prom was their practice wedding." Zander jokes.

"No point having a practice wedding when the groom leaves you at the altar with nothing but a broken heart and memories." I add as I take a deep breath while willing my eyes to stay dry.

"Yeah, guess that's pretty shitty. Well, if you ever need a replacement groom. You have my number." he adds as he pretends to straighten his non-existent tie.

"I'll keep that in mind," I reply as I give him a little push.

We spend the next hour chatting before he kindly gives me a lift home after I receive not one, but two annoyed calls from my sister asking when I'll be home.

"Thanks for today; I really needed it." I admit through the open window as I'm saying goodbye.

"Anytime wifey. Kick ass tomorrow." Zander says with a playful wink. Before revving his engine and driving away.

# Chapter Twenty

# Gabe

The last few weeks have been a blur. All I've done is work, smoke, drink, get high, or run around being Marko's little fucking lap dog.

My phone buzzes in my pocket and when I pull it out I see it's a reminder. A reminder telling me it's prom today, and that I need to go pick up that stupid little wrist flower thingy, the one I let Nate talk me into ordering. There was also something for me too if I remember correctly.

My heart ruptures all over again. It doesn't matter what I do or what I try, nothing eases my pain. Heck, in a moment of weakness, I even considered reaching out to Kelly just to see if that would give me a moment of peace. Thankfully, even in my drunken state, I had enough self control and sense to not break that one last barrier. I may be a total asshole, an asshole I'm sure Riley hates right now, but I'll never betray my girl that way.

My alarm buzzes again and my anger about this whole fucked up situation rises. I think back to how excited Riley had been all the times we spoke about prom. How excited she'd been to find the perfect dress. How she'd demanded I rent a suit saying jeans and my leather jacket just wouldn't cut it. Heck, even I was fucking excited and nervous to finally get to show my girl off to the world.

*Well her school I guess but still, it might as well be the world. But thanks to Marko, that's nothing but another lost dream. A dream that for now at least has to stay far out of reach. But one day, one day I will get to see Riley in a beautiful dress while I wear my fanciest suit. Even if that's in another life, for her, it'll be worth the wait.*

Opening up my drawer, I roll up a joint and smoke it to escape my thoughts for a moment. It doesn't help much though because permeating through my high is Nate's sickening voice on the phone with Isabella cooing about how excited they both are.

*Fuck them! Fuck them and their simple, perfect, motherfucking, relationship!*

The sound of their pathetic giggling continues, and unable to put up with it for even a second longer, I hop on my bike and drive as far away as I can.

I continue driving until I end up back at the last place I should be, back where my whole life fell apart. Not just once, but fucking twice.

I jump off my bike, drag open the rickety door, and head inside.

"I HATE YOU!" I scream into oblivion, not even sure who or what I'm referring to. "I hate you. I hate you. I HATE YOU!!" I scream over and over falling to my knees.

*I hate this shitty barn, I hate that it was here that I lost the last of my innocence when I took a life. I hate that I walked in here a child, and walked out a monster. I hate that this was the first and only place my father ever seemed proud of me.*

"FUCK YOU!" I scream again. "I hate you!" I scream again but with less strength. I slowly get back up and just look around this decrepit old waste of space. The place that often plays center stage in my nightmares.

*Fuck you! Just standing here, my own personal hell. A haunted house of misery; watching as the only man who ever cared enough to be a father to me, probably took his last breath. Fuck you for forcing me to watch as my girl was almost raped with a motherfucking knife.*

I spot a discarded piece of wood on the floor, pick it up, and begin swinging. I hit the hay bales, getting out a little frustration, but nowhere near enough. Next, I begin smashing the windows, not that there's much left since this place was abandoned years ago. Either way, I revel in the sound of the glass smashing. It almost serves as a release of sorts.

I don't know how long I spent beating the fuck out of this shithole of a building, but long enough that I'd subconsciously removed my jacket and my t-shirt and was covered in sweat.

Finally feeling exhausted, I grab a cigarette and light it up. I'm sitting on the floor outside, soaking up a moment of sunshine, almost finished my second smoke when a wicked idea pops into my twisted mind. I head back inside, take out my lighter, and set fire to some of the dried up hay bales. I even find one of the Sinners' discarded balaclavas, from that fateful night. After covering it in some of the gas from my bike, I throw that into the flames, watching as that small fire soon turns into a raging blaze. I stand back watching long enough to know that the whole fucking building will soon be up in smoke, then I get the fuck out of there, quick, before those flames alert someone to my presence.

## Riley

I slide on my dress and walk outside, as soon as Gabe sees me his eyes light up. That hungry and possessive look in his eyes lets me know he wants to drag me back to bed and punish me for wearing such a revealing dress. His hand finds its way to my throat as his lips crash down on mine. "Such a beautiful little slut," he purrs as he picks me up and throws me down onto the bed. I lie here, suddenly naked, ready to accept my pleasure, or punishment, whichever comes first. Gabe's body crashes down on mine, I reach up to run my hands through his hair but as I do, my hand finds nothing. I bolt upright as my bedroom slowly comes into focus through the darkness. *It was just a dream! A wicked, soul crushing reminder of what I had and lost.*

I feel the tears begin to burn my eyes as I pull the blanket tightly around me and begin to silently sob into the darkness.

*Why is my mind so cruel? Why can't even sleep bring me the much needed peace I so desperately crave?*

I've lost count of how many times I've been woken up from a dream about him. Sometimes they are naughty, reliving my fantasies. Sometimes they're sweet, replaying old memories. Those just destroy me all over again when I realize they're just my own memories haunting me. But the worst are the nightmares I have; the ones where instead of walking in on Justin with another woman, it's Gabe with some random girl on her knees in front of him.

I slide out of bed and walk up the stairs to the kitchen to pour myself a cup of coffee. Not wanting to head back to my room and risk waking Harper, I slip into the sunroom for some time alone with my own thoughts.

I sit, scrolling on my phone, getting angrier and more hurt as I see post after post from the girls at school all cooing over how excited they are that it's prom in the morning.

I look at my screen, it's 2 a.m. I need to go back to bed if I'm ever going to make it through the torture that is today. *Maybe I could just run away? I could disappear until prom is over. Would that be so bad?*

I put my empty mug in the sink, make my way back downstairs, and climb back into bed. Instead of trying to go back to sleep, I decide to torture myself one last time. *Since clearly, I'm a glutton for punishment.* I open the app at the top of my phone, the one that is filled with pictures and ideas for how I had wanted prom to go. It has pictures of me and Gabe together, ideas for hair and makeup, little screenshots of the lacey black lingerie I was going to surprise Gabe with, and so much more.

*I can't do this!* I think to myself as I shove my phone under my pillow, unsure if I want to scream, cry, or fucking steal my parents' car and go give Gabe a piece of my mind for breaking my heart.

I reluctantly roll over, close my eyes, and desperately try to fall back to sleep. The next thing I know, I'm being forced awake by the girls and dragged along to Francisco's to get our hair, nails, and makeup done for tonight. I'm still hurting, but I try to push it out of my mind and plaster on a fake smile. My friends have been looking forward to this for months and they don't deserve me ruining it for them.

"Hey Riley, hair still looks amazing, I see," Brooke compliments as we all make our way over to the chairs.

"Yup, it definitely helped me get my fire back. Thanks again."

*Maybe Brooke can work her magic again and fix the aching in my heart; make me feel strong, brave, and worthy of some happiness.*

"So, what are we doing for everyone?" another one of the hairdressers asks.

The girls all describe how they want their hair done, but I just shrug. "I dunno, maybe some curls or something."

"Curls or something?" Brooke gasps. "It's Prom and the best you can give me is, curls or something?"

*Dude be glad I'm even here, I'd much rather be curled up in bed with a tub of ice cream, eating away my sorrow.*

"I'm only going because these bitches..." I say turning my attention to my friends, "...are forcing me to go."

"Oh shut up Riley; we're not gonna let you miss Prom all because of a certain asshole," Harper says, her voice laced with disdain. *She never liked Gabe even when we were together but now that we're not, that dislike has morphed into pure hatred.*

"Oh which asshole is this? The ex? Lexi's brother? Or do you have another guy on the go now?" Brooke jokes trying to lighten the tension.

"What? Are you talking to Justin again?" Ava and Harper both shout as they lean forward in their chairs to look at me.

"No. We had one fucking interaction when I was at Lexi's. I'd rather become a goddamn nun than let that lying, cheating bastard anywhere near me again."

"Oh thank god!" they both sigh before sitting back.

"Wait...another guy? How many guys are you messing with Riley? We know about the guy from the cinema, but who else is there?" Ava questions, as she leans forward to look, or should I say frown at me.

"The guy from the cinema?" Izzy questions. "Is that the one from the boat?"

"What about the other ones, those you were flirting with at Jake's party?" Lexi questions.

"Wow! You girls slut shaming much?" I snap back. *Why does it feel like everything I do is wrong in their eyes? Whatever happened to having your girl's back?*

"Seriously, how many guys are there?" Harper asks, the disapproving and judgy tone of hers more than evident in her voice.

"Wow. You're all making out like I'm a goddamn whore." I all but scoff.

*Seriously what the fuck is everyone's problem? I'm eighteen and single for the first time since I was fifteen. So what if I want to talk to some guys to make myself feel better after having my heart broken? Even if they were all different people, which they're not, and I was sleeping with all of them. It wouldn't justify how they are speaking to me. They need to back off! Can't they see how much I'm still hurting?*

I let out an angry and frustrated huff. "There's Gabe, my fucking ex who broke my heart, who you all know...well apart from you, I guess." I say as I look up at Brooke.

"Then there's my friend Zander, the guy from the boat, the cinema, and the party I went to with you and Lexi. He's also just a FRIEND. And not that I need to goddamn explain myself to any of you, but every single time I've seen him, I've also been surrounded by his friends as well. So to answer your fucking question, there are literally two fucking guys, neither of which I'm dating, for Christ sake!"

"Oh," most of the girls say before we all fall into silence.

Harper reaches out, presumably to apologize or comfort me but I'm too angry, so instead, I move my arm away. Refusing to even look at her, or any of my other so called best friends, who are too busy looking down at me from their high horses to see that all of this; the new friends, the distant behavior and drinking, heck even the flirting in general is all just my way of keeping myself from drowning in misery, my cry for help.

The girls all begin talking amongst themself, while I scroll through my phone. But before long, the annoyance and awkwardness eases and we all fall back into our usual playful banter as we finish getting our hair done. Then we choose nails and makeup. Wanting the outside to match how I feel inside though, I decide on dark smokey eyes, fake eyelashes and after a little bit of persuasion, some red lipstick.

Once done, Ava drives us all home to get changed and informs us that the limo will be here to pick us up in a few hours. But pretty much as soon as we get home, me and Harper get into another argument. This time over the fact that I'm texting Zander.

*This apparently makes me a giant whore because god forbid a man and woman can be friends.*

"I'm going, screw your limo, I'm getting ready at the hotel instead." I huff as I grab my dress bag and my little overnight suitcase.

"Wait! I'm sorry, I don't want to fight with you, I was just trying to say not to go wild. Think about how your actions affect others too." Harper says as she attempts to touch me.

*Seriously, what the fuck is this bitch's problem, what happened to being beside me through thick and thin? Clearly, I'm only worthy of her love when I'm doing as she wants. And she wonders why I'm spending all my time with Zander and the guys? At least they don't judge me just for being myself.*

"Harper you literally said and I quote. "You need to calm down with the flirting before he gets the wrong idea about you and thinks you're easy." I retort.

"No, I said, before he thinks he can get with you easily." Harper counters, but I don't care to listen either way she basically just called me a whore. And I'm sick of it. Just because she's happy being single forever, doesn't mean I am.

I storm out the door and see my dad hovering at the top of the stairs. "Can you drive me to the hotel?" I ask.

"How about I take you in a bit, maybe you and your sister can calm down a little first," my dad offers.

"I'm leaving now so either you take me or I walk, I don't give a damn which." I snap back, far more rudely than my poor father deserves.

"I'll grab my keys," my father says, clearly realizing now is not the time to argue.

"I'm sorry," I say, turning to my father as we're driving.

"It's fine. I learned long ago not to try and get in between a hurricane and a tornado," my father laughs.

"We're not that bad are we?" I laugh.

"Most of the time no, most of the time your mother and I love how close you girls are…. but when you go wild.. phew… we've learned to take cover," my father teases.

"We get it from you." I laugh back.

"No, your temper, and potty mouth you may get from me, but that attitude is all your mother."

"Well, that's what you get when you live with four women." I laugh.

"Four?" my father questions. "This best not be your terrible way of telling me I'm about to be a grandpa," my father says as he turns his head and eyes me suspiciously.

"Fuck no! The only thing this tummy is full of is food," I laugh, rubbing my tummy for extra effect. "I was talking about Honey."

"Don't fucking do that to me; I damn near crashed the car." my father exclaims.

"Sorry Daddy," I say in a childish and innocent tone.

"Don't you, 'sorry Daddy' me. I'm half tempted to turn this car around, and lock you in your room till you're thirty-five." My father says as he lets out a long sigh.

I flash him a very toothy grin, which is only met by a shaking head in response.

We finally pull up outside the hotel, and I head inside. "Hello, I have a reservation under Riley Foster," I tell the woman behind the desk.

"Oh here you are room 101." the woman says as she scans a key fob on the side of her till. "Now will you need one card, or two?"

"Just one," I reply with a forced smile.

"First floor." she says as she points me toward the stairs.

I find the room easily, I mean it's pretty much the first door on the right. I head inside and place my dress on the closet door, then put my pajamas and clothes for tomorrow in a drawer, before making my way to the bathroom. I throw my hair up in a loose bun, careful not to completely destroy my curls, and then turn on the bath. Finally I have some peace so that I can shave my legs, and rid myself of some of this tension.

*Harper was crazy when she suggested that I get up extra early to shave them before our early hair appointment. Does she even really know me?*

As I'm waiting for the bath to run I put in my earphones and after some searching find the perfect song; something to boost me up and make me feel like the bad bitch I know I am.

# Chapter Twenty-One

## Gabe

Now that Declan has finally stopped sulking enough to let me back in, I'm sitting in Saints drowning my sorrows, while furiously checking my phone to see if there are any reports about the barn fire. My phone rings, but it's a number I don't recognize. At first I don't answer, fearing the worst, but when I receive another call from the same number, less than fifteen minutes later I decide to answer it anyway. "Hello, Mr. Scott? This is Cheryl from Beautiful Blooms. I'm calling because we close in half an hour and we still have the corsage you ordered here uncollected."

"The what? I didn't order a goddamn corset." I say in frustration.

A slight chuckle can be heard before the woman on the other end of the line adds, "Not a corset silly, a corsage; the floral wristband you ordered presumably for a prom or special occasion."

"Oh yeah that flowery thing," I reply while rubbing the back of my neck. *What the fuck am I going to do with this thing? What can I do with a flower bracelet? It's not like I'm going to wear it.*

"Yes, well your flowery thing is sitting here waiting to be collected and we close in half an hour. I can stay a little later, but have to be gone by six o'clock. Can you come and collect it please? Otherwise, you are going to have a very sad girl."

I start, telling the woman to shove her flower where the sun doesn't shine; but wanting an excuse to see Riley, or at least let her know I'm thinking about her, I tell the woman I'll be there soon..

"Here you go," the woman says as she hands me a little white box. "Black and red roses like you requested," she says.

"Cheers." I say as I take the box and leave. Carefully placing it under my seat, I make my way towards the hotel, deciding that I will drop it off with Reception at the hotel for her.

"Hello, do you have a Riley Foster staying here?" I ask. Desperately hoping I have the right hotel.

The woman taps away on her keyboard before asking. "Are you Mr. Scott?"

"Err yeah, yeah I am." *How the heck did she know my name?*

"Brilliant, well here's your key, it's room 101, first floor," the woman says as she points toward a large staircase.

"Oh, okay, thanks." I say as I take the key and make my way to the room. *Riley must have booked it in both our names.*

I make it to the room and knock. Just in case she's already in there, even though the plan was originally to pick her up from home. When I don't get a reply I let myself in. I go to place the box down on a little table near the door, but then I realize she may not see it there so instead I walk in and place it on the nightstand.

I spot a discarded shirt on the bed and decide to head over and give it a sniff, wanting to smell the familiar scent of her perfume. *Mmm smells like heaven.*

I'm just about to leave when a door opens and out comes Riley wearing nothing but a thin lace thong.

"Gabe?" Riley gasps as her hands fly up to cover her naked breasts.

"Fuuuck!" I say slowly as I take in every inch of her, my dick waking up, almost like a rebirth, all of a sudden

"Close your eyes" Riley snaps as she looks around for something, anything to cover herself with.

"Not a fucking chance," I growl, taking a step closer. I reach for her hands and gently pull them away. "You look, wow," I say as my eyes scan every single inch of her, committing this sight to memory.

"Stooop," Riley wines as she tries to pull her hand out of my grip. But I'm still holding both of her arms tightly so that they are outstretched. I take a step closer and kiss her. One hand releasing hers so that I can pull her closer. The hand I released finds its way into my hair as she lets herself melt into my arms. I release her other hand so that I can scoop her into my arms. Her arms and legs wrap around me as I walk us over to the nearest wall to push her against it. Once there I push my rock hard erection against her core, causing her to let out a slight moan.

"I've missed this. I've missed you." I admit as I stop kissing her and thrust harder against her.

"Me too," she pants back. I carry her over to the bed and sit down so that she's cradling my lap. I move my lips down to her neck, causing her to throw her head back, giving me better access to her neck and chest.

I move my mouth to her nipple and begin to lick and suck at it as she grinds her pussy against me. Reaching up, I pull out whatever the fuck that mass of hair is, sitting on the top of her head, wanting to pull and tug her hair. But as I do, flashes of red and orange fall around her face.

"What's this?" I question as I grip a piece of the offending hair.

"I dyed it, do you like it?" Riley asks as she shakes her head causing more colors to flash through like it's on fire.

"Are they supposed to be flames?"

"Yeah!" she says confidently. "You always said I was fiery, so I felt like proving it," she says. That stubborn brattish tone of hers coming out.

"I don't know if I want to punish you for changing your beautiful hair, or reward you for turning me on even more by proving what a spitfire you truly are." I admit, all the while wanting nothing more than to plow into her from behind.

"I'll take both," she admits coyly.

"Anything you wish for, baby." I reply before I push her down so that she's sprawled out over my lap. I give her one sharp spank, causing her to cry out in surprise, and then thrust one finger inside her already dripping pussy, and begin playing with her until her soft moans grow louder and louder. But before she has time to cum, I remove my fingers and give her another slap.

"Heey," she groans. As she shuffles off my lap.

"You said you wanted both." I remind her as I look her square in the eyes and suck my fingers, letting out a small moan of my own as I taste my girl on my tongue.

I watch the way her eyes rest on my lips and know that watching me taste her is turning her on. "Want a taste?" I ask. And see a little frown form on her face.

"Not of you baby, I mean me," I smirk.

Her eyes dart down to the bulge in my pants as she bites her lip. I unbuckle my jeans and shimmy them down my waist, letting my cock finally spring free. My beautiful girl wastes no time, she slides off the bed and drops to her knees between my legs. She starts off slow, teasing almost. She grips my rock hard cock, but rather than taking me into her mouth, she slowly licks from the base to the shaft, paying extra attention to the sensitive parts underneath. Next, she begins to slide her hands up and down in rhythm with her soft licks.

I fist her hair, trying to encourage her to take me in her mouth but I can see from the slight smirk on her lips she's enjoying torturing me too much.

"Open your mouth," I growl. But like the stubborn brat she is, she just shakes her head. Instead, she increases the pace with her hand, only allowing the tip of my cock past her lips, milking every drop of precum.

*Such a stubborn little Firecracker. You want to play? Let's play.*

I reach out and grasp her firmly by the throat, not missing the excitement and lust in her eyes.

*That's it baby, submit to me, the way I know you secretly love to.*

"Now stand. I'm gonna fuck that sassy mouth of yours."

Like the good little slut she is, she obeys. Slowly climbing to her feet, the whole time never breaking eye contact.

I release my grip on her throat, and she lets out a small frustrated huff as I do so. "Sit." I demand. "Now open your mouth and show me how much you want my cock." I say as I grip my dick and rub the head of it against her lips.

She opens her mouth and in one swift movement, I push the whole of it inside, enjoying the soft gagging sound she makes as my cock hits the back of her throat. Next, I grip her hair to hold her head still as I begin thrusting in and out of her mouth.

It doesn't take long before she grabs my hips as she takes more and more of me inside her beautiful mouth. I allow her to move me at the pace she wants, as she begins to take the lead.

I see the way she tries, but fails to rub against me, chasing the much needed friction, so I spread her legs open and begin rubbing her clit with my finger, causing her to moan. The sound and vibration of those moans sends my dick into overdrive. I have to bite the inside of my cheek so I don't end this too soon. *God, how I have missed this and her. I don't ever want this to end.*

I continue to rub her hard nub, harder and faster as she continues to suck. I feel that familiar tingle, letting me know I'm close when suddenly she surprises me further by reaching between my legs and palming my balls. I erupt, shooting my load down her throat.

"Wow," I pant as the final twitches of my orgasm subside.

Riley pulls back, allowing my exhausted dick to pop out of her mouth, a satisfied and cocky smirk forming on her beautiful lips. She rubs her mouth with the back of her hand, having swallowed every single drop like a goddamn queen.

"Such a messy little slut." I say as I take my thumb and wipe away some of the smeared lipstick from under her bottom lip.

"Shit! My makeup," she shrieks before running to the mirror, her eyes widening when she sees how much our fun has messed up her beautiful face.

She grabs a clean pair of underwear from the drawer and then runs toward the bathroom.

I give her a couple of minutes, just in case she's actually using the bathroom before I push the door open. When I do she's standing on her tiptoes, reapplying her makeup.

"What happened to the red?" I ask as I realize she's now wearing darker colored lips.

"It's currently all over your cock." she smirks, before smacking her lips together like a fish.

I rest against the door watching as my beautiful girl finishes doing her makeup. She uses her fingers to fix and smooth her wild hair. But mostly I stare at her almost naked body. Her huge boobs bounce around as she moves her body around. And her bare ass is just begging to be spanked again. Once she's finally happy with whatever she sees in the mirror, even though she looked goddamn perfect already, she leaves the room.

"I have a present for you." I purr as she walks past me. Her eyes dart down and I can't help but smirk. "Not that my greedy little slut." I laugh. I retrieve the little box from behind my back and hand it to her.

"What is it?" she questions, as her brows furrow.

"Open it and find out."

She slowly opens the box, almost as if she's expecting snakes to pop out or something, but as she does, her eyes widen. "Gabe, it's beautiful."

She carefully removes it from the box and with a little help from me, manages to slide it onto her wrist.

"Is it okay? I didn't know what to get. I didn't really think big white flowers or pretty pink things were really you." I mumble. "This seemed more you, more us. Dark, and dangerous, but somehow beautiful."

"It's perfect." Riley reassures me as she cups my face and then stands on her tiptoes to give me the softest kiss. "It will look perfect with my dress," she adds before stepping away

She reaches for a big bag hanging on the wardrobe door and unzips it showcasing a bunch of black shiny material. She crunches it together and goes to step into it.

"Wait? What about a bra?" I say as I realize her tits are still bouncing freely.

"Can't wear one with this dress," she laughs. As she shimmies her legs and hips into the dress.

"So you're gonna go out and just let them be free all night?" I ask as I feel a little bubble of possessiveness mixed with irritation rising at the thought that anyone else may get a glimpse.

"Yep, why? You worried you won't be able to control yourself?" she asked. As she shimmies the dress over her boobs and puts her arms in the thin straps.

Next, she bends down and attempts but fails to put her shoes on through the long dress.

"Come here," I smirk as I scoop her up and sit her on the bed. Before collecting her shoes myself.

Riley lies herself down and lifts one leg in the air so I can slide her shoes on. "And the little straps" she orders, all the while looking at me with hungry eyes.

I try to figure out how to put the buckle up as her leg hangs in mid-air. Riley shuffles herself down the bed slightly and rests her foot against my chest. "Better?" she purrs.

*I've never been a fan of feet, or shoes for that matter. But somehow this is surprisingly sexy.*

Once both of her shoes are on and secured, I take her hand and help her stand. She bends over, just enough to check her hair and makeup one last time in the little dressing table mirror but as she does I notice the huge gaping cut out as the front of her dress widens even more.

*Seriously, is she trying to get me sent to jail for attacking any guy who dares look?*

Stepping closer, I wrap my arms around her, slip them both inside the opening, and roughly squeezed her breasts. "See, such easy access. You need to change, or wear a bra or something to cover up." I say as I get jealous at the thought of anyone else touching her like this.

"Good thing I'll have you around to protect my modesty then isn't it?" Riley laughs as she slaps my hand.

"Well I won't be there when you leave this room, will I? You'll be surrounded by horny fucking teenagers all night," I grumble, even as the thought of leaving her alone with them, kills me.

Riley pulls away and spins around so quickly she almost causes me to stumble. "What the fuck do you mean you won't be there?" she snaps.

"Downstairs, when you go to the disco, prom, whatever you call it."

"Wait…" she says, her eyes widening in anger. "You're telling me you came all this way, and you're still not taking me to prom?" she snaps.

"No, I mean I can't risk anyone seeing us together…" I begin. But she cuts me off.

"So I'm good enough for a quick hotel fuck, but not good enough to be seen in public with? Is that what you're telling me?" She seethes.

"No, it's not like that…" I begin but again she cuts me off.

"Just leave Gabe. Now!!"

"I'm not going anywhere till you let me explain." I snap back.

"Fine, I'll leave then." she says as she grabs her phone and key and storms out.

I chase after her all the way down the stairs and out the door.

"Please, come back upstairs and we can talk." I beg as I look around desperately praying I won't see Marko or any of his minions.

"Fuck you Gabe! I hope you enjoyed whatever the fuck that was because that is the very last time, you and me will ever be together."

"Don't be like that. Let me explain." I say as I grab her arm.

"Get the fuck off me Gabe, or so help me god I will scream my lungs out." she huffs.

Not wanting to cause an even bigger scene than I already am, I released her.

"Come inside please," I beg.

"I need a minute."

"Okay I'll wait," I go to say before she adds the nail in the coffin by adding "without you."

I give her the space she asked for, make my way inside, and head straight for the bar. I order myself a whiskey to get my head back on straight. I sit there for over twenty minutes waiting, before deciding to head back out to her, but as I'm making my way there I spotted Nate and Tucker coming through the door.

"What are you doing here?" Nate questions.

"Just wanted to see you before you go to your prom. It's a big night for you," I lie.

"Yeah sure," Nate says, clearly not believing my lie for a second.

Tucker wanders off and leaves me and Nate alone to talk, but it's only for a few minutes before Princess fucking Isabella appears.

"Looking good, Princess," I say as I notice for once she actually looks like an attractive woman rather than a Barbie doll.

"Thank you," she says, clearly in shock at my unusual niceness.

"Fucking enjoy that," I smirk, smacking my brother on the back. "What are you doing here anyway, psycho?" Pocket Rocket snaps as I walk past her.

"Thought I might crash a high school dance," I fire back with a sneer, before climbing on my bike, revving the engine, and driving off.

## Chapter Twenty-Two

## Riley

I purposefully hid, or should I say blended myself within a group of people from school when I saw Gabe coming, and thankfully he didn't spot me. Instead, he pretty much just hopped straight onto his bike and drove off, leaving me feeling stupid, used, and abandoned.

*I thought it felt bad having so-called friends and family make out that you're nothing but a whore, but being made to feel like a cheap whore by the man you love feels so much worse.*

Once the coast is clear, I make my way back inside to find the rest of the group. "Can we talk?" I ask as I pull Harper away from her conversation with Izzy and Nate.

"I guess," she shrugs, still clearly pissed off.

We talk and then both apologize and within minutes, just like always, we make up.

*We may drive each other crazy at times, after all, our personalities are like oil and water, but she's still my twin flame. And nothing will ever come between that.*

"So what was Gabe doing here? Did he give you that?" Harper asks as she eyes me suspiciously. "I'm not looking for another fight, but please tell me you're not giving him another chance or getting back together. Not after all the pain he's caused you recently"

"No, we are definitely over, one hundred and ten percent over." I say. "Doesn't mean I don't deserve pretty things though. He paid for this, I might as well enjoy it." I add as I look down at the flowers on my wrist, trying my hardest to sound indifferent even though it kills me inside having to admit it.

*How can he give me such a sweet, thoughtful gift like this, only to turn around and reject me all over again?*

"Thank god for that." Harper says with a smile, almost giddy, before linking my arms and guiding me inside.

*I'm glad that YOU'RE happy sis because I'm silently dying inside, over here!*

The next couple of hours go okay I guess, I try my hardest to enjoy myself. Laughing along with the rest of the group. Chatting to classmates from school and sharing, 'Do you remember when,' stories, like we weren't just together in class a couple of weeks ago. But none of it is real. Just a fake mask I'm putting on to hide how I'm really feeling inside.

"I'll be back in a sec, I just need some air," I say as I make my excuses to leave.

I head outside and spot a couple of kids, the ones who spent their whole lives in detention, huddled together around the side of the building. *Fuck it!*

I make my way over and spot one of the girls, Jas, someone who often cheated off me in chemistry, but who I barely know, and strike up a conversation.

"Thank fuck we've seen the last of Mr. Bates."

"Right, that asshole was always riding my ass" she groans.

"Wait, which one of the twins are you again?" Scott coughs, as a bunch of smoke flies out of his mouth.

"Riley," I say with an eye roll. *Seriously we've been in the same school since kindergarten, our moms literally carpooled us together.*

"Wanna drag?" he adds, as he thrusts a joint towards me.

"I'm good," I add with a fake smile. "I'll take a cigarette if anyone has one though."

Another girl, one I don't even recognize, reaches into her pocket and hands me one. "I didn't think, little Miss Drama Club, would be a secret smoker," the guy hanging around her neck adds.

"That would be my sister," I sigh.

"Oh, are you the one who did all those Spelling Bee's?" another guy asks.

"Nope!"

"So what did you do then?" the first girl asks.

"She stole my sister's boyfriend," Whitney, my ex friend, turned complete bitch adds.

"Oh get over it whiney. Justin and Courtney dated for like a month junior year."

"Oh yeah, I remember you." someone suddenly says while others nod their agreement.

*Great, so even to basically strangers, I'm only known for being a whore. Am I the only person who can't see this apparent, neon flashing sign above my head?*

"Anyway thanks for the smoke," I say, before walking away.

I continue my smoke in peace and as I'm walking back inside, I spot the staircase leading to the bedrooms and I am seriously tempted to just head up them, sneak out of the prom, and pretend none of it is happening. Unfortunately though, as I stand planning my escape, I feel someone link my arm and then I'm being dragged by two girls from class onto the dance floor. Ava, Harper, Izzy, and even our friend Sophie are already there, so before I know it I'm thrust into some sort of dance circle. Every time I try to leave, one of the girls shouts, "Oh my god, this is my song," and it starts all over again.

I try my hardest to pretend I'm having fun. Plaster on a fake smile, and dance the night away. But I'm just not feeling it. What I feel is hollow. Hollow and goddamn stupid for yet again believing in Gabe, believing that he wanted me, and giving myself up to him on a silver platter only for him to still refuse to acknowledge me in public.

*I thought we had overcome this bullshit!*

I finally manage to break free from the dance and fun police so I go and sit down to rest my feet, since these stupid fucking shoes seem intent on trying to cripple me. I take off one shoe and begin massaging my achy foot, then pull out my phone, hoping to use the light to confirm I still have five toes since I'm sure one must have been chopped off to cause this much pain.

But I'm pleasantly surprised to see a text message waiting for me. *Who's this from? Literally, all my friends are here.*

**Zander the Great**

> Hey hot stuff! Hope you're living out your very own fairytale at Prom, lol. Try not to turn into a pumpkin at midnight.

**Me**

> Remind me which fairytale I'm living again, since all I want to do is murder every fake ass preppy person here?

I don't expect a reply, especially since his message was sent almost three hours ago. But surprisingly he replies just a few minutes later.

**Zander the Great**

> Hmm, Carrie perhaps? Not a fairytale, but pretty sure it happened at prom. If you suddenly develop demonic powers or the urge to throw pig's blood over your friends, run!

**Me**

> Nah my feet are hurting too much to walk, let alone run. Fuck it, I'll die alongside them.

**Zander the Great**

> Can't be worse than being forced to listen to Jamie's girlfriend murdering Rihanna

> on karaoke, now that is worse than torture!

I'm finally smiling, genuinely smiling for the first time all night. That is until Harper flops down beside me. "Who are you texting?"

Feeling in no mood to start world war fucking three, I lie. "Oh just mom, you know what she's like, wanting to know who's wearing what, who I think Prom Queen will be. Typical mom"

"God I know. I swear she still thinks she's in high school herself at times." Harper agrees.

"Are you coming to dance?" she says cheerfully.

"Nah, my feet are killing me." I say as I hold up the torture devices formally known as stilettos.

"Leave them off them. We are." she says as she lifts up the bottom of her dress and showcases her bare feet. *Why didn't I think of that hours ago??*

I reluctantly slide my phone back into my bag, dump my shoes on my chair then follow her back to the dance floor.

Finally the band announces that this is the last song and the lights begin to come on letting us all know the night has come to an end. Everyone says their goodbyes and hugs their friends as though they won't all see them again. The friends they will probably see again tomorrow. The room begins to empty as everyone either heads to after parties, their rides home, or like we're doing, disappear upstairs to their rooms.

I make my way upstairs with the rest of my friend group politely waving goodbye to Izzy and Nate as they get the elevator up to the second floor. "Come on sluts, off we go", Ava chimes as she links arms with me and Harper as we all walk towards the stairs.

"You sure you don't wanna come back to my room?" Harper asks.

"Nah, I'm fine, I'm too tired to move all my things" I lie. Not wanting to admit that I actually just want to be alone away from her and everyone else for a bit.

"Okay. Well you know where I am if you change your mind," she says as she walks into her room.

Tucker and Ava walk with me to my room then once my door is open, they run past giddily. As soon as the door is closed, I drop my mask, remove my stupid dress, and throw my shoes, before climbing into bed, not even bothering to find my pajamas, and cry myself to sleep.

## Chapter Twenty-Three

## Riley

It's been almost a month since the Prom and yet it's still pretty much all the girls want to talk about.

*As if I didn't already feel depressed and single enough; I could go without hearing about everyone else's super romantic or spice filled evening. Heck even Harper ended up sharing a sneaky kiss with a guy she's been crushing on for months and basically living out my own bookish fantasy after her crush ended up locked out of his room, due to his teammate bringing a friend back to their shared room.*

"Oh my god, Harper, that sounds wild. So you gonna see him again?" Ava chimes, as she spoons a scoop of ice cream into her mouth. "Mmm, this is sooo good, how have I never been here before?"

"Good right? Nate and I have been coming here forever. Nana used to bring us all the time growing up." Izzy agrees wholeheartedly.

"Aww, so what's your favorite flavor?" Harper questions, trying to change the subject.

"Nope! Don't even try distracting us. Spill the tea now." Ava counters.

"There's not much to tell, it was just a kiss. Let's talk about something else" Harper says as her cheeks blush the brightest shade of crimson.

"Harper Louise!" I say, happy to finally use that same authoritative older sister tone she's used on me my whole life. "You spent the night with a boy, a boy you've been crushing on for ages and you really expect us to just brush over that like it was nothing?"

"Oh shut up." Harper whines as she covers her face, getting more and more embarrassed by the second. "I had a spare bed, he was locked out of his room with nowhere to stay, I was just being polite."

"Yeah yeah, is that what it's called nowadays?" Ava teases.

"What? We did! We literally just chatted, had a little kiss then slept. I'm sure you'd have done more though." Harper fires back and, Ava being Ava, falls for Harper's little distraction hook line and sinker, because for the next ten minutes Ava goes off on a tangent telling Harper exactly what she would have done, and trying to talk Harper into messaging the guy. *The one she still refuses to name.*

Everyone is just chatting happily, all desperately trying to either play matchmaker or trick Harper into revealing more about her mystery man, when my phone buzzed on the table.

Zander the Great

> **Hey hot stuff, what are you doing today? A couple of guys and I are going to go-karting if you wanna join us. Let's see if you're fire behind the wheel too.**

Me

> **I'm with my sister and some friends atm but how does in an hour sound?**

Zander the Great

> **Sounds good. Text me your address and I'll pick you up.**

"Shall we head back to mine? Pretty sure Nana was baking when I left." Izzy asks.

"Always." Ava replies.

"Sounds good." Harper adds.

"What about you Riley?" Izzy asks, when I don't reply straight away.

"Can't today sorry; I've got plans with someone else already."

"Someone else? Like who? Boat guy perhaps?" Harper smirks.

*I swear to god if I didn't know better I would think she's almost jealous. Every time she knows I've got a text from him, she makes a point to say something rude or sarcastic in response.*

"No actually, it's with Brooke and Lexi." I lie. "They're gonna show me around campus and try and help me get settled in there."

"Oh that's good. Make sure they show you where the library and all the best places to eat are." Harper says with a proud smile. *One that almost makes me feel guilty.*

"Need me to drop you anywhere?" Ava says as we walk out.

"Nah, Lexi is picking me up in about ten minutes." I lie again.

"Have fun." Izzy adds as they all walk in one direction and I walk in another.

I'm standing waiting on the corner, just like Zander told me to when I hear the sound of loud music booming through the streets. I turn to see where it's coming from just in time to see a bright red convertible, zooming towards me. "Jump in," Zander shouts from the back seat.

*Jump in? Where?* I quickly scan the car and realize it's already full. I see Jamie, Zander's friend from the party, sitting in the passenger's seat but I don't recognize the other two guys.

When I don't move quick enough, Zander opens the door and gets out to greet me.

"Everything okay?" he says quietly enough that nobody else can hear.

"Yeah, 'course," I say, shaking my head. "I just didn't realize I'd be crashing guys' time; we can hang out another time if you want." I offer.

"Nope! It's fine, come on, it'll be fun. Plus it will be funny to see the smile wiped off Enzo's face if he gets beat by a girl." Zander adds with a smirk.

I briefly weigh my options; head back to the girls and be forced to listen to how perfect everyone else's life is and how it's all falling into place while mine is still crumbling around my feet, or spend the rest of the day bored and alone. Deciding neither sound appealing I just think fuck it and I allow Zander to guide me to the car.

I climb inside, but it soon becomes obvious there is very little room for the three of us in the back seat. Between Zander's muscular build, and that of his friend who looks like a goddamn beast, I feel like a rose stuck between two very large thorns.

"Nice to see you again Riley; hope you're ready to get your ass beat." Jamie says as he turns around to look at me with a playful and friendly smirk.

"Oh yeah? And which one of you is gonna be beating my ass?" I joke back, but as soon as the words leave my mouth I realize the double meaning.

"I'd happily beat that fine ass any day." The guy beside me says in a way that I get the feeling he uses to try to pick up girls.

"Don't be such a creep, Enzo," the guy driving snaps. "Sorry about my brother, he was clearly dropped on his head as a baby or something. I'm Lucas by the way" Lucas says as he gives me a little half wave.

"Nice to meet you. I'm Riley," I say politely.

"Sorry, how was I supposed to know she'd be a prude?" Enzo grumbles beside me.

Feeling the need to prove I'm not some innocent little flower, and also feeling kind of pissed off with Enzo's pathetic macho behavior, I just can't hold back my so-called brattish attitude.

I turn my attention solely to Enzo now, but make sure my voice is loud enough that the whole car hears. " Oh honey, that's cute, but I've had bigger, badder boys than you beating my ass, and damn did I enjoy it."

The whole car, minus Enzo, who looks a little stunned, bursts into fits of giggles.

"Damn girl, I felt that fire from here," Lucas laughs.

"Told you!" Zander laughs from beside me. I look over at him and he has a kind of proud smile on his face.

We continue driving and I shuffle uncomfortably in my seat. Zander notices and tries, but mostly fails, to move over to give me a little more room. Enzo on the other hand has his legs spread wide taking up his foot space and mine.

"Dude, move over," Zander says as he gives his friend's leg a slight shove.

Enzo pretends to move it slightly, but it does absolutely nothing.

"Here," Zander says as puts his arm around me and pulls me towards him, giving me a little extra room as my body rests against him.

I lean against him, taking in his masculine scent for a moment. I look up at him, ready to tell him that I'm not ready for whatever he's thinking, but instead of a hungry expression, I'm met with a sincere, friendly one. So I allow myself to rest against him, enjoying a much needed moment of comfort in strong arms. *Even if they're not the arms I'm trying to pretend they are.*

We drive a little further, before pulling up at the go-kart track. We all head inside and spend the next few hours racing. Jamie and Lucas seem great. I get on well with both of them, having lots of banter and giggles, but Enzo on the other hand is a different story. He's not bad, nasty or even rude per se, but he's got this chip on his shoulder.

*It's almost like he believes that he can get any girl he wants or is tougher than any guy around. It's not quite confidence he exudes, but I don't quite know exactly what it is.* Gabe had loads of confidence and bad boy energy yet on him it worked, it was hot. But Enzo just rubs me up the wrong way, and I can't help but try to knock him down a peg or two.

The whole day we've had this kind of half friend, half enemies energy between us. Like when he tried complaining that he needed all the legroom in the car because he has a humongous dick. I couldn't stop my mouth from replying that big dick energy is usually a compensation for having a small one. Or when he remarked about being used to hearing girls screaming and begging him to go faster, my sassy mouth had to remind him that if girls are begging for it faster he's obviously not hitting the mark right the first time.

"I don't know about you, but I need a beer and a cigarette after all that," Jamie pants, as he places his helmet on the table.

"Yeah, that was so much fun, thanks for inviting me," I reply honestly.

"So my flat is literally fifteen minutes away. I've got beers, smokes, and snacks. You want to come back with us? We can grab a pizza or something?" Lucas asks. I must give him a questioning or suspicious look as he quickly adds. "The guys will come, I just mean I can drop you home, or you can come with us.

"Are you trying to steal my girl?" Zander jokes as he comes over and throws his arm around my shoulder.

I shuffle from under Zander's arm. "Yeah sure, sounds good." I reply to Lucas before turning my attention towards Zander.

"Here, carry this," I say, thrusting a helmet into his arms. "You can help me take these back."

Zander follows me and takes back all four of our helmets. "Hope you had fun, be sure to come again," the guy working the register says.

"I'm sure we will. Thanks," I replied with a smile. *I'm happy! I'm actually happy. It seems like forever since I felt happy. Usually, I'm just faking it so people don't start bad mouthing Gabe again or telling me it's good that things are over.*

"Zander, can I have a word?" I ask as we're walking back.

"Yeah of course. What's up?" he asks, sounding concerned.

"Look I like you, you're becoming a great friend, and I'm definitely in need of some friends right now," I admit, "but that's all. You know that right? I'm not looking for a boyfriend or anything."

"Of course. I understand Riley. You've just got out of something, and you're not interested in jumping into anything else. That's fine. I may be a guy, but I can manage a friendship without all the fun extras," he jokes.

"Good. I just don't want to hurt anyone or lead you on."

"Riley, look I'd be lying if I said I didn't find you attractive. Of course I do, I have eyes. But I'm also not some love sick puppy expecting you to fall head over heels for my amazing body, kick ass personality, and killer eyes." Zander jokes again, giving me a playful shove.

"Good, glad we're on the same page." I say with a smile. "Although your body is alright I guess, the personality is kinda weak, but I'll give you a five for the baby blues," I tease back, glad that the humor is easing any awkwardness.

"There she is, there's my girl, all attitude and savageness." Zander adds with a small chuckle.

"That's another thing," I add, my voice getting a little more serious, "please don't call me 'your girl'. You can call me anything else, your sass pot, your buddy, your little demon spawn, heck even your bitch. Just please don't call me your girl." I add, a hint of sadness probably evident in my voice.

He gives me a knowing nod as he throws his arm around my shoulders, "He really did a number on you, huh?"

"You have no idea," I admit, lowering my head in what feels like defeat.

"Don't worry, I'll find a new name for you. Don't blame me if you hate it though, you brought it on yourself." Zander adds as he gives me a reassuring squeeze.

"There you guys are, thought you'd slipped off for a quickie," Enzo teases. "Although you don't look very satisfied, so perhaps you need a round two with me?"

*God this guy is such a creep.*

"You couldn't handle me," I reply with a smirk.

"Think you've met your match with this one bro," Lucas laughs back.

We make our way back toward the car. "Do you want to sit in the front? Might be a little more room." Jamie offers kindly as he holds the door open for me.

"What and you three are going to squash in the back?" I laugh as I motion my hands to the three guys who are all clearly a fan of the gym.

"Good point," he adds back with a chuckle.

"You're welcome to park your fine ass on my lap, baby" Enzo adds as he climbs into his side of the back seat.

"Too bad she's already sitting on mine, isn't it?" Zander adds as he gives my shoulder a little squeeze before he climbs in, and motions for me to join him.

*Fuck it, better than being crushed between them both again.*

With an internal shrug, I climb onto Zander's lap and let my legs drape over him so they're still taking up the space in the middle, if for no other reason than to stubbornly stop Enzo from having any extra space.

"Really? His lap over mine? You're clearly tripping," Enzo says, putting on a playful tone.

"Yep, I didn't wanna waste my time with big dick energy when I had the real thing." I snap back, letting my brat flag fly high.

I feel a slight squeeze to the hips from Zander, as well as what I can tell from the corner of my eye is a smirk.

"Is that right?" Zander whispers against my ear. But no one else hears it over the music and sound of the engine.

I lean back slightly so that my mouth is close enough to his own ear, that only he will hear. "If I feel it, I'm chopping it off."

"No promises."

We pull up outside an apartment block and get out. "Sorry about that, hope I wasn't too heavy," I say as I stand beside the car door and wait for Zander to climb out.

"Baby, I'm happy to be used in your little battle of the wits against Enzo anytime. It's about time someone put that cocky asshole in his place."

We all make our way towards one of the ground floor apartments. "Make yourself comfortable, it's kind of a shithole but my house is your house," Lucas says as he unlocks the door and steps aside for me to walk in. The guys head straight in, walking straight towards the living room, clearly knowing the layout.

I follow behind and find Enzo and Jamie sitting in armchairs and Zander chilling on the sofa. I park my ass at the opposite end of the sofa. Lucas comes in a few minutes later carrying a case of beer.

"So you can either have a beer or one of these," he says, pulling out some bright orange bottle from his back pocket. "Liv won't mind you having one," he offers.

"What is it?" I ask as I take it from his hand. I examine the bottle realizing it's some sort of fruity punch type drink, one I have no desire to try. "Can I just have a beer?" I ask.

"My sorta girl," Jamie adds as he passes me the one he had in his hand and reaches for another for himself.

Lucas looks around at the lack of seating space and then pulls over a small gray bean bag looking thing "Here, swap." I say as I stand from the sofa.

"No it's fine," Lucas offers, but it's clear he's not really fine.

"Seriously, it's all good. Swap."

Zander throws me a cushion and I place it behind me and am pleasantly surprised to realize the bean bag is actually pretty comfy.

"So who wants to play a game?" Enzo suggests about ten minutes later as he reaches into the drawer on the table beside him and pulls out a pack of Cards Against Humanity.

Three hours later, we're all tipsy and laughing hysterically, realizing we're all equally as sarcastic and savage as each other at this game.

"Oh my god, I've actually done this," Enzo laughs as he throws down his card.

"What? You've found yourself naked in another guy's bed?" I laugh, as I hold back the tears.

"Kinda, but not in some sort of gay way," Enzo says rapidly.

"Then what other way is it?" I tease.

"Well, I was having a one night stand and woke up to take a piss. When I was walking back to the chick's room, I must have gotten confused because instead of her room, I ended up in her roommate's room. The lights were off so I just ended up climbing in bed with her roommate and her boyfriend. Believe me, it was terrifying and there were confused screams all around. I almost took a punch for it."

"Oh my god, that's so funny." I say as the tears roll down my cheeks from laughing so much.

"Oh yeah, like you've never had a terrible one night stand moment," Enzo says as he throws a cheese ball from the table at me.

"Actually, I've never had a one night stand," I admit.

"You've never had a one night stand?" Enzo asks dubiously. "You've never met a hot guy in a club or something and gone back to his house for a wild night of fun?"

My mind flashes back to Gabe, and some of the crazy moments we had, when we thought it was nothing but fun. The night we met in Saints, when I would have happily followed him home, and our time on the roof, when I openly handed him my virginity on a silver platter. Both times he saved me from Justin although I wasn't ready, I could have easily had sex with him in a hotel room.

"Well, kind of. But he became my boyfriend pretty soon after so it doesn't really count."

"Great, all that attitude and under all that we have little Miss Innocence!" Enzo says, a hint of bite to his voice.

"I'm hardly innocent. Just because I don't fuck anything with a pulse, unlike some people clearly, doesn't make me innocent." I snap back. *Who the fuck does he think he is?*

"Prove it," Enzo sneers.

"Never have I ever..." I begin before the next hour is spent drinking and taking shots while me and the guys all play Never Have I Ever.

"Never have I slept with two people in one night." Enzo and Lucas both take a shot.

"What?" Lucas laughs nervously. " My ex and I were together for almost two years, when she cheated on me, I kind of went a little wild. Plus it's college!"

"I get it," I say with a shrug because I do. I do get it, I mean, heck half the reason I'm here pointlessly flirting is because I'm hurt that Gabe is with someone else.

"Never have I ever spanked someone or been spanked," Lucas asks, before he goes to take a drink.

"Hey you can't say it if you've done it," I laugh.

"That would be a boring game, plus I wanna get drunk too," Lucas says.

"Okay fine, you can ask and drink I guess," I shrug, not really caring anymore about the rules.

"Exactly, so, never have I ever spanked someone" Lucas repeats. Every single person in the room takes a shot.

"Damn, Rileys a lil minx" Zander says. "I'm assuming you were the one spanked rather than the spank-er." I look up to see him peering at me with a glint in his eye.

"Well duh," I laugh as I playfully roll my eyes.

"Okay then, let's ramp this up. Never have I ever...been tied up or tied someone up." Zander asks, and although the question is aimed at everyone I can feel his eyes glaring at me.

Again I take a drink, as does everyone but Jamie. "Really?" Jamie questions as he looks around the room. "I don't think I'd like that whole power dynamic or being at someone else's mercy."

"That's the fun of it," both me and Zander say at the same time.

"Okay then, how about this, never have I ever... had sex outdoors." I ask. This time it's just me, Zander, and Enzo that drink.

"Details," Lucas demands.

"A few times, back of nightclubs, that sort of thing." Enzo says with a shrug.

"Ex-girlfriend, picnic in the woods," Zander adds.

I feel all eyes on me now. "Erm.. I don't wanna say." I admit

"Oh come on" all the guys groan. "No judgment here, we're all friends," Lucas adds.

"Okay." I say as I screw my face up. "I lost my virginity on a rooftop, had sex on a hotel balcony, and....." I add as I place both hands over my face to hide my embarrassment. "...may or may not have had some mind blowing moments on my ex's bike."

"Daaaamn, you are a kinky 'lil shit!" Enzo cheers as he cracks open another beer and hands it to me.

"Different guys or the same one?" Zander questions, and although he's saying it with a smile, I can hear a hint of annoyance, or perhaps desire in his tone.

"Same guy." I admit as I take a huge swig of my drink.

"Never have I ever..." Enzo says with a smirk, clearly thinking he's found something to call me out on. "... been completely and utterly dominated. I'm talking choking, gagging, blindfolds, handcuffs, the whole nine yards."

I reach for my drink but before I even get there Enzo is whooping, "Daaaamn, you really are a freak in the sheets. I bow at your feet oh Spicy One," he laughs as he pretends to bow.

"Sit down you idiot," Zander snaps as he pulls his friend back by the shirt.

"Where's the bathroom?" I ask as I attempt to stand from the giant marshmallow I'm trapped in.

"Through there, down the hall, and second left," Lucas says as he points towards a door.

I use the bathroom, wash up, and walk down the hall ready to head back when I hear voices behind the door. So feeling inquisitive I press my ear against it.

"Zander is gonna have the time of his life with her. I can't wait to hear the stories," a voice, one that I'm guessing is Enzo says.

"Shut it, I like her. I think she's great. She put you in your place, didn't she?" another voice laughs, but I can't tell if it's Lucas or Jamie.

"I'm just saying she seems like a ride and a half. I'd love to give her a test drive if Zander ain't got the balls to make his move," Enzo says.

I don't want to hear anymore, after all, Zander is my friend. These guys, in their own weird way, are kind of friends, well except Enzo perhaps. And I need that. I love Nate, Tucker, and the girls. Of course I do. But with everything that's happened with Gabe and the fact they all know him, I can't really express myself and be as free and open as I am here. And I need that. I need some harmless flirting and some banter. This is the first time in over a month I've been able to think or talk about me and Gabe without wanting to burst into tears.

I loudly begin turning the door handle, making a point of the fact I'm coming back in. "Sorry, the door was a bit stuck." I lie as Enzo turns to look at me. Jamie and Lucas's eyes dart to me from across the room, I look past them to where Zander was but he's nowhere to be seen.

"Outside, having a cigarette," Jamie says, answering my unasked question.

"Hey, you okay?" I ask as I make my way out to Zander.

"All good baby girl, just taking a breather," he replies as he turns to look at me.

I walk over and stand beside him, "You want one?" he offers as he holds out his pack to me.

"Absolutely," I reply as I take one and place it in my mouth. Zander lights it for me and I take a long drag feeling the familiar taste in my mouth.

*I've never really been a true smoker, not one who needs to smoke at least, but there's always been something kind of intriguing about the taste. But since being with Gabe and tasting it on my tongue almost every time we kissed, it's become my new favorite thing.*

The two of us stand silently enjoying our cigarette but not really saying much. "So, I never did find out, did you drink or not drink for the last question?" I say trying to make a joke on the strangely serious vibe we have going on here.

"That would depend on who it was asking the question I guess, to whether or not they'd get the answer they wanted," Zander replies, being oddly cryptic.

"Well clearly I asked the question," I reply a little dumbfounded.

"Then for you, yes," he replies as he butts out his cigarette on the wall and walks back inside. Leaving me to finish the rest of my cigarette alone.

# Chapter Twenty-Four

# Riley

I head back inside and notice that most of the beer bottles and shot glasses have been tidied away.

"So, fancy carrying on this buzz and heading to another party with us?" Enzo asks.

I look down at my super basic looking jeans and a cut off band tee combo. "I'm not exactly dressed for partying."

"Nah, you're fine. It's not that sort of place. It's super chill. Just good music, lots of cheap booze, and it's just off campus." Jamie adds.

"I dunno, it's not exactly the best place to take her, maybe we should head into town instead," Zander suggests. And while a small part of me appreciates the fact that Zander obviously thinks wherever the boys are going is too rough for me, my stubborn brattish side wants to go even more now.

"Sure, give me like ten minutes." I say as I reach for my handbag and walk towards the bathroom, praying there's some sort of makeup inside, to make me look semi presentable.

I rummage through my handbag and find some concealer, mascara, and an old lipstick. I feel a little cheeky but I open one of the drawers looking for a comb or something. The first drawer I open is mostly condoms and a few other boyish things. But the second one clearly belongs to whoever brought the fruity drink Lucas offered me earlier. It has a small hairbrush, some makeup, and lots and lots of bobby pins. I quickly brush my hair and use two or three of the pins to style my hair. I then take out the eye shadow pallet and swipe my finger over one of the almost empty shades. *Whoever she is she'll never know.* I then borrow some of the spray deodorant. Deciding this is the best I'm gonna be able to look, I close the drawer and head back to the guys.

"Are you ready to go now?" Lucas asks as he grabs his keys.

"Wait, you're not driving, right?" I snap.

"Nah, I'm putting my house keys somewhere safe so I can get in later." he laughs. "Uber will be here any minute."

"Oh," I reply feeling a little silly and relieved.

We climb in the Uber and I'm grateful that this car is bigger and more spacious, so nobody is sitting on anyone's lap this time. We pull up to what can only be described as some back alley bar, we head inside and almost instantly, I'm greeted by half naked women in tiny shorts and a bra handing out drinks.

"We can go somewhere else if this isn't your vibe?" Zander offers as he looks... *Embarrassed?*

"Pretty sure butts and boobs ain't gonna scare her off, right?" Enzo says as he gives me a little poke in the side.

"Nah, of course not." I laugh. Just as a scary looking dude in a biker jacket walks through the door in front of me and the sound of loud music booms from behind him.

I see the guy eye me for a moment, but Zander throws his arm around my shoulder and pulls me closer. "Stay close to me," he says, in a forceful but protective tone.

*Damn, I've missed hearing that sort of tone. And just like the compliant little whore I am, I obey and allow him to walk me inside.*

We walk inside and make our way to the bar, order our drinks, and then head out onto the dance floor. I say dance floor, but basically the whole place is just one sticky dance floor other than the bar. We're all dancing, letting loose when a dark haired girl comes bounding over and throws her arms around Lucas. " Hey baby," she chimes.

"Riley, this is my girlfriend, Liv."

"Hey, I'm Olivia but everyone just calls me Liv," the girl chimes as she surprises me by throwing her arms around me.

"Hey, I'm Riley, I'm erm..."

"Zander's girl right?" she questions.

"Actually..." I begin but Zander cuts me off.

"No, not my girl, just a friend," Zander says. "Well I guess she's all of our friend now," he adds a little too quickly.

"Oh cool, well do you want a drink, new friend?" Liv asks as she frowns at Zander.

"Erm, sure." I reply. But before I have a chance to tell her what I want she disappears within the crowd.

"Liv works here," Jamie explains when he sees the confused look on my face.

We continue dancing and not long later, Liv comes out with beers for all the guys and some sickly sweet drink for me. "Thanks, I say." even though it's nothing like I'd usually drink.

I hold my drink for a while longer, taking reluctant sips every now and again as we continue dancing. The music seems to get louder and louder with each song.

"Smoke?" Zander shouts over the music as he makes a smoking gesture with his hands. I nod my head in response and he takes me by the hand to lead me through the crowd. Lucas has disappeared somewhere with his girlfriend, but the other two guys follow behind. Once we are outside and can finally hear ourselves think, we find a corner to chat and smoke by.

"I'm going for a piss, keep an eye on Riley, will ya?" Zander says before moving me slightly so that I'm closer to Jamie.

"Will do!" Jamie replie, as he accepts his role of protecting the poor innocent little princess.

I take a sip of my drink and shudder, "Drink that bad?" Enzo laughs.

"It's like drinking unicorn piss" I laugh.

"Here." he says, taking it off me and placing it on a makeshift table beside him. " What's your poison? I'll get one of the girls to bring it for you." Enzo offers.

I'm about to reply when I feel strong masculine arms wrap around my waist.

"She'll take a whiskey."

# Chapter Twenty-Five

# Gabe

## Two Hours Earlier

I jump off my bike, pull my hood up over my head, and turn down the dark alleyway toward Desire. *That's right, goddamn Desire.* I head in through the side entrance, the one I asked Cruz to leave unlocked for me.

Once inside I make my way straight to his office, careful not to catch eyes with anyone as I try to discreetly make my way there. As I do, I pass the side rooms, the ones I know are filled with drunk guys getting lap dances and probably a lot more.

I knock on the door, and once I hear, "Come in" I make my way inside.

"Gabriel, long time no see," Cruz says smoothly.

"Looking gray, old man," I tease.

"Asswipe, I should shoot you right out of your shoes." Cruz snaps as he picks up a gun from on top of his desk and points it at me.

I see his two bodyguards' hands twitch as they inevitably prepare for whatever their boss says next.

"Who are you kidding, bet you can't even see me without your glasses, old man," I reply with a laugh.

"Too true," Cruz laughs as he places his gun back on the desk. "Damo, go get us both some whiskey. Me and the boy wanna talk alone," he snaps towards one of his men.

Both men nod and then walk away leaving us alone. "Sad news about Johnny boy, real sad news," Cruz says as he shakes his head.

"I know, but as I said on the phone, that's what I wanted to talk to you about," I say.

"Not yet," Cruz replies. We engage in small talk. The typical 'when was the last time I saw you', 'you've changed so much' bullshit that people say when they see old friends.

*Although friends is kind of a strong word.*

Cruz, John, and my father were all part of the same crew back in the day; back when they were all just punk kids getting into shit. My father of course wasted his life with drugs and booze. John built his own little small town thug empire. But Cruz was always the head honcho. He was the one with the ideas, the money, and the ruthless drive to make it big. He has a shit ton of small bars like this that are a front for drugs, prostitution, and money laundering. He's also into some other shit that I don't even want to know about. But out of a mutual respect, an honor amongst thieves, kind of respect, he and John have stayed relatively tight.

Cruz allows, *or perhaps I should say allowed,* John, to run his little affairs inside Cruz's territory, but John ensured to never step on his toes and also shared a percentage of any of his profits with him.

"Here boss," one of the guys says as he walks in with a bottle of very expensive whiskey and two equally expensive looking glasses.

"Now leave and make sure no one disturbs us," Cruz snaps.

We sit in silence for a few seconds after the door closes, to ensure we're all alone and then Cruz pipes up. " So tell me everything…"

Knowing I'm in way over my head and need help to escape this whole messy situation I sing like a mother fucking canary. I tell him all about them kidnapping me, about them basically killing John, and about them using 'someone else' as leverage.

"This girl, is she worth it? Is she worth everything you're going through? There are millions of easy women in the world; you sure you're willing to go through all this for this one?" Cruz questions.

"What girl? Who said anything about a girl?" I ask. *Shit, did I fuck up? Did I mention Riley by name somehow? I thought I was being really discreet by just saying someone.*

"Really?" Cruz laughs. "You take me for a fool? You want to insult me by making out like I was dropped on this earth yesterday?"

"No, of course not. But how did you know?"

"Oh Gabriel," He replies with a throaty chuckle.

*The way he uses my whole name despite the fact he knows I hate it grates on me; but I guess if I'm trusting him with this secret, and trusting him with my life in essence, I have to trust him enough with my whole name.*

"I know you boy. The only person you care about is that brother of yours... but, no man, brother or not, is falling to his knees offering his life up in exchange for another man's life. Family or not. So my question stands. Is. This. Girl. Worth. It?"

"She's worth everything and more." I admit honestly.

"Then I will help you keep her safe." Cruz says with a nod as he pours us both another glass.

"Are you willing to do whatever it takes, anything I ask, without question?" Cruz asks as he points one of his wrinkly fingers in my direction.

"I'll do anything it takes to keep those I love safe," I confirm without hesitation.

"Then here's my plan...."

Cruz goes through his whole plan, one that won't be a short fix. It will require playing the long game of lying, cheating, double crossing, and murder. But one that hopefully, if it works, will allow me to get back everything I lost.

"Anyway enough business now, time for some pleasure," he laughs as he opens the door again and guides me back down the corridor. As we go his two bodyguards join us silently. "Send me Tammy and Destiny," he says to one of his men before guiding me through another, previously locked door.

The room is small, with a semi circle shaped seating area, a pole, and a small stage, but nothing else.

"Sit down, and relax." Cruz demands. I do as requested and moments later in walk two women, through another door, each wearing nothing but underwear, or even describing it as swimwear is generous.

"Blond or brunette?" Cruz purrs from beside me.

"It's fine." I say as I take a sip of my drink.

"Pick one." Cruz says a little more forcefully.

"Erm, brunette," I say, knowing full well that while she's hot enough, brunettes have never really done it for me, I've always been attracted to blondes.

"Good choice," Cruz says as the blond tops up both of our drinks further, and then her and her friend each climb onto our laps. "Tammy hit the window," Cruz commands. The blond bends over and presses a button, which turns part of the wall opposite into a window.

"Don't worry, it's multi-layered, even with the lights, we can see out but they can't see in," Cruz informs me, as I look ahead at what appears to be most of the bar. I see people dancing away to music I can't hear, just as slow sensual music begins to play around me.

The brunette does her best to entice me, grinding her crotch on my lap, shoving her small but perky tits in my face, but my eyes are more focused on the view of the strangers in front of me.

"Enough," Cruz snaps. Both girls climb off our laps and disappear behind where we're sitting.

"Damn you got it bad huh?" he asks. I turn my head to look at him but don't reply.

"Destiny is one of our hottest girls, and you're looking at her like she's some sort of swamp creature," Cruz laughs.

"Sorry, she's great and all, but…"

"But not who you want her to be?" Cruz finishes.

"Exactly!"

"I had that once…" Cruz says as he walks over to the window and looks out as if admiring his empire. I follow him to the window and am looking out listening to Cruz's story about a girl he once loved, when I spot something. *Or rather someone.*

"Is that?" I say out loud, seconds before my question is answered as my beautiful, perfect, Little Flame walks closer to the window, before disappearing out of sight.

"I'll be back," I shout as I literally run out of the room. I find the dance floor easily, but can't see my girl anywhere. I'm looking around when I see a large mirror on the wall wobble slightly as a bang comes from behind it.

*Damn, you really can't see into that room. So if that's where I just was, then Riley must have gone that way.*

I turn my attention to a door barely propped open with a brick. I see her with her back towards me talking to three other guys. I take a moment to breathe now she's in my sight and look around looking for any of her friends. But I quickly realize this isn't the sort of place any of them would be seen dead. One of the guys she's talking to pushes her towards another and then turns around and walks right past me. I spot Riley shuffling slightly from foot to foot, letting me know she's uncomfortable. She takes a sip of her drink, one that I notice hasn't left her hand in the few minutes I've been watching her. But then the other guy, the one she's instinctively leaning her body away from, takes it from her hands.

*That's it, I'm going over!*

The guy places her drink on the table behind him. *At least he's not doing anything, yet.*

"What's your poison?" the guy asks just as I'm right behind her. "I'll get one of the girls to bring it for you."

I wrap my arm around Riley's waist and don't miss the way she jumps slightly at the contact. "She'll take a whiskey," I growl beside her ear, so she knows exactly whose arms she's in.

"Ga.." Riley attempted to say but I cut her off by bringing my glass up to her lips.

"Drink," I demand as I pull her waist tighter against me. Riley opens her mouth slightly and allows me to pour some of the liquid inside. "Such a good girl," I praise against her ear.

Everything is going perfectly, if only for a second, until one of the guys clears their throat, and just like that, whatever moment Riley was having with me is broken as she moves out of my arms so fast it's like my touch burns her.

"Fuck off Gabe!" Riley says as she spins around to look at me, anger and stubbornness in her eyes.

"Baby wait," I moan as I take a step closer but she pushes me away.

"No, fuck you Gabe, we are done. Stop fucking with me," she says before turning to storm away.

I go after her, but it's as if her anger is jet powering her because her speed of retreat is not like I have seen from her before. It gets to the point where I almost have to jog to keep up with her. I see her run inside and I have to push the half closed door open to fit through. When I finally get my sights back on her, I'm met with a nightmare I didn't expect to see in a million years. Riley locking lips with another guy.

*What the actual fuck!!!*

## Chapter Twenty-Six

## Riley

"No, fuck you, Gabe! We're done; stop fucking with me!" I shout, before turning and storming away.

*He will not see me cry! I refuse to allow him or the other guys to see me like this. See the effect Gabe still has on me. See how easily I melt for him. Every. Single. Time.*

I hear Gabe's heavy footsteps behind me closing in on me. I slide through the gap in the door, not wasting time opening it fully, and as I do, like a Knight in Shining Armor I see Zander, walking towards me.

"Kiss me," I beg.

"Wha..." he attempts to ask but I don't give him a chance to. I practically pounce on him as I crash my lips onto his.

Zander wastes no time kissing me back, wrapping his arms around me as he pulls me closer. I'm beginning to get lost in the moment until I feel another set of hands grab me and physically pull me out of Zander's grip.

"Get the fuck off me!" I bellow as Gabe lifts me off the floor and pulls me away like a child.

He places me a couple of inches back down till my feet are on the floor and then releases me. "Who the fuck are you?" he seethes as he pushes Zander with enough force that he causes him to stumble back a step.

"I'm her fucking boyfriend." Zander replies as he holds his ground. I see Gabe's fist fly back but I put myself between them.

"Move Riley." Gabe seethes as his nostrils flare and he glares beyond me towards Zander.

"Who the fuck does he think he is? Putting his hands on what is mine?" Gabe seethes, but underneath the anger, I can hear sadness and insecurity too.

"But I'm not yours, am I Gabe?" I reply in a half shout, half sad tone. I take a step towards him and place my hand on his chest. "Not anymore. You made sure of that." *Don't cry. Don't cry.* I chant to myself as I feel the moisture pooling in my eyes.

"You'll always be mine," he replies in a possessive but less forceful tone.

"Not anymore. You lost me." I admit sadly as I break not only mine but clearly his heart too, if the look on his face is anything to go by.

*I don't get it. Why does it bother him so much that I'm here with Zander when he was the one who left me? It's like there's something he's not telling me.*

"Come with me," Gabe says as he tries to pull me.

"Riley?" Zander says as he reaches out and grabs my arm to stop me.

Gabe lets out a furious huff as his hand grips mine far too tightly, almost to the point of pain as his anger rises.

"I'll be right back," I say to Zander as I allow Gabe to lead me away. He guides me outside and to a quiet little alleyway.

"What do you want, Gabe?" I ask after a few minutes of standing in complete silence.

"You." he admits, his voice barely louder than a whisper.

"What did you say?" I ask again, even though I heard him.

"I said...you! I want you!" he informs me and for a second the butterflies flutter in my tummy at his words.

"You had me Gabe. I gave you every single part of me. And still, it wasn't enough for you." I reply, hating how my voice now has a bit of a wobble, as my anger subsides and my sadness takes over.

"Don't say that; don't ever think that. You were always enough, you were more than enough. You were my wildfire, my angel, my brat, my girl. You were always mine. And you will always be mine." Gabe says as he cups my cheek and places the softest kiss on my lips. So soft in fact that I barely felt it touch me.

"Don't forget your slut," I add, trying to add a little humor to distract from the pounding in my chest.

"Oh baby, I loved the times when you were my little slut." Gabe moans back, arousal evident in his tone.

"Oh I bet you did," I flirt back biting my lip. "I'm sure they are the times you remember most when you're alone."

"No, the times I got to call you my girlfriend are the moments that run through my mind on a loop." Gabe admits before his lips find mine, much more forcefully and passionately this time.

His hands drop from my chin to my throat in the most delicious way imaginable as he holds me and kisses me, just like he used to. On instinct, my hands tug at his messy hair as his other hand snakes down my bare skin and he grips my hip to hold me in place.

"Riley?… Riley, you out here?" Zander calls from somewhere close by. I unwind my hands from Gabe's hair and with my other hand, I gently move his hand from my hip so he's only holding me by the throat as we stare into each other's eyes.

"Riley?" Zander calls this time from much closer. I turn my head and see him standing staring at us from just a few feet away. I step back so Gabe has no choice but to release my throat but as I turn to walk away he stops me.

"Is it serious?" he asks.

"Is what serious?" I question.

"You and him," he says motioning to where I know Zander is standing. "Is it serious? Do you love him?

"No. Never." I reply honestly.

*Sure Zander is a nice guy, a good friend even. But I could never feel about him the way I do Gabe. Even if I did just force him to kiss me out of stubbornness.*

"Is he good to you? Kind? Caring? Makes you feel safe?" Gabe questions again.

And this time the answer comes easy. "Yes," I admit nodding. Because he does. He's never been anything but nice to me, even when I've told him time and time again that I'm going through stuff, he's always been kind to me.

"Okay," Gabe admits, his voice sad and hollow. "But if he ever hurts you, I'll fucking kill him," he adds through angry gritted teeth.

"Gabe, you're the only one who has ever hurt me," I add softly.

"I'm sorry. I wish I could explain."

*He looks defeated. Like he's waging a war but with whom? I don't know. It's like he's carrying the weight of the world on his shoulders and is just...resigned.*

"I don't need your apologies or explanations; you left me. You hurt me. But now you have to let me go," I admit as I lean forward, kiss his cheek, and then walk away.

# Gabe

And just like that, she walks away from me. Again. Straight into the arms of another man. A better man. One who is clearly more worthy of her than I am. He throws his arms around her and walks her away. He turns back, just long enough to throw me an angry look but then looks back down at her.

*Fucking pussy! He clearly saw me all over his girlfriend and didn't even have the balls to fight me. He should have at least punched me for laying hands on his girl - his girl. Urgh! She'll never be his girl! She's MINE! But still, he saw the girl he is apparently dating in my arms and didn't even come to take her back. What a goddamn pussy.*

I head towards my bike, climb on, and let the feel of the open road beneath my tires distract me.

*"You hurt me! You lost me! I'm not yours anymore!"*

Her words run through my mind on a vicious, hell-like loop; one I cannot escape. I pull off down a secluded dirt road, remove my helmet and just scream into the night air. "Fuuuuuuuuuck!!!!"

Feeling slightly more level headed after my outburst I suddenly remember, not only did I leave Riley, but I also ran out on Cruz in the middle of a meeting. *Fuck. fuck. Fuck!*

I pull out my phone and dial his number. "Yeah?" Cruz snaps when he answers.

"Look, I'm so sorry, shit went down…"

"I saw," Cruz replies, his tone clipped.

"Look man, I'm sorry. I'm out of town but I can turn around and be back with you in about thirty minutes."

"Gabe, I'm currently balls deep in one bitch and I'm about to enjoy the other. Sort your shit out and I'll call you the next time I need you," he says before hanging up.

*Well at least he isn't that mad!* I think to myself with a shrug. Because the last thing I need is another powerful enemy. This time one that would be more than capable of ensuring I end up six feet under.

## Chapter Twenty-Seven

## Riley

I walk inside, thankful for the fact Zander is physically holding me up as it feels like my legs want to give out. "Are you okay?" he asks.

"Honestly? No!" I admit as we finally reach the pub and stand outside.

"I'm guessing that's the ex? The one who broke your heart." Zander says sympathetically.

"Yup. Ripped my heart out, crushed it into pieces, and then stomped on it for good measure." I reply as I snake out from under his grip and sit myself down on a nearby wall.

"For what it's worth, it seems like he still has feelings for you," Zander gently says as he sits himself down beside me.

"Yeah, not enough though, clearly," I add with a sigh.

"He sure looked murderous when he saw us kissing." Zander laughs as he knocks his shoulder into mine playfully.

"Oh my god. I'm so sorry. I can't believe I just attacked you and forced you to kiss me." I say as I throw both my hands over my face. *You really are a pathetic bitch. Bet he thinks you're a complete freak after tonight.*

"Being kissed by a gorgeous girl..." Zander says as he rubs at his chin, "...I've had worse nights." he adds with a smirk.

"He could have beat you up or anything. I wouldn't put it past him." I say as I peer out between the fingers of one hand.

Zander reaches over and pulls my hand away from my face. "Seriously, it's fine. I may look like my beauty has been chiseled from glass..." he adds as he pretends to pose, "but I'm more than capable of taking a punch or two. These guns were not created just to make me look good you know." he laughs as he flexes his biceps.

"Oh my god! You are so vain." I say as I give him a playful shove.

"You know you love it. Why else would you agree to be my girlfriend?" he asks, adding emphasis to the word girlfriend.

"Why did you say you were my boyfriend though? You could have just as easily been just some guy in a club I kissed," I question.

"You seemed like you needed some help, plus, I assumed from his temper that he was the ex. So I thought I'd give him a taste of his own medicine. Boyfriend says you've moved on way more than a drunken kiss with a stranger." he says with a shrug before climbing on the wall and reaching out for my hand to help me off too.

"So what does forcing my friend to kiss me, to make my ex jealous say about me then?" I laugh.

"That you're friends with a guy so hot that you just couldn't keep your hands off him... duh."

"You're so fucking big headed..." I laugh, giving his hand a playful slap, "... but you're a really great friend." I smile, before taking his hand, even though the wall is only a few feet high.

We head back inside and find Liv, another girl and the guys all sitting around a table on the patio. We both find an empty chair and sit down. Zander takes out a smoke and hands me one without me even asking. *I really need to start keeping cigarettes on me. I can't keep stealing all of his.*

"Thanks," I say with a smile as I take it, then lean forward so he can light it.

"Here, you look like you need it," Jamie says as he hands me a glass of what I soon realize is whiskey, although nowhere near as smooth as the one Gabe gave me earlier.

"What is it?" Zander questions as he reaches for the hand the glass is in and smells it.

"Whiskey." Enzo replies. "A not so little birdy told us, it's her drink of choice... or is that only when someone else is tipping it down your throat?" he says in a sarcastic but playful tone.

"Too soon man," Jamie says as he hits him in the arm.

"What? She can take it. Right, Riley?" Enzo laughs.

"Yeah," I say with a mock annoyance. *Really I'm quite enjoying the banter. Better than them all trying to soothe me or tippy toe around me like a little wounded bird, the way the rest of my friends do. I'll take humor and teasing over sympathy and pity any damn day.*

"See, I knew you were a good girl," Enzo says with a smirk.

"Fine, fine, get it all out," I say, holding my hands up in mock surrender.

"He's only jealous," Lucas says as he fires mock daggers at his brother.

"Jealous and horny! That shit was hot! Pretty sure I'm still sporting a semi," Enzo says as he makes a show of adjusting himself in his pants, causing a round of disgusted groans to echo from everyone around the table. "Talking of semis, how are you doing, Zander? That looked like one hell of a kiss."

"Why don't you come over here and find out?" Zander says as he licks his lips dramatically and leans back pretending to go for his button.

"Eww, you ruined it" Enzo groans.

"You okay though?" Lucas whispers from beside me.

"I will be," I reply as I take another drag of my cigarette.

The night goes by in a blur and before I know it, we're all being kicked out and the sun is beginning to rise.

"I don't wanna go home yet. My parents will kill me," I slur as we all stand outside the bar wondering what to do next.

"Well we're off," Liv says as Lucas begins ordering an Uber.

"And we are too," Jamie says once he finally pulls himself away from his new girl's face long enough to speak.

"That's two," Lucas says as he continues tapping away on his phone. "What about the rest of you?"

"I'm crashing at yours," Enzo says with a decisive head nod.

"And what about you Riley? Do you need an Uber too?" Liv asks.

"Erm, what are you doing?" I say turning my attention towards Zander.

"I live within walking distance so I'm all good," he says with a smile.

"Err, yeah I guess so," I say as I let out a small sigh. *The last thing I want to do is go home, probably to either be told off by my parents when they find out, like I'm a little kid, or even worse, a disappointed look from Harper who acts more like my parole officer or babysitter, than my sister lately.*

"Two is fine Luke, the little Miss Party Animal over here clearly isn't ready for the night to end so she can come back with me." Zander says as he rolls his eyes at me and smiles.

I just smile back in return. The Ubers both arrive pretty quick and once they are gone me and Zander take off in the opposite direction. We continue chatting and learning more about each other. Thankfully for my feet, he was telling the truth about it being within walking distance because we arrive at his place in no time.

"Do you live with anyone else?" I ask as I try but fail to be quiet. "Ouch." I say as I hit my leg off a table. Zander quickly turns on a light, which is stupidly placed on the other side of the room.

"Sorry." I mouth.

"It's fine, my roommate isn't home," he reassures me. He leads me to the lounge and encourages me to sit down. "I'll be back in a second," he says before disappearing into another room.

A few minutes later he returns in just a pair of loose basketball shorts. His toned abs are on full display. "Here," he says as he throws a t-shirt and some shorts at me.

"What are these for?" I ask.

"Thought since it's late and you'll probably end up staying here, you might want to get comfy," Zander replies as he runs his hands through his hair. A hint of nervousness or uneasiness in his voice.

"Oh, okay," I reply, unsure what else to say.

"My bedroom is the door on the right." he says, pointing in the direction he just came from.

I grab the items from the sofa and walk into Zander's bedroom suddenly feeling nervous. Until this very moment, likely because of my drunken haze, it hadn't occurred to me that the two of us are alone, in his apartment, and now I'm in his bedroom about to wear his clothes.

*What if he thinks I'm just here because I wanna fuck him? I mean you literally kissed his face off earlier. Shit! What the hell have I got myself into?*

I sit myself down on his bed and place the clothes beside me as I try to decide what to do next.

*Do I go out and tell him I made a mistake coming here and ask him to call me an Uber?* No, that seems rude and is also super embarrassing.

*Should I agree to wear the clothes and just see what happens next?* No, because I may not know what I want, but I definitely know I don't want to sleep with anyone yet.

I must spend too long deciding because I hear a small tap on the door. "Riley? Is everything okay?" Zander asks softly from the other side of the door.

I walk over and open the door, Zander's eyes scan me, still fully dressed and a confused look spreads over his face. "Did they not fit?" he asks. "I've got other stuff I'm sure." he says as he slides past me and begins opening draws.

"Zander," I said nervously. "You know that I'm... I mean this isn't..." I begin to say but he turns around and lets out a slight chuckle.

"Yes, Riley, don't worry. This isn't my super smooth way to try and get you naked in my room," he laughs. " I just honestly thought you'd be more comfy in a baggy shirt and shorts than jeans. But if you feel more comfortable in jeans, keep them on." he says as he turns and walks towards the door. "It's your choice." Then starts to close the door.

"Oh, well then yeah. These jeans are definitely too tight for my beer belly" I joke back.

"Good, I'll go make us both a drink, come out when you're dressed... or undressed I guess," he adds before closing the door completely.

*See, I knew he was just a genuinely good guy; a great friend.* I think to myself before I begin to strip and put his shirt on. I attempt to put the shorts on, but despite my fat ass, and love handles they just will not stay up.

I look down, realizing his shirt is so long it almost comes down to my knees. *Fuck it! This top is so long he'll never know.*

I fold the shorts neatly on the bed and then walk out.

"Here you go. Wasn't sure if you took milk and sugar so they are on the table," he says as I walk towards him.

"Milk and two sugars," I say aloud as I finish making my coffee.

"Glad to see they fit, kind of." Zander says as I come back and sit down beside him on the couch, carefully tucking my legs under me and pulling the shirt down over my knees to stay as covered up as possible.

"So what shall we do now?"

"We could put on a movie," Zander suggests.

The rest of the night goes by with us watching movies, joking around, and some mindless flirting. For a moment I could almost imagine us as a couple, but we aren't. I know that, if I allowed myself to, I could easily fall for someone like him. He's the sort of guy who would treat me like a princess and who I could happily bring around my friends and family, but there's just not that spark here for me.

Zander sees me shuffling around on the sofa and pulls me into a hug, allowing me to use him as my own personal pillow.

*I've missed this. I've missed having strong arms to hold me, I miss having a strong body to lean against. The feeling of being safe and secure in a guy's embrace. Why can't I just fall in love with him? Everything would be so much easier. But it isn't the same as being snuggled up to Gabe. He doesn't smell or feel the same, and my body doesn't ignite from Zander's touch the way it always has for Gabe.*

I almost pull away, not wanting to lead Zander on or have him read too much into this, but when I look up at him, he has such a relaxed and content look on his face, that I just bury myself in his embrace.

*I'm feeling vulnerable and I need someone to ground me. Fuck it, Gabe still hasn't given me an explanation. I really have no reason to feel guilty but my heart will always belong to him, even if it is still shattered.*

I must fall asleep in his arms as the next thing I know, I'm being carried through the air.

"What the..." I mumbles.

"I tried to wake you but you were half dead." Zander says with a chuckle, as he lays me down on a soft bed.

"Mmm," I mumble as I nuzzle into the soft blankets for a second before my drunken brain catches up with the situation.

*You're half naked in this guy's bed!*

*But before I even have a chance to panic I see Zander turn to leave.*

"I'll be out on the sofa if you need anything. Sleep tight." Zander adds as he closes the door.

## Chapter Twenty-Eight

## Izzy

I'm just standing in the kitchen with Nana helping her add the finishing touches to the pies she made for the church bake sale, when the back door all but flies open.

"Sorry," Ava shouts to no one in particular. "Izzy? Nana?" she calls out as she makes her way through the house.

"What the fudge?" I ask as I come out of the kitchen ready to tell her off for storming through my grandparents' house like this. But as soon as I see the worried look on Harper's face beside her, my annoyance quickly morphs into concern.

"Is everything okay?" I gasp, as I wipe the flour off my hands and only my jeans, before giving Harper a hug.

"Have you seen Riley? Is she here?" Harper quizzes as she pushes me away to look into my eyes.

"Riley? No, why?"

"Haven't you seen your phone?" Ava asks.

"No, I've been helping Nana all morning, why?"

"Is everything okay?" Nana asks, coming out of the kitchen to see what all the commotion is about.

"Riley is missing!" Harper says in a panic.

"Okay come and sit down I'll get you a glass of water then you can start at the beginning," Nana says, her tone laced with worry and concern.

"Okay..." Harper says after guzzling the whole glass of water. "So Riley left us yesterday around lunchtime, saying she was going to look around her new college with our old babysitter Lexi since Lexi just graduated this year."

"O-kay." Nana says softly.

"I didn't hear anything from her for the rest of the afternoon. I texted her a few times asking how it went but I got no reply. I tried calling her phone and it was off. So I assumed she'd probably ended up staying with Lexi since she and Lexi are pretty close. I mean it's not unusual for Riley to stay at Lexi's. She's done it a bunch of times, she usually calls to let us know though." Harper says as she rushes to get the words out in a panic.

"Take a breath dear; it'll be fine. It's most likely Riley being Riley." Nana says with a forced easy going tone.

"Anyway, I went over to Lexi's today, to take Riley some spare clothes, and see if she needed a ride back, but Lexi says she hasn't seen Riley since prom night."

"What did your parents say? They must be beside themselves." Nana interrupts.

"They don't know yet. They're on their honeymoon cruise, they left first thing this morning. They're sailing somewhere in the

Mediterranean. And I don't want to worry them. I mean, I practically had to force them to go as they were worried about leaving us while Riley is so fragile and with me and her fighting constantly. I especially don't want to worry them if she's just with a friend somewhere." Harper replies.

"They need to know. I'd be furious if you went missing and nobody kept me informed." Nana says as she strokes my hair.

"I'm not going anywhere; you're stuck with me Nana." I smile. Hoping to soothe whatever worry she is currently playing in her mind.

"Could I have a soda please?" Ava asks politely.

"Of course," Nana replies as she walks away.

"Have you tried Nate and Tucker? I doubt she's there but maybe they've seen her. Perhaps her and Gabe bumped into each other. Wouldn't be the first time she lied to us about spending the night with him, would it? Heck, she could even be with that guy from the boat. Zayden or whatever his name is. You said it yourself, she's always on the phone with him," Ava says quietly as Nana rummages in the fridge.

"I hadn't even thought of that." Harper says, finally sounding a little less stressed.

"Here you go girls," Nana says as she returns with three sodas, one for each of us. "Would you like some cake? Then, I'll help you call around to some other friends to find her?"

"Thank you, but we think we might know where she is." I say as I grab the drinks and we head out.

"Will you be okay? Do you need me to stay?" I ask, suddenly realizing I've completely abandoned her when I was supposed to be helping her.

"Go find Riley," she replies.

We jump into Ava's car and try the obvious places. We call Nate who says he's not seen her and that Gabe was definitely home and alone last night. We head to see Tucker, but he's not seen her either.

Next we drive to that bar, the one that Riley brought us to when we were looking for Gabe. The barman seems friendly enough, kind of helpful actually. He suggests other places he knows Gabe and Riley hung out, but she's not in any of those places either. Finally we drive to the salon, hoping to find Lexi's friend Brooke.

"Brooke!" we call out when we spot her standing at the front desk. "Thank god you're here."

"Everything okay girls?" Brooke says as she looks at what I can only assume are three very sweaty and concerned faces.

"Have you seen Riley?" Harper cries.

"Riley? No. Why is everything okay?" Brooke replies, sounding concerned herself.

"No! She's missing!"

"Missing?" Brooke gasps.

"Possibly missing, probably just hungover somewhere," Ava clarifies.

"Tell me everything," Brooke says, motioning to the chairs in the waiting room.

"We don't have time, I'm sorry." I say as politely, but urgently as I can. "You said before you knew that Zayden guy Riley has gotten close to, from some party or something?"

"Zayden? Oh you mean Zander?" Brooke corrects. "I don't really know him, I have only met him once or twice. Pretty sure he's on the same football team as Noah though. Wait here and I will call him to see if he has an address.

Brooke takes out her phone and calls her boyfriend but he doesn't answer.

"Sit down, I'll get you a drink and I'll try him again in a few minutes, he's probably driving, at the gym, or playing FIFA."

"Here's my number," Harper says, as she scribbles it down on the back of a discount coupon from the table. "We've gotta keep looking but call me if you hear anything."

"Of course," Brooke replies as she waves the number in the air, as Harper practically runs out the door.

"Thanks again." I say, before making my way outside as well.

"Where to?" Ava asks as she starts the engine.

"O'Malley's!" Harper demands.

"I told you Nate doesn't know anything." I try to speak but she cuts me off.

"I'm not going there to talk to him."

"Harper, is that a good idea? Riley won't want Gabe knowing anything." I try saying, but again she talks over me.

"I dont give a fuck what she wants or doesn't want. If he knows ANYTHING I plan to drag it out of him."

We pull up to O'Malleys and the car is barely even in park before Harper gets out and storms towards the gates.

"Hey Harper, what can…" Nate says, but Harper ignores him. "Where's Gabe's office?" she snaps.

"It's that way, but he's…" Nate tries to say but Harper is in no mood to listen, she's in full on mama bear mode.

"Sorry baby," I mouth as me and Ava both chase after Harper who seems to have suddenly become an Olympic level speed walker.

"Where is she?" Harper shouts as she pushes the door open with so much force it collides with the wall causing the small room to shake.

"What the fuck?" Gabe bellows, his face murderous, for a moment, before he looks and registers who we are.

"What are you doing here?" he snaps, his voice sounding more confused than his usual grumpy tone though.

"Where the fuck is she?" Harper huffs as she storms past him towards the little door that presumably leads to a bathroom.

"Who?" Gabe mouths towards me and Ava.

"RILEY!!!" Harper shouts. And in the same way a dog's ears prick up when you say the word 'walk' Gabe's whole body reacts.

"Riley?" he asks. "Why would she be here?"

Harper storms out of the bathroom having not found who she's looking for and marches straight out the door like a frigging hurricane, leaving nothing but dismay and destruction in her wake.

"Never mind," me and Ava say as we turn to leave but he reaches out and grabs my arm, spinning me around to look at him.

"What's going on?" Gabe demands.

"It's just a misunderstanding. Sorry for barging in here."

"Princess, you have three fucking seconds to explain…. One…. two…"

"Okay, okay, get off me though." I snap, as I pull my arm out of his grip.

Gabe releases me carefully, using his other hand to steady me from falling. *Unlike last time when you ended up on your ass in the mud.*

"Explain. NOW!" he demands as he finally releases me.

"We don't know where Riley is. She's probably fine, out partying somewhere. But she didn't come home last night and she lied to Harper about who she was with. And now we can't find her anywhere." I say, the words flying out of my mouth like verbal diarrhea.

Gabe storms out the door, me and Ava give each other a little 'this is going to end badly' look, before we run after him.

By the time we catch up, he and Harper appear to be mid argument in the middle of the yard.

I see Nate rushing over to stop it at the same time as we are.

"Did you fucking know?" Gabe bellows when he catches sight of Nate. We're not quite close enough to hear Nate's response, but are definitely close enough to see as Gabe swings his fist back and clocks his brother on the jaw. Clearly not with his full force, but enough to cause Nate to stumble back in shock.

I run as fast as I can to get to Nate. "Are you okay baby?" I ask while reaching for him. I look between the two brothers and it's obvious that Nate and Gabe are now in a fierce standoff.

"You better hope she's okay because you're dead if I find out she was hurt and you kept it from me." Gabe seethes as he points his finger into Nate's face.

"STOP!" I scream, terrified of what Gabe may do next.

"She's got to be somewhere and us arguing isn't helping," I point out. "Gabe, do you have any idea where she might be?" I say, stepping closer to Gabe and looking up at him with what I hope are pleading eyes.

Gabe looks down at me, the anger on his face soon seeming to ease slightly, "She was at Desire late last night."

"Desire?" All four of us question, almost in synchronicity.

"Yeah, a rough little strip club out of town...."

"A strip club?" Harper all but shrieks.

"She wasn't stripping, I'd have killed every guy in there and dragged her home kicking and screaming if that was the case. It's a space some kids go to when they want to dance and get high, I guess."

"Like that's any better." Harper snaps.

"Okay, so when did you see her? Why were you there? Were you together?" Ava questions.

A pissed off growl leaves Gabe's lips. I instinctively reach up and place my hand on his chest to calm him. Gabe looks down at my hand in confusion, and I quickly pull it away. *But whatever it was, it distracted him enough that his anger didn't explode. Win?*

"Gabe, do you know where she went next? Or even who she was with?" I ask softly.

"No idea, I kind of lost her after she stuck her tongue down some asshole's throat."

"What guy? Does Riley have a new boyfriend?" Ava asks as she looks towards us all for answers.

Again an angry grunt comes from Gabe. "He's no one," I notice the way his fists clench at his side and the clicking of his jaw. Nate clearly notices too and steps forward, drawing an even angrier sound from Gabe's lips.

"Ava, shh," I say, moving again to get more into Gabe's eyesight. I don't for a second think he would hit or hurt Ava, but I know that he wouldn't think twice about verbally assaulting her or hitting Nate if he intervenes since clearly they're both pissing him off.

Gabe turns his attention back towards me, probably mostly because I'm right in his line of sight. He stares down at me, our eyes locked in some sort of unspoken conversation. I hear a phone buzz, "I got it." Harper shouts, holding her phone in the air.

"Got what?" Gabe snaps as he reaches over and snatches the phone clean out of Harper's hand. "Whose details are these?"

"We're hoping, the guy she was with last night," Harper says.

"Come on then." Gabe huffs as he pushes past me and grabs Harper's arm, to pull her away. Harper looks back briefly, a confused look on her face, as she walks quickly trying to keep up as Gabe pulls her along.

"Get on!" Gabe snaps, as he releases Harper and motions to his bike.

"I'm not getting onto that death trap. If you insist on coming, you can go in the car with us."

"The bike's quicker," Gabe huffs.

"The car is safer," Harper counters.

"How about we go and call you when we know something," I offer.

"Yeah, come on Gabe, let the girls go and find her. She's more likely to come home for them anyway," Nate points out.

Gabe turns his attention to his brother, "Will they go to the end of the earth to find her?" then points at Harper. "Do whatever it takes to keep her safe?"

"She's my fucking twin, so yeah, I would." Harper snaps back while poking her finger against his chest in a frustrated and aggressive manner. *She must have a death wish!*

Gabe bends slightly so his face is just inches from hers, Nate launches forward, clearly concerned for Harper's safety. "Would you kill for her? Take a knife and drive it through the heart of any man who may hurt or harm her?" Gabe growls, his voice low and extremely menacing.

"Erm..well.." Harper says swallowing.

Nate grabs hold of his brother's arm, using all his force to try and pull him away, to no avail.

Gabe finally pulls away, giving poor Harper room to breathe. "Because I fucking would, in a heartbeat."

"Oh-kay," Harper mutters.

"Now I'm going. Are you climbing on my bike or staying?" Gabe asks, his tone much softer now, but still with that authoritative current to it.

## Chapter Twenty-Nine

## Gabe

"You'll get this back later." I say as I shove Harpey's phone into my pocket chest pocket.

She tries to refuse, but the revving of my engine drowns out her insistent whine. I flip down the visor of my helmet and take off.

I drive towards the other side of the town, towards the area I recognized from the text, and then pull over so that I can grab the phone out of my pocket.

Unknown Number

> Hey girl, spoke to Noah and he said he thinks Zander lives in one of the houses just off campus. Couldn't narrow it down much but said it's just near a little cafe and laundromat and on the same road as some club they all go to. He's gonna ask his buddy Matty the name of the street. When I know, you'll know. Good luck.

*Who the fuck is this text from? I'm assuming a girl, otherwise if I find out it's a guy, one of the other assholes from last night perhaps, and he left her there, I'll add him to my hit list as well.*

I shove the phone back into my pocket and drive straight towards Desire. That's got to be it since this hole in the wall is the last place I saw her last night.

*I fucking knew I should have dragged her away, forced her onto my bike, kicking and screaming, and gotten her away from them. At least then she'd be safe. Pissed beyond belief, but safe, nonetheless.*

As I'm getting closer, I spot a small building. Its shutters are closed. Just a few feet away, I spot a big neon sign indicating that it's a Laundromat. This is clearly the place they were talking about but there are easily thirty or forty small buildings nearby. She could be in any of them.

Me

> I'm here, any ideas on how to narrow it down? She could be fucking anywhere?

I text back to the unknown number, before realizing I'm supposed to be pretending to be Harper so I remove the cuss and add a little smiley face for good measure.

Unknown Number

> I was just about to call, Matty said it's a house, not an apartment building. It has a green door and some creepy ass huge statue in the garden. Sorry I couldn't be more specific. He says he thinks it's the second or third block after the laundromat. There's apparently a park or kids' play area just down the road. That's all I

> have though, sorry. Call me when you find her.

I take off again and spend the half hour aimlessly driving up and down the streets, beginning to lose hope, when I spot it. A big basketball court full of kids. *Please Mom, if you're looking down on me let this be it.*

I drive down the road slowly, riding up and down, desperately searching for a green door, or scary statue but spot nothing. Before long, I end up back outside of the basketball court. I spot a kid, clearly much less well off than the others judging by his tattered jeans and knock off shoes, and call him over.

"Hey kid…. Yeah you," I shout as the kid looks all around.

The kid barely even old enough to be classed as a teenager sculks over.

"Yeah," he says, a timid tone to his voice.

"How do you feel about making some money?" I ask, the guilt eating away at me as a fearful look flashes across his face. A look I know all too well. This poor kid is deciding what exactly he'd be willing to do for whatever money I'm offering.

"It's nothing bad, kid, I promise," I say more gently. Desperate to ease his fears somehow.

"Here…" I say taking out my wallet and pulling out two twenty dollar bills. "All you have to do to earn this is tell me if you know of any houses around here with a big green door, and a scary looking statue."

"You mean the weeping angel?" the boy questions.

"Huh?"

"Do you mean the weeping angel statue? The one from Doctor Who?" the kid says, a hint of..*what's that*..excitement in his voice.

"Doctor what?"

"Do you have a phone?" the kid asks.

"Yeah, why?" I say, a little more clipped than intended.

"I could show you a picture and you could tell me if that's the one you're looking for." the kid offers.

"Don't you have one? A phone I mean?"

"No. Mama said I don't need one. That only rich kids need them for showing off."

My heart breaks for him. As I look at him it's like looking back at myself when I was a kid. *Well maybe not myself, since I was a rough and tough son of a bitch who would have stolen my wallet and probably keys by now.* But perhaps like Nate, a gentler soul.

I take out my phone and hand it to him. He presses a few buttons and then turns the phone around to show me a Google image. I don't really know what I'm looking at but it is a scary looking statue, so I guess that could be it.

"Well?" the kid asks hopefully

"Is this near here?" I say pointing at the picture.

"Yeah, literally five minutes away. I could walk you there if you want?" The kid offers.

"I've got a better idea, have you ever been on a bike?"

The kid's face lights up as he eyes me and then my bike.

"No, but I would really like to."

"Why don't you go and ask your mom first. The last thing I need is to get arrested for kidnapping." I joke.

But suddenly the kid's face looks fearful. *Oh good job Gabe, not only are you a stranger, a scary looking fucker at that, but now you have joked about kidnapping him. Tone it down!*

"I'm Gabe by the way," I say, holding out my hand.

"I'm Noah, I'm going to be eleven next week."

"I'm almost twenty-two." The words fall out of my mouth, quicker than I can register how dumb they sound. *Why the fuck did I say that?*

"Oh cool. My Mama is twenty-seven, she's a cleaner." the kid responds. *Poor girl, only a teenager herself when she became a mom, much like my own mom.*

I remove my helmet and place it on his head. "Jump on."

The kid tries his hardest, but his little arms aren't long enough to truly get a good hold of me so I come up with another plan.

"I've got a better idea." I say as I carefully slide off and guide the kid to the front, climbing on behind him and reaching forward to control it.

*I've no fucking idea if this will work, I've never let anyone, kid or not, drive my bike. I've only seen it in the movies. Plus, we're only going a few minutes down the road. It should be fine.*

"Hold on here and do not let go, whatever you f..rigging do."

The kid does exactly as instructed and we actually ride with ease until we finally pull up outside a house with a huge ass, freaky looking, twisted angel statue in the driveway. And a green door. Exactly as the text described.

"Run along then, kid." I say, helping him off the bike.

I make my way up the path and bang on the door. At first, no one answers so I bang louder.

Eventually someone comes to the door. I don't recognize him at first, he's definitely not the guy Riley was kissing, that asshole's face is burned into my memory. But he does look vaguely familiar.

"Who is it Enzo?" a voice shouts from inside.

"Erm, Riley's ex I think," the guy replies, but I'm already pushing my way inside, the mention of my girl's name enough to drown out any other sound. The asshole from last night appears, face like thunder.

"You need to leave," he demands.

"Fuck you, where is she?" I bellow back as I try to look past the two man barricade now blocking my entrance.

"She doesn't want to see you; you need to leave." The first guy's voice grows louder.

"Then she can fucking tell me that herself." I snap back as I continue to force my way inside.

"You can't come in." The second guy, the guy who is lucky to be alive after putting not only his hands but also his mouth on MY girl, shouts.

## Chapter Thirty

## Riley

I wake up to the sound of shouting but can't fully place where it's coming from.

"You can't come in," a voice shouts.

"You're not going back there," the voice shouts again a couple of seconds later. I hear a door swing open and bang against a wall, I turn to look at the door to the room I'm in. *Whose fucking bedroom am I in? Wait, whose bed is this and why am I here?*

My brain doesn't have time to piece together the puzzle because the door flies open and I see Gabe standing at it.

*Wait, Gabe? What the fuck is he doing here?*

"If you've hurt her I'll fucking kill you," he seethes at someone I can't see yet.

"Of course I didn't fucking hurt her." Zander snaps as he comes into focus.

"Riley, baby, are you okay? I'm here now. Get your stuff I'm taking you home." Gabe says as he pulls the quilt away from me and lets out an angry growl when he takes in my sleepwear.

"But take that off first." he snaps.

"Wait. What?" I grumble as I sit up and rub my eyes, desperately trying to figure out what the hell is happening despite the fact my head feels like it's been hit by a truck.

"You need to leave." Enzo says as he enters the room.

"Privacy." I snap as I try to cover myself with the bit of quilt not currently in Gabe's hand.

Gabe drops the quilt and allows me to cover myself, even though I'm not exactly naked, just feeling incredibly exposed as all three guys stare down at me.

"Can we deal with whatever the fuck this is, when I'm dressed? PLEASE!?" I snap.

"Yeah, sorry," Enzo and Zander say, turning around to leave.

"And you!" I snap as I widen my eyes at Gabe.

"Me? But I've seen and worshiped every single inch of you." Gabe replies sounding genuinely confused.

"That was then, not now, so you need to leave too," I say as I point an accusing finger in his direction.

Gabe opens his mouth to speak but clearly decides against whatever is in his head and decides to give me this small victory by leaving.

I quickly throw on my jeans from last night, but when I reach for my top, I realize it stinks like stale booze. Either I or someone else spilled a drink over it. My tummy heaves at the smell so I decide to just throw my sleep shirt back on before shoving my hair into a wild bun, using a hair tie currently cutting into my wrist.

When I head out all three men are gathered awkwardly in the living room together. Enzo and Zander are sitting on the sofa firing daggers at Gabe who is standing leaning against the wall.

"There you are," Gabe says when he sees me, before his eyes dart to the t-shirt, that even now when tied in a knot to appear smaller, clearly doesn't belong to me.

"Mine stinks of booze, I think someone knocked a drink over it," I say. Feeling the need to explain even though I have zero reason to.

"We'll stop and I'll buy you a whole new outfit on the way home, just go get your shit so we can get the fuck out of here," Gabe demands.

"She's not going anywhere with you. She's fine here," Zander and Enzo both snap back from behind me.

"I can speak for myself." I shout, equally annoyed with all three of these Neanderthals for somehow thinking they all have any say in what I do, or where I go.

A smug smirk forms on Gabe's lips as he reaches out and pulls me towards him. "I meant you too." I snap, as I pull away from Gabe. Like the frustrated brat I am, I stamp my feet and let out a frustrated half grunt, half scream.

"Baby, calm down," Gabe says as he again tries to hold and contain me.

"No! What the fuck are you even doing here Gabe? How did you even know where I was? And even if by some miracle you just so happened to stumble across me, how did that empty skull of yours compute that I would willingly go anywhere with you??"

"Because I'm here to save you; I'll always come to save you, you're my..." Gabe says.

But I cut him off, anger rising to the point of a full on explosion.

"I'm not your ANYTHING. Yeah we were something once but that's over, we are over. DONE! You had your chance and you ended it so that's it. Forget about me and leave me the fuck alone Gabe. Let me heal and move on for fuck sake." I all but scream in his face.

"Just leave. You heard her, it's over," Enzo mocks from behind me, and like a red rag to a bull, Gabe goes wild.

*Here we fucking go!*

Gabe flies past me at lightning speed and is on top of Enzo on the floor. The two guys throw punch after punch at each other. Unsure what else to do, I scream. And I don't mean shout, or scream in fear, I mean full on childhood tantrum scream at the top of my lungs. Both men stop what they are doing and just stare at me, mouths gaped open.

"Baby?" Gabe questions as he releases Enzo and makes his way to me. "Are you okay? Are you having a mental breakdown or something?" he asks, sounding genuinely worried.

"No." I shout back, "Well yes, perhaps I am having a breakdown," I admit. "But that's only because you won't leave me the fuck alone to heal and recover."

*Why doesn't he get it? Every time he appears or swoops in and acts like a protective boyfriend, it breaks my heart. We were supposed to be together. But HE ended things. HE threw me away. Why is he now professing himself to me every chance he gets but even still, he walks away? He needs to stop!*

"It's okay, baby girl," Zander says as he comes behind me and throws his arm over me.

"No!" I shout again as I wiggle out of his grip.

"Will everybody just leave me alone for a moment to think? All three of you have been pushing and pulling me all morning. And I've not even had a cup of motherfucking coffee yet!" I huff.

"I can make one," Zander offers before scurrying away.

"And you," I say pointing towards Enzo, who is now wiping a bloodied lip on his sleeve. "I don't know where the fuck you came from or why you had to get into an argument that didn't involve you... but I'm really sorry you got punched." I say with my tone stuck in angry shouting mode, despite the fact I was trying to apologize.

"As for you," I put my sights on Gabe, "What the fuck are you doing here and why won't you just leave me be?" I snap, tone laced with fury even as I feel the tears streaming down my face. *However, at this moment, I'm unsure if I'm crying because I'm so angry, or because of every other emotion seeing Gabe brings me.*

"Firecracker, I'm worried," Gabe says sincerely, as he takes the sleeve of his hoodie and carefully tries to wipe my tears away.

"What did you say to her?" Zander snaps, as he comes into the room and sees me crying.

"Nothing. And even if I did, I protect her, not you, motherfucker." Gabe snaps back.

"Seems like you're doing a great fucking job of that," Zander seethes back, as he hands me a steaming hot cup of coffee.

I take a sip and audibly moan as the sweet sweet taste hits my tongue.

"I don't know what's going on baby, but I think you're having some sort of psychotic break or something," Gabe says softly. "Do you need me to call Harpy, or Princess, or even Pocket Rocket maybe?" Gabe offers and for once the fact that he refuses to either use or learn my friends' names fills me full of frustration.

"No Gabe, when will you listen?" I snap. "I just need you to leave me alone. No, I don't need you to call Harper, Izzy, or Ava." I say, making sure to fully pronounce every single name to prove my point.

"But…" Gabe goes to argue but I just fire him a murderous look and he stops.

"Now I'm going to drink my fucking coffee and when I'm done I expect you to be gone."

I take another sip and realize how fucking perfect it tastes. "How did you know how I liked it?" I ask turning my attention to Zander.

"You told me last night. Milk and two sugars," he replies. And for a moment I'm transported back to the night with me and Gabe, when despite the many cups of coffee we had shared, he still had no idea how I took it.

Gabe must have the same thought as a guilty look passes across his face. And wanting to hurt him and drive the knife in a little more, I smile at Zander and add, "Amazing, you have no idea how great it is to know you cared enough to pay attention to the little details; if only everyone else did the same."

"Err, it's just regular coffee, a pretty basic order," Zander replies, clearly a little confused.

"Exactly, so simple and easy to remember" I reply as I stare at Gabe and take another sip.

"Please come home with me. Everybody has been going out of their minds with worry." Gabe says as he gives me his sad puppy dog eyes.

"Well tell them I'm fine. My phone died at some point last night, but I'm fine. And I'm staying right here." I turn around to quickly look at the guys whose house I've basically commandeered. They both give a slight nod of encouragement and I turn back to Gabe, "I'm fine, all I want is for you to leave, please."

"Okay," Gabe says, his head dropped in defeat as he allows me to walk him out.

I watch him walk down the pathway, a mixture of happiness and sadness washing over me as Gabe finally does as I asked and leaves me alone. I close the door and then begin crying for real. No longer angry tears but 'the world is ending' kind of sobs.

Zander comes over and reaches out his arms, offering me a hug. I skulk into his arms and allow him to hold me while I continue to sob. "I'm sor...ry, I promise I'm not al...ways a fucking psy...cho," I say through sobs.

"It's fine, baby girl. Sometimes when shit gets too much we can't help but go a little mental." Zander says with a sympathetic half smile before guiding me over to the couch. Enzo moves to give me the whole couch but Zander sits himself right beside me.

"Come here and lie down." Zander offers as he places a pillow over his lap and pats it signaling for me to lie down.

No longer having the strength to argue, I do as I'm told and rest my head on his lap. Zander begins soothingly stroking my hair as I finally take a moment to relax.

Enzo puts on the TV, choosing some random show I don't recognize but none of us say a word. I continue watching, it's some random show about monsters or ghost hunting. I'm not really paying attention. All I'm focused on is how amazing it feels having Zander play with my hair. I sit up, reach my hands up to the back of my head, and carefully remove the elastic band holding my hair up and then lay back down, fanning my whole head of hair over Zander's lap.

Zander continues to caress and massage my head and hair. I close my eyes for a bit just enjoying the sensation and the much needed peace and comfort it brings. I'm still lying awake but with my eyes closed desperately trying not to have some sort of hair-gasm when I hear banging at the door. *For fuck sake, now what?*

## Chapter Thirty-One

## Gabe

Leaving Riley behind, with not just one, but two horny guys damn near killed me. The anger I feel inside - anger from my crappy situation, from the way I have treated my Firefly, and from her moving on - makes me feel like a volcano ready to spew hot molten lava. Instead of doing something stupid like throwing her over my shoulder or knocking those two Bozos out, I left. I was seriously concerned that if I didn't leave when I did, Riley would break beyond repair. I've never seen her act so out of control. I remind myself of this so that instead of charging back in, I turn and punch my fist into the brick wall trying to release some of these feelings inside of me.

I call Nate and reluctantly speak to him and Isabella. Letting them both know that I've found Riley and that she's somewhat safe. Next, trying to prove I'm not as big of a heartless asshole as everyone thinks, I ask to speak to Harpy.

Isabella passes the phone to Harpy and I let her know her sister is okay and that she doesn't have to panic anymore.

*I may know barely anything about Riley's sister, but I do know what it's like to stay up all day and night worrying about a sibling in danger.*

Next, I drive to the nearest Target and with a little help from Isabella on sizing, I picked up some of those stretchy yoga pants and a plain white t-shirt. As well as a few other bits such as toothpaste and deodorant. If for no other reason than I hate the idea of Riley smelling like another man.

As I'm leaving, I spot some white chocolate at the cash register, the one I've seen her eating many times, and add it to my cart. *See! I pay attention to those small details too!* Then like some sort of love sick puppy I drive back to where I left her with the hope that either she's calmed down and will agree to come home with me, or she will at least be grateful that I cared enough to bring her some clothes.

*What the fuck does this girl do to me? She's turned me into a pathetic lapdog. I teased Nate for being whipped and basically handing his balls to Isabella on a plate, yet now, I'm worse than he is. What the fuck happened to me?*

The whole ride here I've been arguing with, and mocking myself for being so soft and pathetic when it comes to her. I mean look at me, knocking on the door of my girl's new boyfriend's house begging him to let me see her. *What a fucking pussy I've become!*

"What the fuck do you want?" the cocky asshole I punched earlier says when he sees me.

"I'm not here to cause any shit; not this time anyway. I just want to drop these off for Riley."

The asshole reaches out his hand to take them but I pull the bag back out of his reach. "I'll give them to her myself," I snap.

"She's asleep," the asshole snaps back but I don't listen and push my way inside.

When I do, the sight crushes me. Riley is lying across her so-called boyfriend's lap while he plays with her hair. "Riley," I say softly and can't help but notice the way her eyes flutter slightly.

*She's clearly not asleep. In all the time I've known Riley, she's never once stirred at just the sound of my voice. She's normally like waking the dead. So why is she pretending?*

"Riley, I've got some clean clothes for you." I say and she opens her eyes and sits bolt upright.

*I knew it, she was one hundred percent faking it.*

She takes the bag and peers inside, giving me a grateful smile. "Do you mind if I grab a shower?" Riley asks, turning towards the guy I'm desperately imagining choking out right now.

"Course not. It's just through there." he points as he looks at Riley with a gaze filled with desire.

I turn to leave before my twisted thoughts of ramming that letter opener on the table into his heart become a reality. Instead, I step back, allowing her to walk past me towards the bathroom. I am almost out of the room, when the asshole adds, "The locks are broken though, so just close the door; we'll stay in here."

*Nope! Not a motherfucking chance. It was bad enough leaving Riley here with these two pricks before, but hell will freeze over before I allow her to stay here, butt ass naked in the shower with no way to lock the door or protect herself!*

"Okay," she shouts back, not a single hint of bother to her voice as she opens the door slightly and then closes it again.

*Does this girl have a death wish or something? Does she have no idea how guys' minds work? They could storm in there, do anything to her and she'd be completely at their mercy. Not as long as I'm here. As long as there's air in my goddamn lungs I will do everything to keep her safe, even if that means saving her from herself.*

Refusing to leave, I hold my ground as the three of us all stare at each other, nostrils flaring. Between my boiling rage at these jackasses, the fact that Riley is angry with me, and my craving for a cold beer, I'm slowly losing control of myself. Unable to cope any longer I turn towards the bathroom, in need of a whole different type of distraction.

"You can't go back there," one of the guys snaps but I don't even bother looking back to figure out which one. I knock softly, which is met by a gentle, "I'll be out in a minute." I stand outside mentally counting down the seconds but as soon as I reach fifteen I decide that's enough time and just push the door open instead.

"What the…" Riley gasps as she spins around to face me in nothing but a towel. Her face morphs from horror and shock to a stubborn frown as she realizes it's just me.

"Get out of here," she says as she tries to shoo me away with her hand.

"Not a chance," I growl as the blood rushes from my brain, down south, and straight to my cock. I stalk over, wrap my arms around her, and begin kissing her neck from behind. She tries to move away, but clearly, her body is in more control than her mind.

"Gabe, stop." Riley groans, but I can tell by her face in the mirror that she's enjoying it.

"Not until you beg me to," I say as I nip that spot just below her ear. The one I know drives her wild.

"Gaabe... Please . . . Stop," she moans as she gives my head the tiniest of shoves but also moves her neck to give me better access. Letting me know that while her mouth might be saying one thing, her body is craving another.

"Tell me that fucking prick out there, makes you feel like this and I will," I whisper as I use my free hand to wrap around her throat, causing her to moan a little louder.

"Tell me your body aches for him, the way it does for me." I add as I pull open her towel and begin rolling her peaked nipple between my finger and thumb.

*I love having this mirror right in front of me so I can see the way she bites her lip and closes her eyes tightly.*

"Tell me he makes you this wet and ready..." I say as I let go of her nipple and glide my hands down her body, and inside her soaking wet opening. Just as I'm about to get to my happy place, I feel her hips grind toward me, ever so gently.

"Oh Gabe," Riley moans loudly and I move my hand from around her throat and cover her mouth instead.

"Shh, my little Firecracker. You wouldn't want those two dickheads out there to come in wondering what's happening now, would you? I would have to kill them for seeing you like this. This show is only for me." I purr against her ear, loving the way her breath hitches at my words.

Riley shakes her head in response as I work my fingers in and out of her. I pump her slowly, then speed up but when I feel Riley's body start to quiver against me which is her telltale sign that she is getting closer and closer to her orgasm, I stop.

"Gabe...no....more," she says barely coherently. I kiss her on her head and when I see that her breathing starts to become steady again, I start to pump my fingers in and out of her again. I do this two more times and on my next start, I add pressure to her clit with my thumb. Suddenly she throws her head back causing the hand covering her mouth to slip slightly and the next thing I know she is biting down hard on the skin between my finger and thumb as her orgasm comes in strong waves.

I spin her around, pick her up, and place her on the side of the sink. With one hand, I push her to lean back as I take a look at her dripping pussy. I watch as the last spasms slowly stop and look at her face. Her eyes are lidded and she has a smile on her face. I love the flush that goes from her chest up to her cheeks. I then bring my eyes back down to the place that I own on her body and know what I need to do. I'm a starved man and this is my oasis. I lower my head and give a soft kiss to the inside of her thigh, just above her knee. She thrusts her hips upwards and I chuckle.

"You like that baby?"

"More, Gabe. I need more."

I start laying soft kisses up the inside of her thigh and just before I get to her pussy, I give her a nip causing her breath to hitch.

Instead of going to the spot I know she is yearning for most, I place a soft kiss just above it and then kiss down her other leg. I feel one of her hands land on my head and the noise that comes from her can only be from frustration. I feel the tug in my hair as she guides me back to the spot she wants me. Not wanting to tease my girl anymore, I dive in and lick her from the bottom right to her clit. I take her clit into my mouth and swirl my tongue around as I suck it. I love having the taste of her on my tongue. I feel Riley's hand grip my hair tighter, and she pushes me even closer to her core. I first add one finger and quickly add a second as I bring her to orgasm all over again.

Once the euphoria has worn off though, she shuffles off the worktop, slowly puts on her clothes, and then walks back out the door like nothing happened.

*What the fuck?*

"Everything okay?" the boyfriend says as he eyes us both suspiciously.

"Yep, all good." Riley says sweetly.

"Yeah, just enjoying a little snack." I reply with a smirk.

"Shit, food. I bet you must be starving," the boyfriend says as he stands and walks towards what I'm assuming is the kitchen.

"I dunno about that. I asked her but she said she's still kind of stuffed." I smirk. "Sure you don't want to come with me? I'll make sure to have you coming for me." I whisper into her ear, quiet enough that only she hears.

"Goodbye Gabe," she says as she pushes me away, I don't miss the way her cheeks blush and she bites her lip as she does though.

*Pretend all you like Wildfire, I know your body still ignites for me.*

I reluctantly walk away, but rather than the despair I felt earlier, I'm left with a little piece of hope. Hope that no matter what she says, or in today's case, screams, she will always be mine. *Her body still craves my touch even if her brain won't allow her to admit it.*

I get on my bike and drive home, thinking about mine and Riley's bathroom fun the whole way home.

# Riley

Zander continues to scavenge around in the kitchen as I slump myself down on the sofa beside Enzo. I let out a deep breath as my mind spins and my body finally relaxes.

*What the fuck was that? How could I give myself to him, again? And here of all places. What's wrong with me?*

"What's up? A little out of breath?" Enzo smirks.

"What?" I mumble, a mixture of surprise and embarrassment running through me.

"Oh, come on, we both know he wasn't in there braiding your hair." Enzo smirks. "I can practically smell the sex wafting off of you," he teases.

"We didn't…" I go to say but he cuts me off.

"I hope you cleaned up at least, cuz I do not want to find any sort of bodily fluid or used condoms anywhere." he says as he gives me a little poke in the ribs letting me know he's just joking around.

"We didn't…" I begin as I hide my face in the neck of my shirt.

"Well something happened," Enzo adds with a smirk before sitting himself further back into the sofa, a shit eating grin on his face.

"I hate you," I huff quietly.

"What are you whispering about?" Zander asks as he comes in carrying plates of grilled cheese sandwiches.

"Just catching up." I lie, as a second wave of guilt washes over me.

*What the fuck am I doing? I've got a nice guy here, one who would probably treat me like a princess if I let him, but my heart, body, and soul are too fixated on the guy who broke my heart. Yet, like the whore I clearly am, I keep offering myself up for him in a heartbeat. But why does he keep coming back? It's like he wants to be with me in those moments. Is there something I'm missing?*

"Yeah, Riley was just giving me all the ins and outs," Enzo adds with a chuckle.

"Yep." I smile fakely, "After all, it's the closest this guy will get to any ins and outs for a while."

The three of us spend the rest of the evening hanging out, and just chilling together since the last place I want to go is back home. *While I'm here I can pretend I'm someone else, pretend my life isn't a disaster, and just be me.* Unfortunately though, it soon begins to get dark, so Zander has to drop me back home to face the music.

As soon as I walk through the door I'm met with interrogation after interrogation from my whole family. Mom and Dad called from their trip and tried grounding me, even though I'm far too old to be grounded. Harper guilt trips me over the fact that not only did I disappear for almost two days, but I also lied to her and had the whole group worried. *In reality it was less than twenty-four hours, but whatever.* I try explaining I was just blowing off steam, but nobody is in the mood to listen, or willing to try to see it from my point of view.

"Whatever!" I shout as I storm down to my bedroom. Slamming the door behind me in temper.

I throw myself on my bed, continuing the argument in my mind. *I can't ever fucking win!*

When I was at home heartbroken and depressed, they complained and demanded I reenter the world. Now I've finally found the confidence to go out and do shit for me; to try and put Gabe behind me and move on. *Whether that be in a friendship way or perhaps one day more.* Instead they berate me for being too carefree and not keeping them in the loop.

Then there's Harper. She is the worst. She complained about me dating Gabe, saying I was too young to be so heavy with a guy, and an older guy at that. Yet now I'm out, acting like a carefree nineteen year old, getting drunk, hanging out with friends, and flirting with hot guys and she's telling me to grow up and stop being so immature.

*Fuck her! Maybe if she got her hole filled once in a while she'd be less concerned by who is filling mine!*

A slight chuckle falls from my lips as even I can't help but giggle at my own attitude.

Harper comes into the bedroom, grabs her pajamas, and blankets and then storms back out, clearly still as pissed at me as I am at her.

# GABE

As soon as I get home, cock hard as steel from all my thoughts on the drive home, I make my way to the shower.

I turn on the water, remove my clothes, and step under the warm, soothing shower. My hand goes directly to my cock. I run it up and down lazily and as I grow even harder, I pull on it rougher and faster. The image of Riley's face in the mirror as I thrust my fingers into her plays like a movie in my mind. I feel the familiar tingle at the bottom of my spine and a guttural moan leaves my lips as I relive the way her body shuddered and shook in my grip as I brought her to orgasm. The taste of her juices on my tongue as I drew out a second wave of pleasure from her. I feel my cock begin to pulse under my grip as I imagine bending her over that same sink and thrusting my cock into her causing her to moan loudly. I would have held her tightly by her hips and as I thrust harder into my hand, I imagine fucking her dripping pussy harder and harder. The feeling in my back intensifies and I feel my balls tighten just as my cock explodes, covering not only my hand but the fucking shower tiles in cum. I reach out and plant an arm on the wall as I try to calm my breathing down. I watch as my cum drips down the tiles towards the floor and drain.

Fuck sake. I was so engrossed in my own dirty fantasy that I didn't even bother aiming. *This is what that girl does to me. Normally I jack off fast and aim for the drain. With her, I lose my mind.*

Once I'm sure all the evidence is gone, and every inch of the shower has been blasted by the water, I climb out and wrap a towel around myself. I'm just drying off my hair with a hand towel when the sound of my phone vibrating against tiles catches my attention. I bend down and retrieve it, noticing it's a number I don't recognize. But worrying it may be Riley, perhaps using one of those asshole's phones, I answer immediately.

"Gabe, it's Cruz, ninety minutes, the alley off Fifth Avenue."

"What?" I ask as I try to piece together the odd call.

"The back alley, off Fifth Avenue in ninety minutes. Don't be late and don't tell anyone where you are going. For fucks sake, don't get followed." Cruz snaps before the phone line goes dead.

I look down at my phone, *that cryptic call barely lasted fifteen seconds.* I rush to my room, throw on a clean pair of jeans, and a shirt then head straight to my bike. The call may not have lasted long, or given me much info, but it was enough to let me know Cruz is in no mood to be kept waiting.

I pull up, hopefully finding the right dark and secluded back alley, just behind a tattoo parlor.

I park my bike, looking down at my phone. *One hour and thirty-three minutes.* I'm about to hit redial when the headlights of a parked car flash signaling my attention.

*Here we go, I guess!* I make my way over, mentally kicking myself for my own stupidity. *I mean who agrees to a middle of the night meet up in a dark, secluded alley with a known murderer?*

I reach the car and the door flies open from the inside. "Get in!" a voice snaps.

I climb in, spotting Cruz instantly. "Sorry man, I wasn't sure if...." but my words are cut short, as I feel the blood drain from my face and my whole body stiffens in shock as my eyes land on a very familiar face sitting beside him.

"Hello, son!"

# Chapter Thirty-Two

# Gabe

I can barely believe what I am seeing. *Is this a dream? A nightmare? A goddamn hallucination?* My mouth flies open, but the words don't come out.

"I know it's a shock..."

"A..shock?" I stutter. "I saw... I saw you die."

"Well, it seems like the devil himself didn't even want me." He laughs, blowing cigar smoke into my face.

"This can't be real," I mutter, more to myself than anyone else.

"It sure is son," John says, before reaching into his pocket and offering me a cigar, but I shake my head slowly, still unable to process what I'm seeing. I reach into my jacket pocket and retrieve a joint.

*This can't be real! It just can't be.*

"I'm gonna give you both some privacy," Cruz says as he climbs out of the limo.

I light my joint, and take a large drag, hoping to calm my racing mind for a second. "How are you alive?"

"Sheer luck and a paranoid friend" John chuckles.

I look at him silently, willing him to elaborate.

"Where do I start?" John mutters to himself, as he takes a deep breath as he runs his hand through his thinning hair. "Those fucking assholes jumped me outside work, threw a bag over my head, and tossed me into what I'm assuming is the bed of their truck. Next thing I know, I'm being dragged out of the back and thrown onto the ground. I fought back, of course, got a few good wacks in, but I'm in my sixties, no match for a group of strapping teenagers."

I can't help but roll my eyes. *Teenagers. We're all in our twenties.*

"Anyway, I was soon being pinned down and gagged. Either the punches or the lack of oxygen getting to my already fucked lungs must have been too much because suddenly everything goes black. The next thing I remember is the sound of a gunshot ricocheting around me. I was sure they were going to kill me so I lay there silent, in the pitch dark, waiting for the pain to register but it didn't." he says as he reaches over, takes the joint from my hand, and takes a drag himself.

"It was then I heard your voice, or shouts should I say. I'm ashamed to admit it, Gabe, but for a second I thought you may have been involved. That's why I stayed silent, needing to know for sure whether or not it was you or someone else who had betrayed me and orchestrated the attack. After all, you were my head honcho, who else would these monsters follow blindly?"

"I would never..." I attempt to say but he cuts me off.

"I know, son, I know. You're a grumpy son of a bitch, but you ain't no snake." he replies, handing the joint back to me and giving my knee a little reassuring tap.

"I heard everything, Gabe. I heard exactly what they were doing, I tried to move, get up, help you in some way, but my body was betraying me. I couldn't move. I don't know what happened next, it's still kind of a blur, but the next thing I remember is waking up in the hospital.

"The hospital? How did you end up there?"

"That's where the good but paranoid friend comes in. You see, I was supposed to be meeting Mike so when I didn't turn up, he came to work, saw my truck doors wide open, and naturally assumed the worst. He'd forced me into downloading this find my phone, tracker thing a while back and was smart enough to use that to find me. Doctors said if he'd not found me in time, the stroke could have killed me. Thankfully the old fucker was able to drag me into his truck and get me to the hospital. He stayed with me all night until I recovered enough to move to somewhere safer. By the time I recovered enough to come out of the hospital I was already missing, and Mike had found and dumped by car at the bottom of a lake so I'd be presumed dead.

"But it's been months. Why didn't you reach out sooner? Shit your daughter, how could you do that to her?" I gasp.

"Rebecca was an unfortunate victim. I didn't realize she was here until it was too late. I was too weak to do anything then."

"You say you were taken to the hospital, but I called every hospital in the area, praying you somehow survived after I went back and found your body missing. None of them had any record of you." I say, still trying to piece together this fucked up puzzle.

"You can thank Cruz for that, he had some people, off the book people, who were able to care for me in secret, moved me over to Seattle to get the proper care. I needed months of grueling physical, occupational, and speech therapy. They think I'll always need this stupid cane to walk" John explains as he lifts up a small cane from the seat beside him.

"But you're back now, ready to take over again?" I say, hoping and praying for some normality in my life.

"Nah kid, I'm dying, I've been dying slowly for a long time. Won't be long before I kick the bucket and become food for the worms. This, as fucked up as it was, was my chance to finally escape."

The sound of a gentle knock at the window sounds, seconds before the door opens and Cruz slides in. "You tell him the plan?"

"Nah ain't got there yet."

"Keys!" Cruz demands as he holds out his hand.

"What?"

"Bike keys, give them. One of my guys will drive it back while we head somewhere to talk.

The last thing I wanna do is give someone, anyone really, the keys to my baby. After everything that's happened recently she's the only thing I have left, but the frustrated scowl on Cruz's face lets me know this isn't a request.

"Take good care of her." I say as I place my bike keys into his hand.

Cruz taps the privacy screen and hands the keys to someone up front. "Meet us at the Edge," he says before dropping the keys into the stranger's hand.

*The Edge? The edge of what?*

"Yes sir," the voice says before climbing out.

I hear the distinctive sound of my baby's engine purring as we drive away.

Roughly two hours later, we're sitting in what I'm assuming is a safe house, basically in the middle of nowhere on a cliff edge overlooking the sea.

"So you understand the plan?" Cruz asks, as one of his men hands me yet another glass of whiskey.

"Yep."

"And you know that no one else can know about me, not even your brother?" John adds.

"Of course."

"Good! Then take this." Cruz says as he opens up a drawer and hands me a gun, a burner phone, and a huge stack of cash.

"And once this is done, I'm out, right? No catch? Nate, Isabella, and Riley are safe too?"

"You have my word." Cruz says, as he stands and reaches out his hand. Sealing this deal with a handshake.

I stand myself and reach out my own hand, then turn my attention to John.

"I'll walk over and kick your fucking ass right where you stand if you tell me you expect a handshake as a promise from me." John snaps, sounding genuinely hurt.

"You wouldn't stand a chance, old man." I laugh, before bending down, and for the first time in my whole life, I hug him first.

"Who the fuck are you and what have you done with Gabe?" John gasps before pushing me back, a look of shock in his face, before he pulls me back into him and hugs me tightly. "I'm proud of you son. Your mother would also have been proud of you." he whispers in my ear before letting me go.

Cruz clears his throat, breaking this unusually emotional moment. "My men are outside to take you home."

"What about my bike?"

"It'll be in the back of one of their vans. Can't risk you dying before getting your payback, can we?" Cruz says, as he pats me on the back. "Now fuck off, the men need to talk." he says with a forced sense of authority.

"They're ready for their sponge baths," I say loudly as I walk out the door.

I hear a deep throaty chuckle from behind me but don't look back to see which of the old fuckers it belongs to.

# Chapter Thirty-Three

## Gabe

## A Few Days Later

I get home from work, kick off my boots, grab a nice cold beer from the fridge, and slump down on the sofa. I'm too tired to even move to reach for the remote, so instead I just sit, making the most of the much needed silence.

I'm almost finished with my beer when Nate comes bounding through the door, mumbling away to himself. I'm half tempted to go see what he's stressing about, but that requires moving, so I just stay put.

Nate continues mumbling away to himself. I finally find the energy to turn around and catch him repeatedly smiling at his reflection in the mirror. "Thank You... It's an honor..."

"Are you practicing your acceptance speech for the Oscars or some shit?" I joke.

"Fucking hell Gabe, you scared the crap out of me." Nate snaps as he puts his hand over his heart.

"What are you doing sitting in silence?" he asks.

"Why are you breaking my silence?" I fire back. "All I can hear is you mumbling away to yourself like some sort of psych patient. What's so important anyway?"

"Okay... but don't laugh," Nate says as he slumps down on the chair.

"I'm stressed about tomorrow," he admits.

*Tomorrow? What's tomorrow?* I rack my brain trying to think of what he could be talking about then it hits me, his graduation. *I knew it was soon but I could have sworn it was next week instead.*

"Your graduation?"

"Yes, my graduation. You are still coming right? You're the only family I have, I don't wanna stand up there all alone," Nate stresses.

"Of course I'll be there." I reply, trying my hardest to act like I hadn't forgotten.

"Thank god. I was really worried I would have no one there for me. After all, I've got no mom, no dad, and no other friends or family, other than the ones graduating with me. There will be nobody standing up for me if you don't come." Nate says and I hate how sad he sounds. But more so, I hate that our little family is so small. *Nate deserves to have the world cheering him on.*

"Don't worry I'll be there, cheering louder than any other fucker. Just you try and stop me," I promise. "Get the remote, and grab us a drink; some TV will help you relax"

"I'm going for a run," Nate says. "I need to work off some of this tension."

"I know a much better way to ease tension." I shout but he just gives me a glare, before throwing on his running shoes and heading out the door again.

Once he's gone and I'm thrown into silence again, my mind drifts back to my own graduation.

*Sure it wasn't a proper high school graduation, it was just me collecting my GED but still, I drove myself, didn't tell anyone, picked up my certificate alone, and then came home to an empty house. It was barely even worth doing.*

Hating the thought of Nate going through the same, I go against every simple fiber in my body and pick up my phone and dial a number I swore I'd never use.

"Hello?" a voice on the other end of the phone says.

"Hey, it's Gabe .. Gabe Scott, I need something, something for Nate."

# Isabella

# The Next Day

The last few weeks have been awful. It feels like our whole friendship group is falling apart and with the end of school just days away, it's the last thing we need. If our friendship is going to survive the next few years of separation at college, we need to be stronger than ever. Unfortunately, though, we're not. Harper and Riley have been at each other's throats constantly, to the point that Riley has almost completely pulled away from our group.

As a desperate attempt to fix things, me and Ava arranged to meet her alone yesterday, hoping we could talk some sense into her, but she was too preoccupied with her new friends to want to listen to anything we had to say.

We tried to join in with them, hoping to somehow heal the rift and extend a hand. I mean, maybe if we got to see the side of them she does, we'd like them too. *After all me and Nate were strangers to the group not so long ago, and now we'd be lost without them.*

But it just felt weird. I didn't really feel like I belonged. Plus it kind of left me feeling a little torn. Like I was betraying Gabe and Nate somehow. Forced to lie to Nate about how much time she's really spending with that new guy, especially when she's his brother's ex. *It's just awkward.*

Plus on top of all that, my anxiety is through the roof as I think about what the future holds. *What college am I going to end up at? What will that mean for my and Nate's relationship?*

But I can't worry about any of that now, I've got to finish getting ready, I'm running behind as it is, and I know my Pops hates when I make us late. I put on one more layer of lipstick, then rush downstairs, where I know my grandparents will be eagerly waiting for me.

*Today is too important to waste it worrying about everyone else. Today is going to be a good day, I'm sure of it.*

We pull into the parking lot, the one full of proud family members and I make my way to find my friends.

The sun's shining and it's a beautiful summer day so the ceremony is being held outdoors on the school's football field. I proudly watch as my friends and classmates take their seats patiently, waiting for their names to be called. Tucker goes first and I listen with pride as I hear his mom, dad, and older brother scream and cheer as he makes his way to the stage to receive his certificate. Tucker, the jokester that he is, takes a super dramatic bow after receiving his certificate and posing for a photo.

"Harper and Riley Foster!" Mrs. Cross calls out proudly.

Just like Tucker, the girls are greeted by cheers, shouts, and even a few whistles from the crowd.

*I'm sure those whistles are purely because our school is happy for them and have absolutely nothing to do with the fact that as Riley takes her bow, she flashes half the front row since she's wearing a very revealing dress, and her gown just so happens to come undone.*

Finally it is Nate's turn. I sit with bated breath knowing that, unlike the rest of us, he probably won't have anyone cheering him on. Especially since no one could find Gabe this morning. He apparently took off late last night and still wasn't back when Nate woke up this morning. Me, Nate, and Tucker have all tried to get a hold of him, but he's not replying to any of our messages. I catch Tucker's eye from the stage, and we wordlessly share the same thought.

"Nathaniel Scott," the principal calls out loudly. I'm about to cheer when I'm stopped in my tracks by loud clapping and cheering. I turn around and see that behind me, both Nana and Pops are on their feet cheering, as are Tucker's parents.

*Obviously, Tucker must have asked them to, like me, fearing the silence.*

But what shocks me the most is that Gabe is here, just a few rows back. He's clapping, cheering, hollering, and whistling like a proud father. Beside him, I recognize a few of the guys from O'Malley's, especially my favorite, Texan Davis.

On the other side of Gabe, I see a couple who both appear to be in their late 50s, but I've never seen them before. The man is clapping half heartedly, but the woman is wiping tears of joy.

*Who are they?*

Nate is so caught off guard by the noise and trying to crane his neck to see where it's coming from that he stumbles on one of the steps and has to catch himself before he ends up face down on the floor. Despite a few giggles from the crowd, he quickly recovers, jumps up, and continues his walk across the stage, as the cheers and hollers just get louder. Nate collects his certificate and handshake from Mrs. Cross the whole time beaming from ear to ear, before finally sitting down.

I see him looking for me in the crowd and as soon as he spots me, another huge smile forms on his face and he blows me a little kiss.

The wait seems indefinite while everyone else's name gets called, the whole time staring up at the man of my dreams. Realizing that the thought of leaving him to go to college physically feels like having my heart torn in two. Our years apart were the worst of my life and I just don't think I'm strong enough to withstand it again.

Finally, towards the end, it's my turn. *Why the heck does my last name have to start with a W?*

"Isabella Williams?" Mrs. Cross calls and, of course, it's met by cheers and hollers from my grandparents. My mom has even come and seems happy and carefree, but my dad is nowhere to be seen.

"I'm so proud of you, Bella," Nate says as I walk past him and find the seat he naturally saved for me, right beside him.

"One last round of applause for the graduating class of 2024," Mrs. C cheers. The whole audience erupts in claps as we all throw our caps in the air.

Everyone rushes off to greet their own family, Nate kindly escorts me to mine, but I can see he is eager to see his own.

"Go ahead baby, I'll catch up with you later." I say as I stand on my tiptoes to give his cheek a little kiss.

"You sure you don't mind, Princess?"

"Go!" I encourage him, even though I don't really want him to.

Nate immediately releases my hand and rushes off to greet his brother. I hear the guys from work cheering again as they all begin high fiving him.

"Thanks so much for coming," I say politely to my mom, even though being at your only daughter's graduation is pretty much a standard expectation.

"Wouldn't miss it," she says, hugging me. "Your father would have loved to come too, obviously, but something came up." she adds, clearly disappointed and covering for him, yet again.

"It's okay, I understand," the air around us becomes heavy with our lies.

*Just once I wish my useless excuse for a father would realize that being there for his only child should come before work. Just once I wish I was a priority.*

My family continues talking and congratulating me, I smile and nod along, pretending I'm listening but the whole time my gaze keeps wandering over to where Nate is.

*Who are those people he's talking to? I know everyone in Nate's life but I don't recognize them.* I look past Nate now, unable to miss how awkward and uncomfortable Gabe looks beside him. *It's obvious he's not involved in whatever conversation the other three are having.*

"Go see him," Nana whispers to me. "Anyway, how about we go inside and get some refreshments?" My mother and Pops both make agreeing sounds and they all wander off.

Now that I'm alone, I make my way over to where Nate is deep in conversation. Initially I walk alongside them, not wanting to be rude or interrupt them. But as soon as I get close enough, and without breaking his conversation, Nate reaches out his arm and pulls me to his side.

"I want to introduce you both to my beautiful Bella. Bella, these are the Jacksons," he says, pointing to the two strangers.

*Now I understand why Gabe looked so uncomfortable.*

I don't know everything about their time in foster care but I've heard enough stories to know Gabe didn't last long. And that there was no love lost between him and his foster family.

It does make me wonder though, since Nate hasn't really mentioned speaking to them since he moved away, other than the odd text here or there, how they knew to be here today. *Nate never mentioned inviting them. Did he?*

Nate continues chatting, reminiscing about memories and people I've never heard of, but instead of giving the conversation the attention it deserves I can't help being distracted by Gabe. Poor guy looks so uncomfortable; like just standing here is taking every ounce of self restraint he has. I also don't miss the way nobody really seems to be including him in the conversations.

*Poor guy is looking more and more like an outsider peering in through the window to a family he doesn't belong to.*

"I'm going to get something to drink," I say, excusing myself. "Feel like joining me Gabe," I say, fully expecting a grunt or a rude comment, but to my shock, he gives me a grateful nod before walking up beside me.

We both head towards the drinks table, walking side by side but in silence, before finding a nearby bench to relax on. Gabe doesn't say anything at first but also makes no attempt to leave my side. "Are you okay, Gabe?" I finally ask.

"Define okay?" he says with a sad half-grin.

"Did you know they were coming?" I ask, moving a little closer so we can talk undisturbed. *Well, as undisturbed as you can be with hundreds of people around anyway.*

"Who do you think talked them into coming and drove half way down the fucking highway to meet them and show them the way?" He shrugs as he continues to look into his drink as if it's about to perform magic.

"You did that? Why?" I ask, a little surprised by his revelation.

"It's what Nate deserves. Everyone deserves to have their family with them at times like this, right?"

I think this is one of the most honest and raw conversations I've had with him lately. He'd started to come out of his shell with me back when he and Riley were together, but since then he's basically given me a wide berth. I'm almost afraid to say anything that might cause him to shut down again.

*I wonder if anyone ever came to his graduation?*

As if he can hear my thoughts, or maybe he sees it in my face, he replies very quietly, "I didn't have anyone to come to my graduation. And looking back, it felt kind of shitty."

"Can I give you a hug?" I ask cautiously.

Although he doesn't say yes, he doesn't say no or back away either, so I lean over, put my head on his shoulder, and give him a little hug. "You're a great big brother, Gabe," I say before letting go of him.

"We need to get back," I hear one of the construction workers say as they make their way over to us. And just like that, gone is the fragile and open Gabe, his walls back to being sky high.

"Thank you so much for coming," I say, hugging Davis goodbye.

"Gabe didn't give us a choice, he threatened to staple our balls to our beds if we didn't come with him," Davis laughs. "Luckily the baby was already awake when Gabe came knocking. Otherwise it would have been a showdown between Gabe and my wife, and between you and me, I don't know who I'm more afraid of." He laughs before joining his friends to leave.

"I think we'd better get back before Nate thinks we've run away together," I joke, getting up to leave.

"Maybe we could wait another minute," Gabe says. At first I think he's cracking a joke, but his eyes are clearly begging me to stay, so I sit back down and wait in silence.

A few moments later Nate comes over, "There you both are, I was wondering where you got off to." He says as he weaves his way between us and sits down in the gap. "The Jacksons had to leave, but they told me to say goodbye," Nate says, looking over at Gabe.

"Sure they did," Gabe snorts as he stands up and walks away.

"What the hell is his problem?" Nate asks.

"Cut him some slack, babe. He loves you and he ventured out of his comfort zone today."

"What do you mean?" Asks Nate, clearly not understanding what I'm trying to say.

"Well it's not really my place to say anything but, just ask yourself who came to support you, and how they knew to be here today." I say, leaning against him as he puts an arm around my shoulders.

"I think I should go check on him," Nate says as he rests his head on mine.

"I think you should too," I reply and give him a soft kiss on his cheek.

Nate stands up and reaches out his hand to help me up. "Are you sure you're okay with me leaving you alone?" Nate asks thoughtfully.

"Yeah, I'm fine, I want to try and catch my mom before she goes back anyway," I smile.

"I love you Princess," Nate says, kissing the top of my head.

"I love you even more," I say, lifting my head to kiss him on the lips.

I walk over to my family. Nana and Pops are engrossed in conversation with some other grandparents, all raving about how proud they are of their grandchildren. "And here she is now, our pride and joy," Pops beams to the group.

"Pops, you're so embarrassing," I blush.

"What's embarrassing about telling everyone in this room that we're proud of the wonderful woman you've become?" He says louder, obviously trying to make a point.

"Shh," I say, covering his mouth, "that's exactly what's embarrassing."

I hear quiet sniggering from the rest of the group. *Apparently, they find mine and Pop's playful exchange funny.*

"Where's Mom?" I ask, looking around without seeing her.

"She had to leave," Pops says, and it's clear from his saddened tone that he feels guilty having to tell me this.

"It's okay, Pops," I say, faking a smile.

"It's not okay, and I will be speaking to her soon."

# Chapter Thirty-Four

# Gabe

Even when I'm good, give my all, it's never good enough. I drove all the way to meet the Jacksons, kept my mouth shut, and was as polite and accommodating as possible all motherfucking day, and yet the bastards didn't even have the decency to show me the same courtesy by at least saying goodbye.

*Not that I gave a fuck, not really.*

But Nate looked at the both of them like they hung from the moon. Smiling gratefully, and thanking them immensely for turning up, yet had it not been for me they wouldn't have even known.

*But of course, I got no thanks. No, 'I'm glad you came, Gabe. Thanks for supporting me, even though none of us were here to support you bro.' Nothing! How is it the only person who seemed to have even noticed I was here, was goddamn Princess Isabella?*

"Didn't expect to see you here."

I turn around and see my perfect little Firecracker standing in her cap and gown. "It's a special day for those I love, I won't miss it."

"I'm sure Nate is grateful..." Riley begins.

"I wasn't just talking about him." I admit sheepishly.

A little smile and blush colors Riley's cheeks. *It's unlike her to be this shy and easily flushed though.*

"Well, I'm glad you came." Riley says softly, but her choice of words causes a little fire to ignite in my core. I step closer, pulling her into my arms so that to anyone watching, it looks like I'm merely giving a friend a congratulatory hug.

"How about we get out of here, and I make you cum instead?" I purr into her ear.

I hear Riley's breath hitch slightly, so I quickly add, "But first, I think you need to be punished for being a dirty little slut and driving every guy wild by showing them what's mine."

A small whimper leaves Riley's lips, but I tease her further by releasing her and stepping back. "Really proud of you Riley," I said it loud enough that anyone passing by could hear.

"You suck," Riley mouths, as she begins straightening her gown, letting me know that if I was to put my hand inside I'd probably find her wet and ready.

"That's your job, baby," I replied with a cheeky smirk.

"Good job Riley, you made it on and off the stage without falling on your face," a random boy teases.

"Oh shut up Martin, I was like twelve." Riley laughs. "At least I didn't wet my pants," she fires back.

"I was four," he gasps. "And Miss Steward was an evil bitch who refused to let me go to the bathroom before the Christmas play started."

"Yeah yeah, excuses, excuses." Riley laughs, as the boy walks away, leaving us in peace.

"So, how about me and you leave this place, head for a drive, and find a way to celebrate properly."

Riley's eyes glide down from my face to my dick, and I don't miss the way she licks her lips before they find their way back to my face. "I can't. Harper, my parents, and I are going out for dinner."

"Just the four of you? Or will your so-called boyfriend be joining you?" I say with a hint of venom in my voice.

"No, not today." Riley smiles, but it doesn't reach her eyes. "I'm meeting him tomorrow instead."

I know she's lying, from the way she twists her hands, and leans away. *She'd be terrible at poker.*

"If you were my girlfriend, I wouldn't let you out of my sight, I'd be here cheering you on in front of your friends and family, then eating you out when we were alone."

Riley throws her hands up to cover my mouth but it's too late, the words are already out and I don't care who may have overheard.

"You're such a perv," she says through gritted teeth.

"But you fucking love it." I reply as I glare into her eyes, enjoying watching as they darken with desire.

"Riley are you coming?" her sister shouts as she makes her way over. I see the 'don't you dare say it' look that Riley gives me before she releases my mouth, and walks away.

My phone buzzes in my pocket and when I pull it out I realize it's a call from Phoenix, a call I've been expecting all morning.

"Gabe, get your ass to Saints now, we've got a problem," Phoenix barks.

"I'm actually kind of busy now, maybe I could come over later." I reply, purposefully trying to annoy him further.

"You'll get your ass here now. Or so help me…" he bellows down the line. And even from here, I can practically hear that vein in his neck throbbing in anger.

"As you say boss," I say, hoping the smirk on my face isn't evident in my tone.

I make my way towards Saints and into the cellar. The one that's mostly just used for storage. The same one Marko commandeered as his own personal clubhouse. As soon as I begin making my way down the steps, I can hear Marko's fuming.

"How could this happen?" he snaps. "Someone here is a mole. I fucking know it…. Is it you?" He bellows as he points to one new recruit, one I don't even recognize.

"Nah boss, honest. I wasn't even down at the docks, that was Levi's crew."

"Is that so?" he says, turning his attention to another guy, presumably Levi.

"Yeah, but I wasn't in charge of transportation, that was Jacob."

I continue leaning up against the wall, loving the chaos in front of me.

"And YOU, where the fuck were you?" Marko snaps as he turns his attention to me.

"I was at my brother's graduation, feel free to ask any of the guys from O'Malley's."

"Arggh! This can't be happening!" Marko seethes as he storms past me and up towards the bar.

I follow after him, playing the dutiful sidekick, and find Deeno, Micheal, and Phoenix outside, drinks already in hand.

Marko practically throws himself down on one of the chairs, snatching a bottle of rum out of one of the guy's hands and taking a gulp. "How the fuck does this keep happening?" he practically screams.

"Anyone wanna fill me in on what the fuck is going on since you dragged me all this way?" I snap back, as I play my usual role of asshole, while desperately hiding the smile that wants to break free.

"You had something to do with this! I'm sure of it." Marko barks, as he raises his hand, ready to throw the bottle at me, but Phoenix grabs his arm.

"He had no idea. He wasn't given any info, you know that." Phoenix reminds him.

"Yeah, apparently I'm not trustworthy enough to sit at the big boys' table anymore, despite the fact it's my fucking table, to begin with." I snap back, faking anger.

"Then who the fuck is it?" Marko snaps as he gulps yet more rum from the bottle.

"Maybe if someone fucking brought me into the loop, I'd be able to help." I remind them.

With Marko's nod of approval, Phoenix then fills me in with some of the shit that's been going down recently. Apparently in the last few months; three different shipments of drugs have been seized. Two of his guys have ended up inside, probably singing like canaries, and multiple deals have gone sideways.

"That's what happens when you hire every Tom, Dick, and Harry who fancies themselves as a tough guy." I reply nonchalantly as I take a drag of my cigarette.

"It's expansion, you wouldn't understand. You and John were small time. I'm thinking bigger." Marko fires back in frustration.

"Small time? Perhaps. But we never ran the business into the ground. Our men were loyal, our bills were paid, and most people feared the name." I add, continuing to smoke, like I don't have a care in the world. "You, on the other hand, have your fingers in so many pies, it's no wonder you keep getting burned."

*I know this guy is unhinged and pushing his buttons isn't a good idea, but it's sooo much fun!*

"Fuck off Gabe, you have no idea what I'm trying to accomplish, your tiny brain couldn't even comprehend the magnitude of what I have planned. This time next year, not just the town will fear us, but the whole fucking state too."

"Ooo evil genius in the making." I mock.

"Oh fuck you!" he snaps as he picks up a glass and throws it at the wall behind me, narrowly missing my head. "Go shake down O'Conner, he owes us 5G's" he snaps before practically ushering me away.

I do as I'm told and leave. I chuckle and smirk the whole fucking way back to my bike. *This is going to be easier than I thought.*

Phoenix was right, they have been careful, keeping me away from the big deals, purposefully excluding me from team meetings. Refusing to tell me who our clients are or where the bigger deals are going down. *Since clearly they don't trust me, and rightly so!*

What those morons have failed to consider though, is that by hiring pretty much any tough guy who asks, including fucking high school bullies employed purely to push drugs, is that those punks have no loyalty. They'd sell out their own grandma for a couple of hundred dollars. Not to mention, throw a pretty girl into the mix, a few local hookers I've known from around and about, and they have no loyalty to their new employer. Those idiots will brag about every deal going down.

Thanks to Cruz, we even have a local cop on the payroll, one willing to arrest people when we say and turn a blind eye when needed. Taking down the Sinners, causing chaos in the rank, and even getting a few of Cruz's competitors locked up or killed while we're at it. It's a no fucking brainer.

*And best of all as far as anyone else is concerned, my hands are completely fucking clean.*

## Chapter Thirty-Five

### Riley

The summer holiday is almost over, just two more weeks and I'll officially be a college student. Izzy, Nate, and Tucker have all decided that college isn't for them but Ava was lucky enough to get into a college a few hours away that has an amazing dance program. As for me and Harper, although we're going to the same college, it's going to be anything but the same experience. This is why I'm so glad that Zander is going to still be here. At least I'll have someone other than Harper and her disapproving big sister vibes, to surround myself with.

"Why don't you come out with us? Celebrate the end of the summer in style?" I all but beg.

"Because I've got better things to do with my final month in town than party, drink, and do god knows what else you guys get up to." Harper huffs.

I hate this. I feel like I'm being torn in two; torn between two different worlds. Like I have one foot in each but am being split in half trying to balance. On one side I have Izzy, Nate, Ava,

Tucker, Harper, and her new boyfriend Josh. *All of which I adore, well apart from Josh who I think is as dull as watching paint dry.*

But all they want to do is cute coupley things, leaving me as the desperate, lonely, outsider. I've tried bringing Zander, just so I'm not alone, since he's basically become my best friend. But that's just awkward.

Izzy and Nate, while always polite and friendly, clearly felt awkward hanging out with my new 'boyfriend', even though I've told them all a million times that we're just friends. Tucker and Ava are nice and neutral and don't really care either way. But Harper is damn rude. *I honestly have no idea what her problem is*!

She hated Gabe. Now I'm no longer with him and she seems to hate Zander even more. He's never been anything but nice toward me. It all seems to stem from her catching us sharing a joint one time at a party. That and the fact she still blames him for 'kidnapping' me. Even though it was me who lied about going looking at colleges with Lexi he knew nothing about it. *Guess it's easier to hate a stranger than your own twin.*

"Whatever, stay here and be boring I'm going out." I snap as I grab my jacket and purse and walk out.

"Take it sour puss isn't joining us?" Enzo laughs as I climb into the backseat.

"Oh well, her loss." Zander shrugs from the passenger side.

We pull up outside Desire, our favorite club. Tonight they're having one of their theme nights. Tonight's theme is murder and mayhem. Everyone has to come as their favorite villain or killer.

Enzo and Jamie have both come as their favorite horror villains. Whereas me, Zander, Liv, and Lucas have on one of those neon purge masks.

The music is pumping and the energy is high. We grab a drink and go right to the dance floor. We get lost in the music and every once in a while, one of us breaks away to grab another round of drinks. As the night goes on, my inhibitions start to drop. I find myself dancing closer and closer with the boys, sometimes even grinding on them.

"You call that dancing?" Enzo teases. "Come to Daddy, let me show you how it's done." he laughs, as he reaches out his hand and tries to encourage Liv to dance with him.

Liv is sweet, but for someone who works in a place with half naked girls walking around, is surprisingly timid.

"You're not afraid of a little dance are you, Little Tempress?" he says, holding out his other hand to me.

"Hope you can keep up." I smirk, before I walk over to him, spin around and begin grinding my ass against him as I dance.

"Daaaamn!" Both Jamie and Lucas say at the same time. Enzo's hands attempt to reach for my hips but before they get there, I twirl myself around, drop into a squat, and slowly pull myself back up, so that I'm mere inches from his crotch. He stumbles back a step. surprised by my proximity.

"Seems like it's you who's afraid of a little dance," I reply with a smirk.

"Hey! No fair. You didn't say you wanted me to practically impregnate you on the dance floor." Enzo whines, as his friends all mock him.

"Really, you just couldn't resist could you." Zander whispers, while also smirking down at me.

"What?" I coyly ask.

"Second chance? You want sexy, I'll give you damn sexy." Enzo huffs as he pulls me back towards him and begins grinding against my ass. He's got some moves, I'll give him that. If I found him even the least bit attractive it may do something; but since I don't, it just feels like my ass is taking a pounding it really doesn't need.

"See, you're loving it. All the girls get wet for me." he boasts.

"Not me dude. I'm drier than the Sahara Desert." I laugh, stepping out of his grip. *Two-nil for me.*

Zander is laughing the hardest, as his friend struggles to maintain his cocky demeanor.

"Oh yeah, like you could do better?" Enzo snaps as he narrows his eyes at his friend, "That girl's practically impenetrable! She probably wears a chastity belt for fun."

"You just gotta know what buttons to push." Zander smirks.

"Oh yeah, and which buttons would they be?" I say crossing my arms in defiance.

"Why don't you come here and I'll show you." Zander says suggestively.

*Fuck him. He knows exactly how to activate my bratty side.*

Me and him have the strangest dynamic, to the outside world I'm sure we look like a couple. We hang out constantly and the flirty banter we share is next to none. And if we let it, there could probably be some fucking amazing fire in the bedroom since our personalities are so alike. But we've never been there. Sure we flirt all the time, but it's playful flirting, we're kind of like friends with benefits.

*But instead of sexual benefits, we have the cutest couple benefits. He's almost like the best girl-friend you flirt with, and grind against to get the free drinks, but you both know it's all an act.*

"Well?" Zander says, his tone almost challenging.

*You're on!*

I walk over, not even caring that I'm basically being pimped from one boy to the next. I go to spin, assuming like every other boy the only way they know to dance is by grinding against you. But Zander surprises me by stopping me and turning me to face him.

"I want to watch you." Zander says, his tone and authority making me a little hot and bothered. The beat drops and I get lost in the music. Running my hands through my hair and swaying my body to the beat, Zander steps closer, and brings his hands to my hips, guiding me to the point that I'm virtually grinding my crotch against his leg as my body is pressed against him. *What the fuck am I doing?*

I turn myself around, needing a break from the intensity. But that break doesn't come. Instead, as I look forward I'm met by an even more intense and hungry look. Standing directly in front of me, but behind my friends, is Gabe, beer bottle in hand, watching me intensely as he leans against the wall.

Zander's hands soon find my hips as he dances behind me, but unlike Enzo who practically dry humped me, he keeps his dick far from my ass. I move my arms around as I sway my body to the music. I can't take my eyes off Gabe, and he doesn't take his eyes off me. The two of us are locked in an intense moment where there's no one else here.

I find myself playing up more, swaying harder, dancing sexier, as Zander's hands caress my hips softly. Gabe continues to watch me, his gaze letting me know, his touch would be anything but soft.

I reached up to grab hold of my hair to get some much needed air to my neck. Zander reaches up and grips his hands into mine, almost holding my hand, before forcing my hand to slowly run down my neck as we both continue swaying to the music. He guides my hands, painfully slowly, down my neck, over my collarbone, and just as it's about to dip into the curve of my chest he stops. And drops my hand.

"And that's how it's done!" he says loudly.

The whole group burst into giggles, this time at my expense.

"Damn, maybe the Ice Queen can thaw after all," Enzo laughs.

"Go suck a dick!" I huff.

"You're the one practically touching yourself for me," Zander smirks.

I look up, hoping to catch Gabe's face, but he's gone. Disappeared. I turn towards the bathroom, needing a moment of alone time to process what just happened.

*I can't believe I almost let one of my best friends touch me, or make me touch myself, should I say, in the middle of a packed club.*

I wash my hands and am just about to leave when I feel a hand link with mine. I look up and see Zander, now wearing his blue purge mask. "Zander?" I question but he doesn't answer; instead, he just pulls me through the crowd and out a door. Once inside this vacant room, he forcefully pushes me down and locks the door behind him.

He turns around to face me, and I don't even need to see his big green eyes shining through the mask to let me know this isn't Zander at all. He may be wearing Zander's mask, but my body doesn't ignite for Zander the way it is now. Despite what anyone who saw our little show on the dance floor may believe.

*Even so, I'm gonna have some fun with this!*

## GABE

*Y*ou *think you're gonna tease me like that? Allow another man's hands all over your body and get away with it? Never!*

*She's lucky all I did was steal that fucker's mask while he was at the bar. It took every single ounce of my resolve not to knock him out. Had I not been so desperate to be inside of her right now, reminding her of exactly who that beautiful body belongs to, her new boyfriend would have been picking his teeth up from the floor.*

She eyes me hungrily and it infuriates me, but strangely turns me on knowing that she clearly has no idea who is behind this mask.

"Dance." I command in a low gravelly voice as I motion to the pole.

"But there's no music." she says, as she looks around, frowning at the complete silence around us. *This room is soundproof, Firefly. And I intend to make you scream.*

I reach for the remote, and suddenly music is filling the room. She looks at me with a hint of confusion in her eyes so I just point at the pole.

*You want to dance? Tease me with the way your body moves? Then dance little slut; dance for me!*

She begins dancing, initially just swaying her hips beside the pole, before her confidence grows as she begins to feel the music and starts to incorporate the pole in her moves, not true pole dancing of course, but more so using the pole as something to dance around and grind against.

*Fuck! What I wouldn't give for it to be me, her ass is rubbing against. My rock hard steel, her hand is stroking.*

Unable to resist and desperately needing to touch her, I use my finger to usher her off the stage and over towards me. She dances over, shaking and swaying her body with every step until she's standing between my legs.

"Yes?" she asks, that stubborn and bratty tone I love, alive in her voice.

Without saying a word, I reach out and unzip the front of her tight leather top, exposing even more of her beautiful perky breast to me.

*Fuck! I've missed her beautiful curves.*

She reaches to cover them up, looking around nervously.

"No one can see. It's totally private." I reassure her. *She may think this is some other asshole she's stripping for, but there's no way in hell I'd risk letting anyone else see her.*

She looks into my eyes for a moment, trying to decide whether or not she should trust me. *Or him I suppose.* But a little smirk of confidence forms on her face before she slowly removes her hands, letting her breasts make their escape.

*I don't know if to be happy she did, or goddamn furious that she obviously has this much trust in that asshole that she'd expose herself like this for him. Doesn't she know that he's not worth it? He's not good enough for her. Neither am I, I guess, but I'd never betray her.*

She goes back to the pole and continues dancing, before long she brings her hands down her body, the way she did earlier on the dance floor, but rather than stopping at her chest she brings them down her tummy, under her skirt, and then shocks me by removing her panties, and kicking them at me.

# Chapter Thirty-Six

# Riley

I can barely take it anymore. The look he is giving me with his piercing eyes is so intense. I can feel my pussy getting wetter and wetter. He thinks he is disguising his voice, but the raspy growl he's doing is just getting me hotter.

I bring my hands down my body, over my nipples, and down my stomach. The burning desire inside of me, crying to be relieved. I watch as his head dips and his eyes follow my hand as it disappears inside my panties. *My soaking wet panties.*

Unable to take the feeling of the lace against my already sensitive nub, I slide them down my legs and kick them towards him. He catches them, holds them to his nose, groans, and stuffs them into a pocket in his jacket. Next, I swing around the pole, this time grateful for something cold and hard between my legs. I continue grinding against the pole, knowing full well that he has a perfect view of my pussy beneath my very short skirt.

*You want this? Come get it then!*

He unbuckles his jeans and his hand dips inside. I watch intently as his hand clearly slides up and down. *But it isn't enough, I need more.*

"Take it out. I want to see you." I whine.

He just shakes his head and continues to stroke.

"Please, I want to watch you." I beg.

"Such a dirty whore" he says, his voice deep and hoarse.

I watch as my masked monster removes his rock hard cock and begins running his fist up and down. I go to step off the stage, desperate to replace his hand with my own but again he shakes his head, eyes still boring into me, staring into my soul as he continues to pump his cock.

"So I'm only allowed to watch?" I groan.

Again he shakes his head. Then using his free hands points to my skirt. *Oh so that's how this is going to go, is it?*

I sit down on the stage floor, arching my back against the pole and spreading my legs, ensuring that Gabe has a perfect view, and then dip my finger inside. Another low guttural moan leaves his mouth as he watches me, which causes me to play harder. The two of us are in a frenzied state, both working ourselves up to orgasm in front of the other.

*This should be embarrassing, humiliating even. If it was with anyone else it probably would be. But the two of us, together, raw and desperate, is exactly what we need.*

"Mmm…. yeah," I moan as my orgasm builds and builds, my fingers rubbing harder and harder as I close my eyes, anticipating my release. But before I get there, my hands are being ripped away and I'm being lifted up.

"What the…" I begin, but I'm cut off as I'm plonked down on his lap and his huge dick pushes its way inside, roughly.

"Fuuuuuck!' I call out. A feeling of pain mixed with pleasure as my body is forced to accommodate his size, especially since it's been months since anything, real or plastic, has been inside me.

*The feeling of his cock inside me, our bodies united like some sort of dirty jigsaw feels amazing.*

Gabe gives me a couple of seconds to adjust to him and then begins thrusting up, as he uses his strong grip on my waist to bounce me up and down as he fucks me roughly. His thrusts feel desperate, possessive… angry even.

"Yes… yes," I pant as my orgasm builds and builds. "Yes…right there… fuck me harder, Gabe" I moan. But instead of giving me what I so desperately crave. He stops his rhythm completely and looks me dead in the eyes, before pushing the mask off his face and onto the top of his head.

"You knew it was me?" he gasps.

"Of course I knew it was you, Stupid." I chuckle. "You think I just fuck every guy who asks."

"No, but I'm wearing…" he begins, his tone confused, but I cut him off again.

"Yep. Zander's mask. How did you get that anyway?" I say more to myself than him.

"I assumed you'd think I was him." Gabe admits a mixture of confusion and relief in his tone.

*So this wasn't just a little role play game, he really wanted me to believe I was fucking someone else? But why? And should I be happy that he was clearly so desperate for me that he'd pretend to* be someone else? Or damn furious that he'd try and trick me into fucking him as he pretended to be someone else?

My face must clearly show my indecisiveness, as he reaches out, grips my cheek lovingly, and plants a soft kiss to my lips. "Please don't hate me, any more than you already do. I just had to have you. And I didn't think you'd want me in return. I just wanted a minute alone with you, away from prying eyes, but I didn't think you would come with me willingly, especially after last time. That's why I pretended to be that asshole out there."

*The vulnerability in his voice breaks me, a few months ago he'd never have let his walls down like this for anyone, yet here and now he's laying everything out in the open for me. Showing me the broken little boy he keeps locked inside. A side I know I'm the only one who gets to see.*

"You don't need to pretend to be anyone else with me. I see you Gabe. I will always choose you, even when I know I shouldn't." I admit, before leaning forward and planting a small kiss to his lips.

"I don't believe you." He says as he shakes his head before removing the mask fully and placing it on a ledge at the back of the bench we're sitting on.

"I knew the second you dragged me through the club and threw me down on this chair it was you." I laugh as I throw my head back, causing his dick, that's still rock hard inside me to rub against me.

"Mmm," I moan, without meaning to.

"Oh you like that do you?" he purrs as he thrusts his hips up, pushing himself even deeper inside of me.

"Yes." I moan as I begin grinding my hips.

"Then who am I to deny my little Firecracker what she desperately wants?"

"One more thing," I moan, as he thrusts inside me slowly, but forcefully.

"Anything for you," Gabe purrs.

I reach out, grab the mask, and carefully put it back in place, giving him a nervous little smile.

"Such a kinky little slut." Gabe growls, before lifting me up, so that he can stand with me, before laying me down on the soft carpet. He must press something as he does because suddenly all the lights go out.

Darkness surrounds us, as the loud thumping of the bass causes the floor to vibrate against my back. My senses are in overdrive, with each and every thrust, all I can see is the neon crosses over his mouth as he pounds into me harder and faster.

There is something mysterious about us having sex in this almost public place, knowing that there's a possibility of someone walking in. Coupling that with the mask he is wearing and the entire ambiance of the room helps to make this one of the strongest orgasms I've ever experienced in my life!

*Shit, I really hope he was telling the truth about this room being completely sound and sight proof. The last thing I need is a room full of strangers to hear or see this from outside.*

"That was fucking amazing!" I pant, as I rip off the mask, needing the softness of Gabe's lips on mine. He clearly craves the same as once the mask is removed his lips crash against mine, but rather than his kiss being hard, fast, and aggressive, like everything else we just experienced. It's soft, loving and reassuring. His hands lovingly caressing my cheek as he pulls me against him.

"I missed this," I admit as I curl into his arms.

"Me too baby, me too."

We stay wrapped up together for a while before I finally break away slightly. "I could really do with a smoke." I laugh.

"Me too, but since when do you smoke?" Gabe says, eying me suspiciously.

"What do you mean?" I ask sitting up. "I've smoked since we first met. That's literally one of the reasons we got talking in the first place because I was too much of a chicken to just kiss you so I stole your cigarette." I laugh.

"What?" Gabe laughs, sitting up himself, and tucking his dick back into his jeans.

"Yeah that first night, after I made you pay for my drinks, the next dare was to come and kiss you but you looked so peaceful with your eyes closed that I hovered too long. You looked so angry when you caught me though, so instead of kissing you I just stole your cigarette.

"That's hysterical," Gabe teases. "You should have just climbed onto my lap, and kissed the hell out of me, I wouldn't have minded."

"Yeah, but then you would have thought of me as nothing more than a bunny, someone to fuck in the bathroom and forget about."

I see a flash of guilt cross his face for a moment before his confident mask slips back into place

"You'd never be just a bunny. You're my whole fucking world."

*Now it's my turn to hide behind my walls. I could so easily slip back into things with him. Fool myself into believing we're back together and life is going to be perfect. But I'd be a fool to believe that. No, now it's my turn to keep him at a distance. I couldn't survive another blow to my already damaged heart.*

"So, back to the smoke. I've smoked as long as you've known me." I say changing the subject before I stupidly open my heart, as well as my legs, to him and he destroys me all over again.

"No, I smoke. You steal. You steal the odd drag here or there from me, just to annoy me, I presume. But you've never been the one to crave them."

"Guess things change." I say as I stand up, retrieve my discarded clutch, and take out the pack I have inside.

"I'm assuming we can't smoke in here so let's head outside," I say, as I bend down and retrieve my underwear from his pocket, zip up my top, and flatten down my hair.

"Hey! I was planning on keeping those." Gabe complains.

"Do you want me walking around in this skirt with nothing under it?" Already knowing the answer.

"Put them on now!" he almost screams in his response.

"You coming?" I say after I have my underwear in place and start walking toward where I hope the door we came through is.

"This way, Firecracker, we can leave here without having to go through the club." Gabe calls as he leads me through a different exit.

I reach for his hand and walk through a narrow walkway that feels more like I'm walking between the walls than anything else, but we soon reach an exit that leads to a balcony.

I light up my cigarette and enjoy the slight burn it causes in the back of my throat, a feeling I've gotten more than used to these last few months since hanging out with Zander and the rest of the boys.

I'm almost finished, still curled up against Gabe, staring down at the alley below, when I spot a familiar face.

"Zander!" I call, and Zander looks around but doesn't see me. "Zander, up here," I call out. Zander looks up and throws his arms in the air before making his way over to the fire escape and climbing up to greet us.

"There you fucking are!" he pants. "I've been looking everywhere for you."

He reaches over and starts hugging me, completely ignoring Gabe. Gabe growls and attempts to pull me back but I stand my ground.

*You no longer get any say in who I can or can't talk to. It's one thing trying to control me when you're my boyfriend, it's a whole other thing doing it when you're my.... Friend? Ex? Friend with benefits? Fuck buddy? Whatever the hell we are.*

"Sorry I vanished; I kind of bumped into someone." I admit, head down as a feeling of guilt washes over me. Not because of what me and Gabe did, never for that. But for possibly leading him on, while we were dancing and then disappearing for god knows how long to have sex with my ex.

"So are you two back together then?" Zander questions as he takes in the way mine and Gabe's hands are intertwined now.

"Err..." I say looking up at Gabe who is looking down at me with an equally unsure face.

"Whatever, good for you. I guess I just assumed after everything you'd told me about him, the two of you were over for good." Zander says, a hint of something, *disappointment, or annoyance perhaps?* In his voice.

"Funny, so did I," a low and menacing voice says from behind us.

# Acknowledgments

I apologize in advance that these are going to be lengthy, but as anyone who's ever had to have a conversation with me knows.... This girl can talk for all of England. I'd like to blame it on my neuro-spicy-ness but, nope, I'm just a 'lil whirlwind of craziness.

That said, this is my book. The book and main characters have been screaming to be written since the start of my first book, Forever Entwined. Those of you who have followed me on the many ups and downs of my writing journey will know that at one point I was adamant this book would never be written. But to those who pushed and pushed and begged and pleaded for me to write Gabe's story, thank you because without your love, support, friendship...and the occasional kick up the ass (yes, Jenn, I'm looking at you here), this book would have never become a reality. But I'm so grateful it did. It may have pushed me out of my comfort zone and forced me to tap into my inner smut slut, but throughout this story, not only did Gabe heal and grow, but so did I.

**To My Family-**

Thanks for loving and supporting me on my journey. Thank you for joining me whenever I was lucky enough to get to travel for signings or book events. I truly appreciate it. Thanks for allowing me the time and space to write, and not going crazy when I would stay up all night or spend my days off writing.

And to my mum, my unlikely biggest fan, thank you for reading book one despite me literally BEGGING you not to. And for asking questions constantly about what was going to happen in books two and three. Who knew bad boys and bikers would take your fancy?!? Haha.

**Kuristien Elizabeth-**

My best friend, partner in crime, soul sister, and twin fucking flame. Thank you for being you, for loving me unconditionally, and for always being my safe space. I love you girly. Your friendship, love, and understanding have been like a pillar of strength, guiding me to happiness even when I had no idea how to get there myself. You taught me to be stronger. You give me the confidence to be unapologetically myself and have taught me that if I want something, I have to be the one to grab it, regardless of all those holding me back.

**Jenn Maryk** -

What the heck can I say about you? Words aren't enough to thank you for everything you've done for me. During my journey, you've been my friend, my PA, my editor, and my walking spell checker.

You're somehow a master with a degree in speaking "C.B" and know exactly when to let me go wild and when to rein me in. You are the perfect balance of firm but fair, and I couldn't have done any of this journey without you ... you're stuck with me now. Locked in the basement and threw away the key level of stuck!

So thank you so much, Jenn for not only being my P.A. and Editor, but for also being a true friend.

**To my Girlies** -

Thank you for all being there to help and support me. Thanks to all of you for giving up your time to be a part of my team. I know I can be alot. But thank you for sticking with me and my madness.

I'm so grateful to each and every one of you for being a part of my team. Your girls are honest to god some of my favorite people.

Thank you to Nurse Julia for being there to answer my medical question, including but not limited to.... "Would you die from a stab to the dick?" ( Come on, who else thought that was the perfect death blow for Marko?)

To Tabatha, Tianna, and Sam- thanks for keeping me awake with all our late night talks and for all the times we went off wild batting ideas back and forth.

To Gemma for always being my first order; no matter what book I write, you're somehow always the first to order every version to add to your bookshelf. I see you, I love you, and I appreciate you.

To Nichole, Ashley, and Amy, thank you all for being my girls from day one. Way before I was even C.B back when I was just a reader with an idea, and an extra thanks to Ashley for making so many of my graphics.

And this will be novel length if I thank every single person individually so to Greta, Ally, Bella, Abbie, Andrea, Jayde, Kaitlin, Laura, Lorelei, Vanessa and everyone else who has been a part of my author journey. Thank you all from the bottom of my heart.

And lastly, thank you to my readers. The ones who have taken the time to read my stories and fall in love with my characters. I love, adore and appreciate every single one of you! Hopefully I'll get the chance to meet or talk to some of you in the future. Feel free to reach out anytime as I love receiving little "hey i just wanted to say..." messages. They make this whole crazy journey worthwhile.

I have one small ask of all of you and it would mean the world to me. If you loved this book and Gabe, please leave a review. Reviews are what help Indie Authors like me and make such a difference.

## About the Author

I am a UK based author who sees herself as a spicy, neurodivergent, crazy person. I love to read, spend time with my kids and family and spend far too much time scrolling on social media.

My two dogs, Kara and Skyler, are my shadows, and whether I'm reading, writing or just relaxing around the house, they will be beside me, making me laugh.

I love connecting with my readers and the people in the book community. If you are ever inclined, send me a message so that we can chat! You can find me mostly on Facebook (yeah, I know it's not most people's first choice, but I'm terrible with social media and just can't work most of them).

I also dabble with TikTok occasionally, although, I'll be honest, it's mostly to watch either dog videos or spicy BookTok videos when I'm supposed to be writing.

But feel free to come chat to me anytime.

linktr.ee/c.b_halliwell

Gabriel's Sacrifice is my second book in the fire and ice series, and I'm hoping to have book three out before the end of the year as I'm sure by now you're screaming at me for all the cliffhangers.

Until then though, If you'd like to know more about the Scott brothers, and get to know more about Nate, Izzy and the rest of the group, you can catch the heartwarming story of Nathaniel and Isabella here

https://books2read.com/u/3yQlZn.

Forever Entwined is an emotional friends to lovers, second chance, small town read that I promise won't disappoint and will definitely have you reaching for the tissues.

Printed in Great Britain
by Amazon